BARRING

STEVEN CADE reputation for investigative Television in Canada. His assignments took him to many remote corners of the world, including a journey across the Sahara where he lived for many weeks with a tribe of Touareg in the mountains of Air in Niger. In recent years he has travelled extensively in Asia and is a frequent visitor to the islands of the Indian Ocean. When he is not travelling he lives with his wife and children in Dartmouth on the Devon coast.

Steven Cade's first novel, *Slade's Marauder*, is also published by Fontana. *Barrington's Women*, like its predecessor, is based on a true event that took place during the Second World War.

Available in Fontana by the same author

Slade's Marauder

STEVEN CADE

Barrington's Women

FONTANA/Collins

First published by Souvenir Press Ltd 1982
First issued in Fontana Paperbacks 1983

Made and printed in Great Britain by
William Collins Sons & Co. Ltd, Glasgow

For my wife, Penelope

1

A bitter wind was blowing down from the Opland Mountains in the north, carrying with it swirls of fine powder snow that hung in ghostly eddies between the tall grey buildings of Oslo's Karl Johan's Gate. Occasionally, when the wind was briefly still, a distant rumble of sound floated up into the sky above the fjord, beating against windows hollowed by the night as though all the great white geese were on the wing. But those who listened in the darkness had no illusions about the origins of the sound. There were no friendly geese passing by; just the sound of freedom dying as the German battle cruisers fought their way past Oscarsborg Castle in the hours before dawn on April 9th, 1940.

On the fourth floor of the Royal Bank of Norway, Lieutenant-Colonel Charles Barrington lit the last of his cigarettes and gazed impatiently towards Palace Hill. He had been waiting in the room for almost five hours and his bad left leg had long since knotted into throbbing strands of pain around the deeply scarred knee. He was a tall, broad-shouldered man with finely moulded features dominated by smoky grey eyes and dark hair greying at the temples. His skin was darkly tanned from ten years in India, and the ribbons on his chest recalled the battles of the last Great War as well as the campaigns in Africa and Burma.

He rose suddenly from his seat by the window, collecting a silver-topped walking cane and starting his hundredth circuit of the marble floor, tapping the cane with irritating regularity until the thin, grey, dejected figure beside the ornate telephone gazed at him with gentle reproof.

'If it takes much longer, Herr Director,' Barrington said acidly, 'I suggest you include the Wermacht in your plans.'

The Director of the Royal Bank of Norway allowed his shoulders to rise and fall and shook his head as though nothing was comprehensible any more. His features were pallid and deeply lined, as though the night had been too long. When the telephone rang he jumped and almost lost his balance on the narrow-backed chair, his mouth twitching nervously as he lifted the receiver to his ear. He listened for a moment, nodding his head once or twice, then slowly replaced the phone.

The British officer faced him across the desk, legs straddled, the walking cane before him. 'Yes or no, Herr Director?'

'The Minister of Finance is leaving the Palace now with the necessary papers.'

'And King Haakon?'

'He has agreed to the transfer of our gold reserves to your country, Colonel.'

'But is he coming with us?'

The Director shook his head. 'There is no time. His Majesty will leave the city with senior government ministers within the next hour, but where they go is a secret.'

Barrington glared at him as though it was his fault. 'He'd be a lot safer with my men.'

The Director nodded politely. 'Of that I'm sure, Colonel, but we still have a Norwegian army and there are matters of State which require his attention.'

'Yes, of course,' Barrington replied impatiently, 'but are you sure he realizes that Oslo will be occupied in a matter of hours?'

'His Majesty is fully aware of every aspect of the situation, including the fact that we have sunk a German battle cruiser less than an hour ago.'

Barrington dismissed it with a wave of his hand. 'Alters nothing. They've got five destroyers and six troop carriers. Once they've silenced the castle defences you've got nothing that can touch them. They'll be tying up in your harbour by noon.'

The Director bit his lip and turned to the telephone, lifting the receiver and tapping the cradle until the switchboard answered. He asked for the vault and then waited, his face grey and weary, until the chief auditor came to the phone. He spoke slowly, with resignation, instructing him to begin transfer of the gold to the British army trucks waiting in the street outside. When he replaced the receiver his hand shook slightly and he picked up a silver letter opener to conceal the fact.

'I shall require your signature, Colonel,' he said. 'The Minister of Finance will be here to witness it.'

Barrington smiled wryly. 'Of course. If I lose it between here and Trondheim you can always take it out of my pension.'

A salvo of guns rolled in the distance, blue light flickering against the dark horizon. The Director flinched and led the way to the elevator in the corner of his office. It seemed overburdened with just the two of them inside. He closed the wrought-iron gate and pushed over an ancient brass gear lever that grated in protest. Distant cogs clanked dismally and they began to sink into the depths of the building, watching each floor rise above them in stilted silence.

The brilliant lights in the vault burst upon them and the Director quickly released the handle, apologising as they sank a foot below the floor. Barrington swung his stiff leg over the step, refusing the Director's proffered hand, and moved briskly towards the group of soldiers standing by the main door. The bank employees were pulling trolleys stacked with the small grey cases of gold bullion with a notable lack of enthusiasm.

Barrington reached the sergeant-major, returning his salute while trying to ignore the shattering crash of regulation boots on marble. 'Get this operation speeded up, Sergeant-Major,' he said quietly. 'I want to be on the road in half an hour. Double up the trucks and kill the lights outside.'

Sergeant-Major Carver's 'sah' rang round the lofty room, ricocheted from pillar to pillar and jerked the dark-suited clerks into frozen attitudes, torn between resentment and panic.

'And let's keep it quiet,' Barrington added as the sergeant-major sucked in enough air to shatter an ear drum. 'There's no point in broadcasting our intentions.'

'As you say, sir,' he replied crisply and went to the men at the door. Within minutes he had two columns of soldiers and civilians passing the grey cases of gold to a double line of trucks.

Barrington donned his greatcoat and stepped out into the street, walking along the line of trucks. There were twenty in all, each to carry twenty five cases of gold and two soldiers. Together with four corporals, a sergeant and the sergeant-major it amounted to forty-six men to guard fifty tonnes of gold bullion.

He winced at the thought, mentally visualising the route over the mountains to Trondheim. A British destroyer was on standby in Flekke Fjord, waiting for his signal, but once the German landings were consolidated in Oslo they would try to cut off both Trondheim and Andalsnes. The fact that at least two generals had assured him a week ago in London that the Germany invasion of Norway was a month away and would be over the Danish border seemed rather academic now.

Whilst he could admire the German strategy of a seaborne invasion up the Oslo Fjord, he could also feel a measure of despair at the kind of tactical minds in London that could ignore such a vast inland waterway. Although Oscarsborg Castle had heavy guns and underwater torpedo tubes covering the straits, a heavy cruiser and five destroyers had been pounding it since dark. Barrington knew it was a matter of hours, but convincing the Norwegian Treasury officials had taken far too long. Finally only urgent messages from London and the intervention of King Haakon had cut through the mass of red tape.

He gazed through the swirling snow at the last two trucks, wondering if he had sufficient time. If the gold fell into German hands it would not just be a tragedy for Norway, but for the British war effort as well.

And yet, less than two weeks ago, he had stepped ashore at Southampton after a restful and extremely pleasant voyage on the *Empress of India* from Bombay. At fifty-one, with a leg that should have resulted in his discharge three years ago, he could expect nothing more than a handshake, a pension, and a farewell dinner from his regiment, the Buffs. The fact that war had broken out did raise the possibility of some civil service post, or even a desk at the War Office, but during the voyage home he had made up his mind to make it a complete break and turn down any offers connected with the military.

He had been totally unprepared for the attitude he encountered in both the War Office and Whitehall. Generals, Principle Secretaries and Parliamentary Private Secretaries blandly ignored his stiff left leg and cane, making it clear that there was no question of early retirement. Everywhere he went there was frantic activity as Britain prepared for the inevitable invasion of Europe, once Hitler had consolidated his position in Poland. An expeditionary force was being formed to support France and Belgium, and the cry was for experienced officers, men with the ability to command. In the space of four days he was offered a dozen posts from Command Supply Officer to a recruit training camp in Surrey.

He was spending the nights at his club where the talk was all of the impending invasion. His own regiment, he learned, was being withdrawn from India to man the garrison in Malta. He felt a deep regret that he could not be with them, but they had a new commanding officer now and his presence would only complicate the situation.

'You just thank your lucky stars there's a war on,

Charles,' said David Lang, an old school chum who had been promoted to Brigadier only a week before. 'Look at me? A year ago I was starting to make retirement plans, sounding out a couple of merchant banks, looking for the old town house in Knightsbridge and then zip . . . Adolf starts goose-stepping into Poland and we're in business again.'

He beamed, rolling the brandy snifter in his hands, leaning forward with a confidential wink. 'Could be a long war. The feeling is that he's caught us with our pants down and old Chamberlain is due for the chop.'

'You mean a coalition?' Asked Barrington.

Lang nodded, dropping his voice again. 'They're pushing Halifax down everyone's throat, but I'm putting my money on Churchill. He's a tough old bird and one way or another he'll get what he wants.'

'Let's hope so. The way to stop Hitler is by hitting him hard the minute he moves against France.'

'Absolutely, old boy,' Lang said without enthusiasm. 'But then it would be over in a matter of months. We'd all be mustered out by Christmas.'

Barrington grinned at his doleful expression. 'Somehow I don't think that's quite the attitude, David.'

'True,' he admitted, 'but fortunately it's not a real possibility. Even if we manage to put half a million men into France, they'll be poorly equipped and under the command of the French.' His eyes twinkled. 'If Hitler's Panzers can't cope with that combination they're wasting everybody's time.'

'You're incorrigible, David,' Barrington replied, shaking his head in mild reproof. 'The last time we fought in Europe it was a disaster. We were both there. You wouldn't want that again.'

'Of course not,' he answered soberly. 'But this time it won't be trenches and bayonets. It's going to be fast, light armour and fighter aircraft dominating the battlefield. We're not ready for that and neither are the French. You'll see.'

'Doesn't sound like my kind of war,' Barrington said slowly. 'In India and Burma the Lee Enfield and the bayonet got us by.'

'Come off it, Charles. We heard about that close quarter stuff along the Sino border. Wasn't that where you got the leg?'

'It wasn't that bad.'

'All the same, your lot know all about moving fast and taking people out with a knife or a wire. Right?'

Barrington shrugged, staring into his brandy and seeing the silver leaves of the moonlit jungle, the sudden flurry of movement as they rose up around the Chinese muleteers. There were no shots, no cries of warning to the camp along the trail. Just the sickening thud of knives going in to the hilt and the wheezing wail of that last breath being sucked into the lungs already filling with blood.

'Our main problem was snakes,' he said quietly. 'You had to watch where you put your feet.'

Lang guffawed loudly and signalled to the steward who immediately lifted the tray of brandy and port and moved towards them.

'Seriously, old chap, you ought to consider that training camp. Once we've had our nose bloodied in France the radicals who are crying out for modern techniques will have their day. All these exciting new ideas for parachute commando, submarine saboteurs, long range reconnaissance groups will be worked out at special training camps and you could carve yourself a very nice piece of the action.'

'I think I shall,' Barrington said thoughtfully. 'I'm seeing Bill Farley at the War Office tomorrow.'

They drank to it and arranged to meet for dinner the following week, but the next morning Barrington was summoned to the Foreign Office for a meeting that changed all his plans.

'You'll be a sort of special envoy, acting directly for the Crown,' said Sir Humphrey Pennington, one of the Foreign Office's more senior civil servants. 'You'll be empowered to give any reasonable assurance to the Norwegian Cabinet and the King, but I can't emphasise too strongly the urgency of the matter. We must get those gold reserves out of Norway before the Germans over-run the country and grab the lot themselves. We've already convinced the Prime Minister and Oscar Torp, the Minister of Finance, but some members of the Cabinet are hanging back. They can't accept that Germany has to invade Denmark and Norway, otherwise they'll always be looking over their shoulder.'

'How much time would you say we have?' Barrington asked.

Sir Humphrey pulled at his lower lip, glancing at the calendar. 'The destroyer will be standing off Trondheim from next Monday. I'd like to see you on board with the gold by Wednesday. That gives you at least a week's safety margin. Jerry isn't going to break through the Norwegian lines in less than a fortnight, even if he invades tomorrow.'

A roll of gunfire beat down through the swirling snow, echoing along the Karl Johan's Gate. They were heavy guns, firing in measured sequence. Barrington pulled up the collar of his coat, wondering if Sir Humphrey was feeling just a little guilty tonight.

The crisp footsteps of Sergeant-Major Carver approached and he turned, acknowledging his salute. 'Yes, Sergeant-Major?'

'We're loading the last two trucks, sir. There's a Mister Torp looking for you. Government civvie, sir.'

'Thank you. Any chance of coffee for the men before we leave?'

'Corporal Mellick organised it, sir. Couple of nice old ladies who live above the restaurant across the street.'

'Well done. Save me a cup and be ready to move in fifteen minutes.'

Barrington went back to the bank, surprised to find how cold he was when he went inside. The Director and Chief Auditor were waiting with the Minister of Finance who gave him a quick, impatient look before opening a briefcase from which he took an imposing sheaf of documents. Barrington crossed to them, noting that the last few cases of gold were being carried to the trolley.

'You are a trusting man, Colonel,' the Minister said with unconcealed irritation. 'I would have expected you to personally check the number of boxes.'

'I'm sure our count would have been the same,' murmured Barrington. 'Anyway, there were five hundred cases last week, so no doubt there were five hundred this morning.'

Oscar Torp cleared his throat and spread the documents on the desk, taking out a gold pen. 'We require your signature as representative of the English Crown and in your capacity as Commanding Officer of the convoy charged with carrying the gold to the vessel waiting at Trondheim. You will see that there is a total of fifty thousand and two kilos of gold listed on the attached sheets by ingot serial numbers, exact weight, and the assay mark together with transfer certificates where the country of origin was not Norway. You may examine them.'

Barrington shook his head and reached for the pen. 'I'm sure the Director and your own staff have been most thorough, Herr Minister. On behalf of His Majesty's government I assure you that as of this moment your gold reserves are the responsibility of Great Britain and, irrespective of events, will be honoured when we are once again at peace.'

'I accept your assurance,' the Minister replied formally. 'Let us hope that day is not too far distant.'

Barrington nodded and signed the receipts, initialling the sheaves of accompanying documents, then waiting whilst Torp and the Chief Auditor signed as witnesses. A set of documents was handed to him, the Minister of Finance locking the remainder in his briefcase. From somewhere the Director produced a bottle of aquavit and solemnly poured four glasses.

'Good luck, Lieutenant-Colonel Barrington,' said Torp, 'and may God be with you.'

* * *

In the street outside the convoy of trucks were starting up their engines, letting them idle as the snow continued to blanket the cobbles in a fine powder. Across the wide thoroughfare, some three hundred yards further along, was a small shop that sold shoes and handbags from Paris and Rome. Above it was an apartment belonging to a retired civil servant who was partially deaf and in bed most nights by nine o'clock. He rented two small rooms above the apartment to a young journalist who spent much of his time covering the political scene for an obscure magazine published in Stockholm. He had been sitting at his narrow window beneath the eaves of the old grey building since midnight, a pair of binoculars trained on the bank and the trucks outside. When they began to pull away he turned to an open suitcase containing a radio transmitter. The aerial was already extended and clipped to a metal conductor outside the window.

Placing a pair of earphones over his head he checked the tuning dial, then spoke softly in German. 'This is Night Owl for Black Eagle. Over.'

The windows rattled as another roll of gunfire blended with the deeper roar of the trucks below. The young man's name was Jan Felder, and ever since he met Vidkun Quisling in Germany the previous spring he had been a dedicated member of the Fifth Column. To Jan the sound of naval guns along the Oslo Fjord was pure music and fulfilled everything he had been told. He knew that within a matter of days, perhaps hours, Norway would fall to the Germans and Quisling would be installed as Premier. The only thing that would mar a perfect victory would be the disappearance of the nation's gold reserves.

'This is Night Owl for Black Eagle, over.' He said again, wincing as static crackled in his ears.

'Hello Night Owl, this is Black Eagle. Do you receive? Over.'

His heart beat in his throat and he squeezed the microphone between his hands. 'Yes, Black Eagle, I can hear you. I have an urgent message for Oberkommando Wehrmacht and for the . . .' His mouth dried out with the enormity of what he was about to say. 'And for the personal attention of the Führer.'

The static surged between them, like distant applause.

'Go ahead, Night Owl. We are linking you with Berlin. Over.'

Jan Felder licked dry lips and turned to gaze down at the last of the British trucks moving away from the bank. 'This is Night Owl for Stronghold. All the gold has been loaded into twenty British trucks and is leaving Sector One at o-three-thirty hours. My information is that the destination is Trondheim and the route is via Lillehammer. The convoy is led by a Colonel Barrington with a detachment of approximately forty men. Weapons seem limited to rifles and revolvers. That is all. Night Owl over.'

He waited, eyes gleaming, head held proudly. After a moment a new voice came through his earphones. 'Well done, Night Owl. This is Oberkommando, Berlin. Do you have an estimate of the journey with present weather conditions? Over.'

'Yes, sir.' Jan replied quickly. 'In this weather I estimate ten hours, perhaps twelve if the snow is heavy in the mountains. Over.'

'Thank you, Night Owl. Remain on station until twelve hundred hours. Berlin Out.'

Jan took the earphones off with shaking hands and crossed the small, cluttered room to the gas ring in the corner. He lit the gas and filled a pan from the washbasin tap, placing it on the flame. From a cupboard beside the small desk he used to write his political reports he took a chipped white mug and a tin of coffee. There was an enamel filter funnel with a wire mesh base for the filter paper and in this he placed two spoonfuls of coffee.

By the time the water had boiled the street below was dark

and still again with only the lights in the Director's office showing in the bank building. He poured the boiling water over the coffee and warmed his hands over the burner as it slowly seeped into his mug. When it was done he stirred in coarse brown sugar and went to the alcove above his desk. A picture of Adolf Hitler was pinned to the wall, a candle on either side as though this was the altar of his aspirations. He sipped the strong black coffee, then placed it on his desk and took one step back to raise a stiff right arm.

'Heil Hitler,' he said. 'Heil Hitler.'

And there were tears in his eyes.

2

The aircraft had begun to spiral as streamers of fire trailed from the engines, twisting and turning in a world of total darkness. The very air had begun to scream, buffeting the men who were trying to crawl towards the open door. There was a shriek of tortured metal and then a crashing along the fuselage as a wing tore itself loose. Flames licked around every window, turning the air into acrid heat that seared the lungs. But the door remained black, a beckoning hole in a nightmare world.

He began crawling towards it, feeling the parachute beneath him. Obscure figures went by, their faces blank, without features, and everything was strangely calm as though they were floating in a gentle sea instead of plunging to oblivion. It seemed an age before he reached the door, gripping the cold metal edge with his hands, feeling the heat of the flames behind him, forcing himself outwards. But something held his legs. Something cold and heavy with enormous strength. He tried to look back, to find out what it was, but the aircraft was spinning so madly that he was being pressed against the floor.

The fear rose with a scream in his throat. Whatever held him would never let go. He tried to move, to push his head out into the cool night air; but it was impossible. The heat became unbearable. The scream of the aircraft a cry of terror that matched his own. He could only wait for oblivion.

The world disintegrated into bright light and the scream of the aircraft became the shrill clamour of the telephone. With a jolt he was back in his room at Kiel, sitting up in bed and knuckling the sleep out of his eyes.

'Yes,' he said, forcing the calmness into his voice. 'This is Captain Lodtz.'

'Oberkommando Headquarters, Captain. We have General Kiestner for you.'

'Thank you.' He waited, holding the phone against his shoulder while lighting a cigarette. His watch showed five fifteen. He felt the first glow of excitement, looking across his room to the map of Norway pinned to the wall.

'Captain?'

'Yes, Herr General.'

'Are your men ready?'

'They have been on standby for almost a week now, General.'

'Splendid. The gold left Oslo forty-five minutes ago in twenty British trucks. Our intelligence confirms that it is going to Trondheim via Lillehammer and should be on the mountain road to Dombas shortly after dawn. Your orders are to stop the convoy and to prevent the gold from leaving Norway.'

'Yes, General. May I ask how long it will be before I have support?'

'The invasion is underway and landings from the sea will take place in Oslo within the next six hours. We expect a period of consolidation, perhaps three days, then supply lines will be extended and further seaborne landings will be made along the west coast. We expect to be in control of the entire country within one week.'

'My congratulations, General. A magnificent plan.'

'Thankyou, Lodtz. You will leave at dawn. The operation is codenamed Stronghold.'

'Yes, sir. I will contact you as soon as I have the convoy.'

'Do so, the Führer himself has asked to be kept informed.'

Lodtz put down the phone, the words ringing in his ears. '*The Führer himself.*' The blood throbbed in his throat and every nerve end seemed to vibrate with the sheer exhilaration of knowing that he, Wolfgang Gerd Lodtz, was in command of an operation that had Hitler's personal attention.

He picked up the phone, tapping the cradle until the operator answered, and asked for the duty room. Minutes later the klaxon began to howl across the airfield. He began to get dressed, donning the thermal underwear, then the dark green battledress followed by the white over trousers and parka. His parachute hung behind the door, its static line neatly coiled and clipped to the harness. On the front of the pack, painted in black and crimson, was the snarling head of a wolf and the words: Sky Wolves.

The airfield was situated on the outskirts of Kiel, some two hundred acres of open fields crossed by two runways. It had been used as a gliding club since 1934 and regular weekend courses for members of the Hitler Youth had provided a good excuse to erect a row of barrack blocks which now housed Lodtz's special paratroop commando unit. There were two hangars beyond the barracks and a further six were under construction on the north side of the field, but so far the only military aircraft were the three Junkers being wheeled out onto the service apron.

In the operations room the pilots and crew were being briefed by Captain Lodtz. The clock above the large map of Norway showed that it was 5.45 a.m. and in the east the sky was just beginning to lighten with the approaching dawn.

'We should sight the convoy on this road at about nine o'clock,' said Lodtz, indicating the winding road that ran alongside the River Gudbrands. 'We will make our drop on the north side, possibly in the valley between Fevang and Arnes. We jump at two thousand feet, in line, and I want it tight.'

He looked round the room. 'Any questions?'

'Visibility may be a problem,' one of the pilots said. 'We may miss the convoy.'

'If that should happen, we will continue to the valley at Vinstra and make the drop there. That will place us about two hours ahead of the convoy.'

'How about containers?' Asked the flight commander. 'Do you intend to drop full field equipment?'

'Not at all,' Lodtz replied. 'Each man goes in with his own supply pack. The only containers dropped will be with our skis.'

He waited, but there were no more questions. He smiled grimly. 'Thank you, gentlemen. We take off in thirty minutes.'

'The grey corrugated fuselages of the Junker 52s vibrated to the roar of the three 575 horse power BMW engines as the mechanics warmed them up in the cold dawn air. Lined up before each aircraft were fifty men, all dressed in white combat outfits with the squat main parachute on their backs and the smaller reserve pack across their stomachs. The men formed two squads of twenty five under the command of a sergeant. The squads broke down in turn into two patrols of eleven men and one corporal. The groups were known as Red, Blue and Green with a lieutenant in command, two medics, a cook, and a radio operator.

The Sky Wolves were the brain child of General Eric von Marenstein who saw the need for an airborne commando in 1938 and created the force two days after Germany marched into Austria. Wolf Lodtz was placed in command with a completely free hand in training methods and choice of equipment. By September 1939 he had a highly trained force of 150 men capable of hitting isolated targets anywhere in Europe within a matter of hours.

The men were experienced skiers, climbers, canoeists and parachutists. Their weapons were the most modern - the new MP40 developed by Schmeisser from the Erma MP38 and probably the most effective machine pistol in the world. Each man also carried the new Mauser automatic, four grenades, spare ammunition and a three-day supply of food. Inside the right boot was a six inch knife kept razor sharp.

As the grey light of dawn seeped over the airfield the Junker transports taxied onto the runway and began revving engines. A wooden tower stood against a copse of trees, the broad windows and radio aerials the only indication that it was anything more than an observation post. A powerful spotlight suddenly flashed on and off, repeating the signal three times.

The first of the JU 52s released its brakes and began to lumber down the runway, its corrugated skin shaking alarmingly as it strained to leave the ground. With less than five hundred yards of runway it began to lift slowly off the tarmac, the three engines at maximum revs as it cleared a line of trees and began climbing towards the dark clouds above. By the time it had reached the cloud base at three thousand feet the two sister aircraft were in formation on each wing.

The fine powder snow that had been falling over southern Norway stopped shortly before dawn and a wind began to blow off the sea, clearing the clouds so that by nine o'clock the sky was deep blue and the sun had put a sparkle on the snow-covered hills beyond Lillehammer. From the air they seemed low and featureless, but they rose quickly to the west where the Jotunheim Mountains dominated the horizon with peaks above two thousand metres and valleys that twisted and turned around frozen lakes and fjords.

Lodtz leaned back in the bucket seat, turning his head so that he could look through the small square window to the crisp white hills speckled with fir trees and outcrops of rock. He knew this country and the memory of it aroused nostalgia in a warm welling tide of emotion. It was twelve years since he skied those hills, but between 1922 and 1928 he had spent two weeks each year with his parents and sister, Inger, skiing cross-country from village to village. At the age of fourteen every day had been a new adventure, each village a kaleidoscope of smiling faces, log fires and smorgasbords that filled long rooms lined with barrels of herring and tables that groaned beneath mountains of food.

His first girl friend had been Norwegian, his first triumph had been to win the cross-country event at Storskavan. At seventeen he had broken a leg, and at eighteen he had fallen in love with a sixteen-year-old whose parents were Laplanders and who did not approve of Germans. At nineteen, just east of Trondheim, his father had died on an icy ridge, his heart failing in the cold with the nearest doctor ten miles away.

Lodtz sighed and reluctantly pushed the images away. At thirty-one he was stocky with square-cut features and pale blue eyes. He was no longer the gawky youth with the likeable grin. In twelve years he had changed beyond recognition. He had become harder, colder. He had become a soldier.

There was a buzz from the ready lamp beside him. He unclipped his seat belt and moved forward into the narrow cockpit. His parachute made movement difficult, but removing it was even more trouble so he edged himself through the doorway and leaned forward until he could see over the shoulders of the pilot and co-pilot. Ahead, running beside the clean white sweep of a frozen river, was the main road between Lillehammer and Dombas.

The pilot took off his helmet and gestured, shouting above the roar of the engines. 'We've just passed Arnes. Should see Fevang in about five minutes.'

'Any sign of the convoy?'

'No, but you still want to drop fairly close, don't you?'

Lodtz nodded, wishing the sky wasn't so clear. If the British saw them dropping they might turn back. He glanced at the altimeter, noting they were at three thousand feet.

'Bring us down to two thousand,' he said.

The pilot gazed at him for a moment, his mouth tightening. The hills already rose up on either side and the valley they were following had many turns. 'If you have to jump in a hurry you could be down to five hundred feet.'

'I know,' replied Lodtz. 'But if we're going to ambush those trucks we can't afford to be seen in the air.'

The pilot looked sceptical, but moved the control column forward and they began to descend towards the floor of the valley. It narrowed half a mile ahead and Lodtz glanced at the map the co-pilot had on his knee. It should be Fevang beyond the hills where they gave way to another valley at least a mile wide. They banked, engines roaring, and swept through the narrow pass with ice covered cliffs rising up a thousand feet on the left, the road and river to their right flanked by a series of ridges rising steeply above them.

The village came at them so quickly that Lodtz almost missed it, but even as he was noting the terraced rows of houses beyond the small square with its grey church and green roofed village hall, the pilot was shouting and pointing along the road ahead. His pulse quickened as he saw the line of trucks, grinding slowly up the hill beside the frozen river. The pilot banked and pulled them away in a climbing turn so that they lifted up over the crest of a mountain to drop swiftly down into the valley beyond. Lodtz slapped the pilot on the shoulder, grinning, and moving back along the aircraft.

Sergeant Driker rose from his seat beside the door as soon as he saw the Captain's expression. Together they turned the locking bars and pulled the door away, placing it down on the floor. The Sergeant clipped his static line to the cable running along the roof of the aircraft and Lodtz checked it before clipping on his own. All the men were on their feet now, clipping on, checking their reserves and the parachute pack of the man in front. The pitch of the engines changed and Lodtz knew the pilot was throttling back. He stepped up to the door, turning to give a thumbs up signal to his men. The buzzer went and the light began to flash repeatedly. He took a deep breath, feeling the surge of nausea that came with the fear, and stepped out into space.

The slipsteam took him like a doll and turned him round and round before flipping him upside down. Somehow he kept elbows tight into his sides, arms crossed over the reserve and knees together. Although he could feel no drag from the parachute on his back he knew it would be steaming out behind him, ready to snap open as soon as the shrouds were clear.

The sky seemed to be full of tumbling bodies as Driker sent the line of men out on the run. The ice cold blast of air howled in his ears, buffeting his body which seemed to be falling forever into a bright blue hole. He tried to turn his head, convinced the parachute had failed to open, then remembered his reserve and fumbled for the handle. Even as he found it, the blue dome beneath exploded into a white canopy and he was tumbling head over heels, clutching at his harness as the world righted itself and he was gazing down at the Norwegian snowscape.

He gulped in air, feeling the nausea settle, then checked the sky around him. He felt a surge of pride as he saw the descending rows of parachutists. His Sky Wolves, falling like leaves on an unsuspecting world. High above the last of his men were still leaving the aircraft, but even as he watched the triple lines ended and a moment later the Junkers were banking away to climb over the hills to the east.

He studied the ground below, estimating he had some two minutes before landing. They were dropping towards the snow-covered hillside at the head of the valley with the road and frozen river two thousand metres away, curving round the hillside into the next valley which would lead to the town of Fevang.

Looking back along the valley he could see the road winding out of the pass with no sign yet of the convoy. He was beginning to congratulate himself on a perfect drop when he saw the lone skier standing on a ridge.

There was no time to do anything more than fix the location in his mind, then he was pulling his elbows into his sides, getting feet and knees together as the white expanse beneath him began to resolve itself into a gentle slope with folds of snow and occasional bushes and outcrops of rock. He reached for the harness above his shoulders, bracing his legs for the shock, and suddenly he was down, rolling through feathery drifts to flounder onto his knees as he pulled the shrouds and collapsed the canopy.

Everywhere he looked white figures were plunging out of the sky, sliding through snow until the parachutes were brought under control. Lodtz unfastened the Schmeisser that was clipped across his chest and checked the action before descending the hillside to a ridge that overlooked the road and valley. He stretched out and took the small pair of field binoculars from his pocket, slowly scanning the road until it went out of sight at the head of the valley. Sergeant Driker sprawled beside him, looking down to the road some fifty feet below.

'Blue Group are ready to dig in, Captain. Green are fitting out with skis.'

Lodtz nodded, carefully focusing the binoculars on the distant pass. 'Any injuries?'

'One man broke a leg, two have twisted ankles that may prevent them from skiing.'

Lodtz gave him an irritated look. Driker grimaced and shrugged. 'There's always someone, Captain.'

There was a shrill whistle from the slope above and Lodtz turned, seeing the stocky figure of Lieutenant Niemens at the front of his column. Lodtz stood up and gave the pre-arranged signal. The officer pushed himself forward with his ski poles and led the way at an angle along the slope towards the road. They would take up positions behind the banked snow on either side to prevent the trucks from turning back.

Lodtz checked his own group, noting that most of them were already on skis. The medic was splinting the leg of the injured man, but there would be little else they could do for him. He swung back to Driker.

'We'll have to bury him in the snow until its over,' he said quietly. 'I don't want anything moving up here.'

Driker nodded, gesturing to a ridge which was no more than twenty feet above road level and in easy range for the machine pistols. 'That position below could be useful, sir.'

Lodtz considered the drifts of snow, then shook his head, pointing further along where an outcrop extended almost to the road. 'We'll set up there. It gives us a better element of surprise and less chance of being in Blue Group's line of fire.'

Driker glanced back up the slope, grimacing in annoyance as he saw that the Captain was right. 'Yes, sir. I should have seen that.'

Lodtz grinned and passed the binoculars to him. 'You can't always be right, Sergeant. I'd get a complex!' He pointed across the valley. 'See if you can spot a skier on the far slope. I saw him on the way down.'

The Sergeant lifted the binoculars and began to sweep the far side of the valley. Lodtz left him to it, knowing that he would spot anything that moved. Driker, like all his NCOs, was hand picked and totally reliable, but there was a rapport between them that set him apart from the other men. During the long months of training the Sergeant had developed an intuitive sense that enabled him to respond to situations almost before the orders were given. As a result he was virtually in command of Red Group when Lodtz was pre-occupied with the development of the total force.

It was an arrangement that suited Erik Driker, for it gave him the power of command without the responsibility of a commission. He was a short man with powerful shoulders and thick legs given to straddling invisible lines with great truculence. His hair was black, curly, and his face set in hard planes that were rarely altered by a smile. Although he was only twenty-nine, he seemed older because life for Sergeant Driker was a very serious business.

He found the skier after sweeping the far slope of the valley three times. He was about half a mile away, descending a series of ridges. As Driker watched the skier stopped, staring towards him. A moment later the sun glinted on binoculars.

Lodtz finished giving orders to the squad leaders and then fitted his own skis as they made their way down towards the outcrop of rock beside the road. Driker came up and squatted beside him, the binoculars dangling from his hand.

'We might have a problem with the skier,' he said.

'You think he's interested?'

'Using binoculars and moving down into the valley.'

Lodtz thought about it for a moment, then shrugged. 'There's not a lot he can do, anyway.'

'Unless he got close enough to the road to warn the convoy?'

Lodtz gazed across the valley, picking out the skier almost immediately as he traversed the ridges, heading east. In a matter of minutes he would be on the valley floor and able to cut across towards the road. He sighed. 'Who's got the Kar?' He asked, referring to the Kar 98K sniper's rifle.

'Wilner,' Driker replied. 'If the skier tries to cross the valley he'll be in range for about five minutes.'

'All right. Tell Wilner to set up if he tries for the road, knock him over.'

Driker nodded and moved back to the ridge, calling for Wilner on the way. Lodtz clipped his boots into the running alpine harness and stood up, sliding them backwards and forwards in the snow. There was no sign of Blue or Green group, but that only meant they were now in position. His own men were cutting along the slope above the road, edging down towards the rock. He began to follow, only to stop as Driker called softly to him from the ridge.

'Yes, Driker?'

'Convoy just clearing the pass, Captain.'

Lodtz slid over to him and took the binoculars, picking out the dark green trucks almost immediately. They were still two miles away, but in the clear air he could already hear the whine of the engines as they began to increase speed. He felt a surge of exhilaration as he counted the trucks, knowing there was no mistake.

'They are eager to meet us, Captain,' Driker commented quietly.

'Like fat English geese,' agreed Lodtz, swinging the binoculars across the valley towards the skier. He found him almost immediately and felt a quick surge of alarm. The skier was shussing hard across the flat snow, angling towards the road about a mile ahead of the trucks.

He turned towards Wilner who was spread-eagled on the ridge, his rifle resting on a log he had swept clear of snow. He was using the Ajax telescopic sight, gazing intently into it.

'Is he in range, Wilner?' asked Lodtz.

Private Wilner rolled onto his side and tugged nervously on his ear. He was no more than twenty with freckled features and short blond hair. Lodtz felt a brief spasm of irritation that Driker had not chosen an older man, but he quelled it, knowing instinctively that if Wilner had the Kar 98 then Wilner was the best shot they had.

'It's not so much that, sir,' Wilner said awkwardly. 'It's just that . . . well, the skier's a girl, sir.'

Lodtz gazed at him with ice blue eyes until he was so pale his freckles stood out like buckshot. 'She is going to warn the enemy, Wilner,' Lodtz said finally. 'So you will shoot her. You will shoot with great care because if you miss I am afraid I will believe that you deliberately chose to miss.'

Wilner's eyes widened with horror and he shook his head emphatically. 'Oh no, sir. I would not do such a thing.'

Lodtz allowed his expression to soften. 'Very well, Private Wilner. It is a pity that your first target should be a woman, but that is the fortunes of war. Go ahead.'

Wilner gulped and nodded and turned back to the rifle, pulling it firmly into his shoulder as he gazed through the telescopic sight. She was half way across the valley now, long blonde hair falling from the woollen cap she was wearing. Her jacket was white with blue markings on the sleeves. He steadied the sight, holding it on her slim figure, noting how well she moved, each thrust of the ski a long fluid stride that covered all of two metres. He tried not to think of her as a person, but she reminded him of his sister, and then he was thinking of his mother and wondering what she would feel if she could see him now. His finger stroked the trigger and he was aware of cold perspiration on his forehead, a tightening in his throat as the horrifying reality came home to him.

There was a hand on his shoulder, the voice of Driker calm and unhurried. 'It's just another kind of target, Wilner. Knock it down.'

He stopped breathing, the rifle rock steady, the sight centring on the girl. His finger tightened, then the butt jerked hard against his shoulder and the tightness in his throat became a spasm of horror as the figure plunged into the snow. He shut his eyes tightly, trying to hold back the revulsion.

'Good shot, Private Wilner,' said Captain Lodtz. 'Better put another one into her.'

He opened his eyes, the words numbing his mind. He tried to swallow but his mouth was too dry. He stared through the telescopic sight, working the bolt action to put another round into the chamber. The streak of crimson on the snow beside her brought the bile into his throat and he felt sure he was going to be sick.

Suddenly the girl moved and crawled to her feet. He didn't know whether to feel relief or alarm. Driker was beside him, telling him to fire, but he was fascinated by the left arm of the girl which was scarlet, gleaming like silk in the sun. He pressed the trigger, jerking with the recoil, watching the snow kick up beyond her. He knew that he had done enough. One bullet, one moment when he believed he had killed her, one searing wave of revulsion and guilt. That was enough.

'Again!' snapped Driker beside him.

He reloaded, his fingers clumsy with the cold. The girl was on the move, pushing herself awkwardly with one ski pole. He centred the cross hairs on her back as she went away from him, then let the barrel drop a fraction as he fired. The bullet sprayed snow ten metres behind her. He worked the bolt again, steadying the sight, feeling relief as she began to drop below a rise in the ground. He fired, watching the bullet kick up snow as she dropped out of sight.

Lodtz lowered his binoculars and turned to gaze at Wilner with dubious eyes. The man fumbled with his rifle, concentrating on reloading the magazine.

'Sorry, sir,' Wilner said when he finally looked up. 'The range was a bit too much for me.'

'A pity,' Lodtz said coolly. 'Your first shot must have been quite remarkable!'

Driker ordered him back to his squad in a flinty voice, then went to stand beside the Captain, gazing across the valley. After a while the skier came into view again, well out of range and moving slowly, but purposefully, towards the road.

'Do you think she can make it, sir?' Asked Driker, gauging the distance as the rumble of the trucks grew louder.

'I don't doubt it for a moment,' replied Lodtz. 'If she can get to her feet after taking a high velocity bullet in the arm, she can probably do whatever she sets her mind to. We'll just have to hope that she doesn't do it in time.'

3

The bullet took Tania Arlberg in the fleshy part of the arm just above the elbow. The impact knocked her flat, twisting her round and sending her ski stick flying. There was never any doubt in her mind about who had fired the shot. She had spent the morning listening to the radio bulletins from Oslo, reluctantly accepting the fact that the invasion of her country was under way and within hours there would be German soldiers in the capital.

She was on her way to discuss the development with her parents in Tretten when she saw the paratroops landing on the far side of the valley. She watched their movements with interest, accepting the fact that they were Germans and only mildly curious about their purpose. It was not until she heard the distant convoy and saw them come into view beyond the Arnes pass that she realized what was going to happen. The decision to warn the soldiers was taken without hesitation.

Lying in the snow she fought back the waves of nausea and tried to move her arm. There was no pain, only a spreading area of numbness. She turned to look at it and felt faint again. Blood was pumping out, streaking the snow, soaking the lower part of the sleeve. She sat up, her head strangely light, taking the scarf from her neck and tying it around her arm. She managed it quite quickly, pulling it tight with her teeth and right hand before pushing herself upright onto her skis.

As she began to move forward the snow ahead of her spurted into the air. She had heard no shot, but it was obvious that a bullet had just hit the snow. The fear rose up, constricting the throat and bringing a shakiness to legs already growing weak from shock. She gritted her teeth and spoke sharply to herself, refusing to acknowledge the waves of dizzines that threatened to swoop in and overwhelm her.

There was a ravine ahead with a ramp of snow leading into it and she took the option immediately, turning as another bullet puffed up snow beside her. She crouched low, edging her skis to slide down the incline. A moment later she was out of sight and able to relax.

The convoy was about a mile away, grinding slowly up the side of the valley from the pass. She paused, checking her arm. The tourniquet was doing its job and the bleeding had almost stopped. She took stock of the ground ahead, estimating the speed she could make across the valley. There was a wide sloping field of snow with a stand of fir trees to one side that would shield her from the Germans. Beyond the trees was an area of hillocks and ridges that climbed gradually to the road. From Tania's position it was less than half a mile, but she would have to travel almost as fast as the trucks to reach it in time.

She set off, using the loping stride of the alpine skier. Her long, narrow skis slid smoothly through the snow, giving just enough hold on rising ground to take her up the hillocks and yet slick enough to let her coast down the other side. She was no longer concerned about the Germans, convinced that she was well out of range. Beyond the trees she began rising towards the road, angling along the slopes, pacing herself so that each rhythmic stride gave her that brief second of respite.

She could hear the whine of the trucks clearly now, see them from time to time as they climbed up the valley. Her breath was beginning to rasp in her throat and her vision was becoming blurred. There was a dull throbbing ache in her arm which was beginning to stiffen, altering her rhythm so that she occasionally floundered and once fell, sliding twenty feet down the hill. The icy shock of the snow brought her quickly to her feet, however, and she edged sideways up the hill until she was back on the trail she had been following.

She paused on the last ridge, her heart pumping, sucking cold air into her aching lungs. A field of deep snow was all that separated her from the road, but the line of trucks was very close and the air filled with the roar of their engines. She started down the ridge, picking up speed, thrusting the skis into that fast, running stride which eats up the snow. But her sight kept blurring and the throbbing pain in her arm seemed to be spreading through her shoulder and across her chest. She fell, the snow filling her mouth. Sobbing, she forced herself upright, leaning on the ski pole, snow and water in her eyes, a burning pain in her side.

She floundered, trying to get into her stride, but she was leaning to the left and her skis kept crossing. The world was filled with the roar of engines as she pitched forward and lay, weeping bitterly, because she had failed.

4

Charles Barrington was dozing beside the driver of the leading truck when the man tapped him diffidently on the arm and pointed to the skier who was floundering in the snow about five hundred yards from the road. He studied the figure as they drew nearer, at first curious, then with growing concern.

'Stop the truck, Baker,' he said, taking a pair of binoculars from their case.

The driver slowed to a halt, signalling to the vehicles behind. The skier had pitched forward into the snow and was making no attempt to get up. Baker squinted against the glare of the sun, then studied the road ahead as it wound along the side of the valley. There was a stillness, an air of brooding menace that brought a prickle of fear across the back of his neck.

'It's a woman,' Barrington said quietly. 'She's had some kind of accident. Blood on her arm.'

Baker put the hand brake on and wished he had the courage to tell the Colonel they weren't supposed to stop for anything or anyone.

Barrington climbed awkwardly out of the truck and went round to the back, lifting the canvas to find Corporal James and two privates playing cards. Some of the bullion cases had been arranged neatly into a table. Money was stacked in front of each player who was staring at the Colonel with varying degrees of guilt.

'First aid kit and snow shoes, Corporal,' Barrington said crisply. 'On the double.'

Corporal James took Private Parker with him, mainly

because he didn't trust him with the cards while he was away. Neither of the men were much good with snow shoes, tripping and floundering through the heavy drifts. Parker fell once and almost disappeared, cursing Norway and Barrington with equal enthusiasm. It wasn't until they were almost upon the skier that the full extent of her injury was apparent.

'Jesus, Corp,' exclaimed Parker, touching the crimson sleeve of her anorak. 'She's been shot.'

'Shut up and cut it open,' snapped James, glancing up the valley. She hadn't been shot long, and from her tracks she had been heading for the road.

The girl's eyes flickered open as Parker unfastened the tournequet, tearing open a field dressing as Corporal James sprinkled sulphamezanine powder over the wound.

'You're British,' she said in English, sounding surprised.

'Right you are, Miss,' replied Corporal James. 'Now how come you got yourself shot?'

'Oh,' she looked up towards the road in horror, 'you must turn back. Quickly.'

'How's that, ma'am?' Parker asked, tying the dressing securely round her arm.

'The Germans. They landed by parachute at the head of the valley. I'm sure they're waiting for you.'

James winced and got to his feet, waving urgently to the Colonel who was watching through his binoculars. He pointed up the valley, pantomimed shooting, then added a Nazi salute for good measure. He turned back to the girl, pleased with his performance. 'How do you feel about us carrying you to the road, Miss?' he asked her.

She nodded, her face as pale as the snow beneath her hair, and forced a smile. 'I'm just a little weak, that's all.'

Barrington was studying the slopes above the road half a mile away. At first it seemed quite normal, unbroken folds of snow with the occasional outcrops, until he saw the ski trails, many of them, running down towards the road. He focused with care and scanned the hillside again. Ski trails, large areas of broken snow, a container lying open with parachute shrouds. He grunted with satisfaction, holding the glasses steady, finding the figures in white stretched out in a line above the road.

'Fancy now,' he said to himself, lowering the binoculars. 'I wonder who you're waiting for?'

He turned and beckoned to Sergeant-Major Carver who marched crisply across, crunching his boot into the snow and producing a 'sah' that echoed to and fro across the valley.

Barrington waited patiently for the echoes to subside. 'We'll be turning the trucks round and heading back down the valley, Sergeant-Major. I want it done quickly, starting with the rear truck.'

'Right, sah,' replied the Sergeant-Major, trying hard to control his curiosity. He had witnessed the corporal's pantomime and put two and two together. He cleared his throat, searching for a suitable remark.

'We've got Jerry ahead,' said Barrington, putting him out of his misery. 'They've come in by parachute, and not so long ago either.'

'Parachutes, sir!' exclaimed the Sergeant-Major, his shocked expression suggesting that such devious tactics were quite outside the rules of war. 'He's got a bit of a bloody cheek hasn't he, sir? Just like that? Dropping on a foreign country?

'I imagine it'll be one of their crack commando units. They'll be expert skiers, climbers, and fighters too I should think.'

'Our lads will soon sort them out, sir,' the Sergeant-Major said with quiet pride. 'Just say the word.'

'The word is retreat, Sergeant-Major,' Barrington said firmly. 'We'll do it with all possible speed, returning to Fevang and from there we'll take the bridge across the Logen River and the secondary road leading north up into the mountains.'

The Sergeant-Major saluted with inscrutable features and

did a smart about face, marching along the line of trucks with his voice cracking like a whip. 'All right you lot get back in your vehicles and stand by to do a smart about turn. Any driver who doesn't execute a perfect three-point turn will feel the pointed end of my stick right where it hurts. Is that understood? Then come along now, come along, let's be having you!'

Corporal James and Private Parker carried the girl for the last three hundred yards, making heavy going of it as they floundered up the sloping bank to the road. Although she was close to fainting more than once, Tania managed to keep her senses and stood unaided when they reached the road.

The officer who came to her was tall and broad shouldered with tanned features and eyes as grey as wood smoke. His hair was black, greying at the temples, and when he walked there was no bend in his left leg so he used a silver-topped cane to ease the weight as he swung it forward. He looked into her face and smiled a surprisingly gentle smile.

'We're putting some blankets in the back of a truck, and then we'll take you to the doctor in Favang,' he said.

'There's no doctor there, and anyway the Germans will know I've warned you. I'd rather travel with you for a while if I may.'

'Of course, Miss . . .?'

She smiled wanly, moving with him towards the rear of the truck. 'Tania Arlberg. I saw the Germans landing across the valley and then I heard your trucks. I thought it was a Norwegian Army convoy.'

'How close to them were you when you were shot?'

She wrinkled her brow and gazed back along the valley. 'About half a mile. I never thought they could shoot that far. I was very surprised.'

'I'm sure you were. My name is Barrington, by the way. Charles Barrington. Let me help you up.'

He lifted her into the back of the truck where Parker and Corporal James had made up a bed with a dozen blankets between the stacked cases of bullion. They helped her to stretch out and then covered her as Barrington pulled himself into the truck and signalled to the Sergeant-Major who was bellowing at the driver behind them.

'You want me to travel up front, sir?' asked Corporal James.

The Colonel looked out as the truck behind them completed its turn. 'Yes. Tell Baker to overtake the trucks where he can. We want to be in the lead by the time we reach Favang.'

'Right, sir,' said the Corporal, dropping over the tailgate and moving out of sight.

Barrington went to sit on a bullion case beside the girl. Parker was looking as though he ought to be somewhere else. The Colonel gestured for him to sit down as they began to move, backing across the road, then turning slowly until they were facing east.

'Where will you go?' Tania asked curiously.

Barrington was unfolding an ordnance map. He glanced up, smiling. 'We need to get to Trondheim. I see that there's another major road about twenty miles north of here.'

She nodded. 'Yes, it's a good road. It goes to Ulsberg and from there to Trondheim. But to reach it you have some very difficult driving over the mountains.'

The truck had completed its turn and was now moving after the convoy, picking up speed as they began to descend towards the pass at the head of the valley. Barrington gazed back along the road, feeling a sense of relief even though there had been little likelihood of the Germans reaching them in the time it took to turn round. He glanced back at the girl who was watching him with a disturbingly direct gaze. She had the bluest eyes he had ever seen.

'How fast could cross-country skiers reach the Ulsberg road?'

She thought about it, visualising the route which she had travelled many times. 'If you knew the way you could make better time than a truck,' she said finally. 'Especially heavy trucks like these. But surely the Germans won't know that you're going to Trondheim?'

'They know,' replied Barrington. He spread the map out beside her, indicating their position. 'Now suppose we take this road across the mountains to Annolsetrene. Is there any way we can cut across to Imsenden?'

She shook her head. 'No. It's all forest and hills, some of them fifteen hundred metres. The only way you can reach the Trondheim road is by cutting back along the other side of this valley to the town of Valebru. Then you have a fairly good road up to Krokhaug and from there you can reach the main Oppdal Trondheim road.'

Barrington stared at the map, his face grim. He knew she was right, but the risks of interception were considerable. The only other alternative was to drive all the way back through Lillehammer to Hamar, but if Oslo had been occupied the Germans could already be coming after him on the same road.

'Why do they want you so much?' Tania asked curiously.

Barrington smiled wryly and tapped one of the cases. She read the stencilled words for the first time, her eyes widening as she saw the crest and 'The Royal Bank of Norway' on the sides.

'It's not so much us that they want,' said the Colonel. 'It's your national gold reserves which we just happen to be carrying.'

'All our gold?' she gasped. 'All of Norway's gold in these trucks?'

He nodded. 'I'm afraid so.'

She pulled the map towards her and stared at it, small white teeth gnawing at her lip. Her colour was beginning to return and he was struck by the delicate pink of her cheeks against the ivory arch of her neck.

'You should be resting, Miss Arlberg,' he said, suddenly filled with guilt. 'We must find somewhere for you.'

'But the gold,' she said. 'You can't let the Germans have the gold.'

'I don't intend to.'

'On the radio it said that the German army was in Oslo. There is to be a parade through the streets this afternoon with the mayor and the German commander in the first car.' She shook a small fist. 'Imagine that! A parade!'

'It's all happened too quickly for anyone to do much about it,' Barrington told her gently. 'The army was expecting the invasion from Denmark.'

'I know.' She glared at the map. 'And so they'll be coming up the road to Lillehammer which means you can't go back. Yet those parachutists have only to cross the River Logen and climb into the next valley and . . .' She gazed at him with anguished eyes. 'They'll kill you all and steal our gold.'

'Oh I don't think we'll allow that.'

She gave him an exasperated look and gestured at the map. 'Colonel, you can't drive back into the German invasion and you can't drive west to Valebru because they'll get there first. You can only go up into the mountains, but the road stops at Annolsetrene. Of course, I'm no military strategist,' she added defensively, her cheeks flushing.

'Don't worry about it,' said Barrington dryly, 'you're doing fine.'

'I'm sorry,' she said quickly, 'you must think I'm terribly rude. It's just that I used to live in those mountains. My parents moved to Tretten two years ago, but until then we lived in a tiny village called Borgas.' She pointed at the map. 'It's probably not even marked.'

Barrington bent closer and studied the area. He found it finally, at the end of a track that seemed to be little more than a footpath. 'It's here. I suppose the road is blocked at this time of year?'

She shook her head. 'No. There's a lumber camp on the edge of the village and they keep the road open so they can haul the logs down to the mill at Annolsetrene.'

He stared at the map for a long moment. 'How many people live in Borgas?'

'About two hundred. Why?'

He made no reply, turning and looking out of the rear of the truck. Baker had overtaken all the vehicles so that they were now in the lead. In the truck directly behind he could see the ruddy features of Sergeant-Major Carver. He made up his mind and gestured to the Sergeant-Major, then turned to Parker who was sitting on cases beside the cab.

'Give Baker a knock, Parker. I want to stop.'

Parker nodded and pounded the back of the cab until Baker got the message and began to slow down. Barrington returned to the map and gazed at it until the truck had come to a stop. He glanced at Tania, tapping the map. 'You're certain the road will be open?'

'It's the only way the log camp can work through the winter, and most of the men are employed there. But it's still a dead end. Sooner or later the Germans will find you there.'

'Perhaps.'

She glared at him. 'Do you have to be so vague?'

'Miss Arlberg, we'll be leaving you at Annolsetrene where I'm sure there will be a doctor to look after you. It's better that you know as little as possible.'

'You don't trust me?' she demanded, eyes flashing. 'I came across the valley to warn you, got myself shot, but you don't trust me?'

'It isn't that,' he said with exasperation. 'I don't want you involved.'

'Well you'll never find your way to Borgas, Colonel. And even if you managed to choose the right track through the forest, you'd only get yourselves bogged down or lost.'

'Indeed?' He gazed at her coldly until her eyes dropped and the blood rose in her cheeks. 'Well you mustn't worry yourself too much about it.'

He folded the map and climbed over the tailgate, dropping down onto the snow-covered road.

'It's not you or your men I'm worried about, Colonel,' she called after him. 'It's all this gold that belongs to Norway.'

He paused, glancing back. 'Then you mustn't worry

about that either, Miss Arlberg. I gave the bank my receipt.'

Sergeant-Major Carver was waiting for him by the side of the road, stamping his feet and slapping his hands against the cold. A white veil of snow had begun to fall, shrouding the hilltops around them and the pass through which they had just travelled. The village of Favang was half a mile along the road, the bridge a grey line across the clean white ribbon of the river.

'It rather looks as though Jerry knew what he was doing, Sergeant-Major,' said Barrington, holding the map between them. 'He's cut us off along this valley and left himself the option of going over the northern ridge to command the only other road open to us.'

'How far back does that mean we have to go, sir?' Asked Carver.

'Lillehammer at least, but ideally Hamar. And that puts us too close to the German invasion forces.'

'A bit of a sticky one, sir.'

'There's another option. If we take the mountain road from Favang, heading north into this area around Annol-setrene, we can drive through the forest to the village of Borgas. We unload the gold, bury it in the forest, take the trucks back down towards Valebru. The whole operation should take about six hours and during that time Jerry could have given up waiting and headed east down the valley.'

'We still have to get the gold out, sir,' the Sergeant-Major reminded him.

'True, but not today. It's going to be up to you to get the men to Trondheim and inform HQ that I'm in Borgas with the gold.'

Carver didn't like it and said so, but Barrington was adamant. 'If the Germans are on the ball they'll have this area sewn up within the hour. I can't risk fifty tonnes of gold. This operation was never meant to be carried out against the enemy, we don't have the strength for it, so get to it Sergeant-Major.'

He snapped to attention and saluted before marching

along the line of trucks, bellowing instructions to the drivers. Barrington went back to his truck and told Corporal James to ride in the rear, reminding him to keep an eye on their passenger.

'Glad to, sir,' he said cheerfully. 'How far will the young lady be travelling with us?'

Barrington hesitated, aware that she would be listening. 'Just down the road, Corporal. Just a few miles down the road.'

5

The fine particles of ice came off the ridge in whirling spirals that stung the face and eyes. Wolf Lodtz lowered the binoculars and pulled the pair of goggles down from his forehead, gazing bitterly across ridges and slopes clothed in deep folds of snow, to the thin ribbon of road five hundred metres below. From this vantage point they could see some five kilometres towards Fevang and three in the opposite direction. Beyond the road was a dark sea of pine forest, crested white, rising in terraced ranks towards the brooding mountains dominated by the peak of Store Kvien in the north.

They had crossed the frozen river as soon as the British convoy disappeared through the pass at the head of Gudbrands Valley, shussing hard in deep snow and stands of pine that made ski trailing difficult. But the men were honed to the peak of physical fitness and traversed many of the steeper slopes on the run, shouting insults at each other, their boots clicking rhythmically in the cross-country harnesses which Lodtz had acquired from Oslo's leading ski manufacturer less than six months ago. Any man who fell on the icy slopes slid down to the timber line accompanied by a chorus of abuse from his companions, but as they got higher the accidents grew more serious. By the time they reached the rim of the valley a thousand metres above the river, one man had died and two more had been left in tents with broken legs.

The northern side of the valley rim proved much easier to traverse with undulating fields of snow and trails that wound down through stands of timber. Lodtz chose a knife-edged ridge half way down to rest and wait for the convoy. It had taken them just under two hours and he was sure that the trucks could not have driven back to Fevang, then along the more difficult Valebru road, in that time. To make doubly sure he sent a patrol down the hillside to check for tyre tracks on the snow-covered road. They reported that no convoy had passed.

That had been two hours ago and as he gazed at the empty road below he felt the doubts gnawing at his mind, teasing him with their logic. The British would run back to Lillehammer, take the long route beside the Glomma River through a hundred miles of pine forest and undulating hills until they reached Tynset to begin the long descent through Orkla Valley to Trondheim.

He crouched down on the ridge, pushing goggles up onto his forehead and spreading the map on the snow. All he knew about the man in charge of the convoy was that he was a British Lieutenant Colonel named Barrington who had spent the past twelve years in Burma and India with his regiment, The Buffs.

Lodtz cursed beneath his breath. It was typical of the Oberkommando staff that all they could give him was name, rank and regiment. They had an intelligence section with more than a thousand pimply faced youths and limp-wristed professors who spent most of their time dancing attendance on the High Command. The moment Barrington arrived in Oslo a file should have been opened on him, and by now Lodtz should have enough detail about the man to predict every move he made. Instead he could only glare at the twisting roads on the map and wonder where the devil he was.

He turned and shouted for Driker who was with the radio operator on the ridge above them. The rest of the men were spread along the hillside in groups of ten eating field rations of liver sausage and hard rye bread. For the past hour the only topic of conversation had been the options open to the British convoy, and whether Captain Lodtz had guessed right. An enterprising sergeant in Blue Group had opened a book on the situation and was currently offering even money that the convoy was half way to Lillehammer, with ten to one against the trucks appearing on the road below.

Sergeant Driker arrived, brushing snow from his anorak. 'Yes, Captain?'

'Where the hell is that 189?'

'It's on the way, sir. Cleared Oslo five minutes ago. Pilot reports good visibility. He'll be in sight of Lillehammer in a few minutes.'

'He's taking his bloody time!'

The Sergeant shrugged. 'The plane left Alborg in Denmark at one fifteen, sir. They had to refuel.'

Lodtz glared at him. 'Sergeant, are you aware of the gravity of our situation if we don't find that convoy?'

'I'd say we were in the shit, sir. Going deeper by the hour.'

'Right, Driker. And all because of that sod of a marksman you picked!'

The Sergeant's cheeks reddened. 'He was the best shot in training, Captain.'

'Shooting at targets isn't shooting at people. I want him sorted out when we get back. I mean right out. Some other unit.'

Driker stared at him levelly. 'He has a sister about the same age as the girl he shot.'

'We've all got sisters, Driker, and some of them will probably die before we've won this war. That man was given an order and I don't think he was trying very hard after the first hit.'

'We can't know that, sir. It was extreme range.'

'Yes, there is no way we can be sure. If there was I'd have him shot right now.'

Sergeant Driker said nothing, his eyes remote, his features giving no hint of his emotions. Inwardly he was seething with rage. Wilner had let them all down, turned a text book operation into something approaching disaster. He had no intention of sending Wilner to another unit. At least not before he had taught him the error of his ways.

Lodtz cursed savagely and slapped the map. 'He should have doubled back on this road from Fevang. Why didn't he?'

'Perhaps he kept on going to Lillehammer, sir. It's the long way round to Trondheim, but he's got no alternative.'

The Captain considered him with contempt. 'If he's gone back to Lillehammer then we're dealing with a fool. He knows our invasion forces are in Oslo, probably putting an armoured column together right now. They'd catch him long before he ever got to Trondheim. No, we're dealing with a fox. I think he's gone north into the mountains.'

'I'm sure you're right, Captain,' Driker replied politely.

Lodtz glared at him. 'Don't give me that shit, Erik. What have you put your money on?'

Driker's lips twitched in a smile. 'I took a twenty-to-one long shot, sir. I always did like outsiders.'

'Which is?'

'The loop road that runs down to Valebru from Annolsetrene.'

Lodtz peered at the map, grunted and slapped it with the back of his hand, grinning at Driker. 'The north road. You're not as stupid as you look, Driker. I've always said so. Now how fast can we cut across country to the edge of Valebru?'

Driker looked up at the sky, across to the rising ranks of pine covered hills, then down at the map. 'Two hours on the run will just about warm the lads up, sir. Especially if we pick up ski trails.'

Lodtz nodded, glanced at his watch. 'All right, get over to Lieutenant Niemens and work out a route with him. Call in the other company commanders if there's any problem. I'll be with the radio.'

The radio operator's name was Lichter, a young man with

dark unruly hair and ears big enough to dwarf the earphones. He was speaking loudly into the microphone when the Captain reached him, repeating the grid reference for their position. Lodtz tapped him on the shoulder and he quickly passed the earphones and microphone to him.

'This is Stronghold,' said Lodtz. 'What is your position?'

The voice that came back was faint and blurred by static so that he had to strain to make out the words. 'Eagle One to Stronghold. Am clear of Lillehammer heading low along main road to Gudbrands Valley. Will be above you in four minutes. Over.'

'Is there any sign of the convoy so far?'

'Nothing, Stronghold. I made three passes low over the town and saw no large group of trucks. The road below me is empty apart from small local traffic.'

'All right, swing right over the river as soon as you have cleared the town of Tretten. We are fifteen kilometres beyond Fevang.'

'Thank you, Stronghold. This is Eagle One. Out.'

Lodtz pulled the earphones down around his neck and settled down to watch the valley to the east. The sky was cloudy, but there was no mist. He felt the tension building in him. They still had the afternoon to find Barrington and his trucks, but once darkness fell they would have lost him.

Lichter suddenly stiffened and pointed towards the east. A faint drone began to build into the distinctive howl of the Focke-Wulf 189. A moment later it had lifted into sight above the trees along the ridge, climbing into the sky above. The aircraft was fast and sleek, its twin booms and twin engines making it the fastest fighter reconnaissance aircraft in the world.

'Hello, Stronghold, this is Eagle One. I have you beneath me. Over.'

Lodtz lifted the microphone to his mouth. 'We see you, Eagle One. Will you head due north about five kilometres beyond this range of hills until you come to a mountain road heading east. Follow the road to grid reference Alpha four-nine, then report. Stronghold out.'

'Heading for grid reference Alpha four-nine. Out.'

The aircraft banked beneath the cloud and went into a shallow dive towards the pine forest across the road. In two minutes it had vanished over the far off ridges. Lodtz sat and tried not to look at his watch. The convoy had to be in those mountains, probably doubling back right now. He gripped the microphone, wondering why the observer had not reported.

'Hello Stronghold,' said the voice, as though reading his mind. 'We have the road, heading east through pretty thick forest. No sign of life, though. Over.'

Lodtz licked dry lips and gazed at the map, a cold wind of fear going through him as he saw the endless valleys and dark ringed peaks. If Barrington was not on that road they would have to search every mountain track between Lillehammer and the Glomma River. It would take days.

'Eagle One, this is Stronghold. Head due east to the village of Annolsetrene. Grid reference Beta five-zero. Over.'

'Heading east. Grid reference Beta five-zero. Out.'

The Captain sat gazing towards the distant hills, listening to static and cursing the woman who saw them land, the private who failed to kill her and the British colonel who should have doubled back into Lodtz's trap.

'Stronghold, this is Eagle One. We are over flying a small village where the road turns south. There is no convoy. Over.'

Lodtz gazed at the map with eyes that smarted and blurred with angry frustration burning in him. Where the hell could he be? What kind of game was he playing?

'Stronghold, do you read? Over.'

'Yes, Eagle One. I read. What is your height?'

'One thousand feet above local ground. Over.'

'Go up to three thousand and circle a radius of ten kilometres. There may be another road heading west in the valley below Store Kvien Mountain. Grid reference Gamma two-nine. Over.'

'Circling to three thousand. Grid reference Gamma two-nine. Out.'

He had to wait again, his mouth dry and the cold seeping up through his legs to join the icy weight in his stomach. '*The Führer himself has asked to be kept informed.*' The words howled in his brain, a chorus of accusing voices that sang the sentence again and again until it had its own rhythm, like some demented canticle.

There was movement beside him and he glanced round to see Driker, eyes hooded, concealing his thoughts. 'We're ready to move, Captain,' he said, softly. 'Just waiting for the word.'

Lodtz glanced down the hill to the slope along the ridge. The men were in their skis, packs on their backs, forming twin columns of hooded white figures. They looked like an army of ghosts waiting for a war.

Eagle One to Stronghold. We can see a road west of us. It seems to link up with the road going north to Annolsetrene. Over.'

'Thankyou, Eagle One. Follow the road west and stay with it if it turns south. Over.'

'Eagle One turning west.'

Lodtz looked at his hand, wondering why it was so numb. The fingers were chalk white, wrapped tightly around the microphone, the tips bloodless and almost frozen. He opened them with difficulty and slipped on his mitten, avoiding Driker's sympathetic glance.

'Stronghold, this is Eagle One. We have your convoy. Twenty trucks, heading south along narrow road through pine forest. Estimate they are two hours from Valebru. Do you need any interception? Over.'

Lodtz closed his eyes and took a deep breath, the exhilaration rising up and threatening to choke him with its intensity. 'Stronghold to Eagle One. We require no interception. Return to base. Stronghold out.'

Lodtz handed the microphone to the radio operator and got to his feet, gazing down at the columns of men. The Sergeant watched him, a smile on his lips.

'You just won your bet, Sergeant,' said Lodtz. 'And I think I've just won fifty tonnes of gold.'

6

The village of Borgas nestled in the fold of a wooded hillside at the head of a small valley through which flowed the river Imsa. In summer the logging camps were busy felling acres of trees to drag them along narrow trails behind horses, or float them down the Imsa to the saw mills at Imsenden. In summer people came from Sweden and Denmark to walk the hills and canoe the rivers, lakes and fjords, staying at the chalet style hotels perched on ridges or crouching in valleys which turned fast-running rivers into broad and gentle strands of water.

In the winter the rivers and fjords froze and the forest-covered hills attracted only the most dedicated cross-country skiers. The villages went into hibernation, the hotels closed, and most nights all lights were out by nine o'clock. The snow fell in thick blankets that festooned the trees, iced the roofs and frosted window panes.

Borgas was slightly different from other villages for the men continued to fell timber after the snow came, either stacking it on the slopes below the village or trekking logs by horse to the saw mill at Annolsetrene. The hotel on the pine-capped ridge above the village was closed, however, and would not open until early May when the snow had gone. Indeed, many people were wondering if it would open at all this year for the Hansens, who owned it, always spent winter with their parents in Denmark. Since last week that had been German occupied territory and no one knew what was going to happen, least of all the Constable who functioned as mayor, police chief and justice of the peace.

When the convoy of British trucks arrived in the square

with its natural spring, now frozen, bubbling from black stone in gleaming rivulets of ice, Constable Jan Hever was just recovering from a lunch of herring in Madeira, country cheese and home cured ham, wholemeal bread and dill pickles. Such a meal required washing down with a minimum of three bottles of lager supported by a glass or two of aquavit. It had been a most pleasant lunch, eaten before the log fire in the village store that smelled so richly of marjoram and dill, of matured cheese and freshly churned butter, of rye biscuits hanging in loops from the old beams, and of Mrs Jacobsen who served him lunch twice a week with hopes of making it a more permanent arrangement.

The convoy of trucks stretched from the square, which was little more than a widening of Kristiansen Street to make room for a grey wooden church and the village hall which served as both school and cinema, to the three-storey redwood house facing Lanikor's garage. Beyond those properties was a wide expanse of snow, then forest all the way to Annolsetrene.

Barrington's convoy made the village of Borgas seem ridiculously small, taking up as it did the only street and dwarfing some of the older single storey homes along the way. The entire school population, some thirty children ranging from six to fourteen, came whooping out into the square to gaze in awe at the heavy trucks still simmering from the climb. A few women stepped out of their doorways to watch, but only Constable Hever actually approached the soldiers.

Lieutenant Colonel Barrington met him half way along the line of trucks, smiling gravely and accepting his formal salute before shaking him by the hand. He expected language to be a problem, but was pleasantly surprised when the Constable spoke in halting English.

'You have the wrong road, Colonel,' he said, gesturing ahead. 'Beyond the square the road goes around the hill and up to the Varennes Hotel, but no further. I am afraid we are, how you say, the dead end.'

'Just the sort of place we need, Constable,' Barrington said cheerfully. 'You see we have something of a problem.'

The Colonel took him by the arm and steered him round to the rear of the truck, pulling back the flap to show him the grey cases with the black stencilled words and the royal crest. With bulging eyes the Constable took in the number of cases, then stepped back to look up and down the line of trucks before turning back to Barrington.

'It can only be one thing,' he said finally. 'But why here? In Borgas?'

Barrington explained about the German commandos, the change of plan, the need to protect the gold at all costs. Within minutes the large iron bell in the church steeple was sounding out over the rooftops, bringing in the men from the forest. The Colonel watched them arrive with interest. They were cheerful, relaxed individuals wearing heavy cord trousers tucked into woollen socks just below the knee. They wore sweaters and thick jackets or fur-lined anoraks, and their faces had the ruddy glow of health from working in the open. Their ages ranged from eighteen to middle and late forties, but there were older men who came from houses in the village in answer to the bell. In all there were almost a hundred, but only about sixty were capable of the work Barrington had in mind.

Lars, logging boss and joint owner with Mrs Tollinson of the only bar in Borgas, translated for those who were unable to understand the Colonel. The discussion ranged from open scepticism that the Germans were dropping into the area by parachute, to positive assurances that the gold would be safe in Borgas until the Nazis were driven out of Norway.

'That's not really the problem,' Barrington said politely, waiting for Lars to translate loudly and with some embellishments. 'The invasion has happened far sooner than either of our governments imagined. At this moment I don't know what the situation is at Trondheim, or Lillehammer for that matter, and with the main coastal road being blocked by paratroops I need to put the gold into a safe place.

'And then what, Colonel?' asked Constable Hever. 'They are saying that Norway will be fully occupied by the Germans within a week.'

'I doubt it,' replied Barrington. 'I'm sure my country will do something, probably with French help. And then there will be your own people. There will be an underground movement, a network of communication and supplies. Once these things exist we can get the gold to the coast and out to a ship. It's only a matter of weeks.'

Tania Arlberg appeared on the edge of the crowd with an elderly man Barrington took to be the doctor she had gone to see when they arrived. Her arm was in a sling and though she was pale her eyes were bright and she was smiling at the villagers, answering their questions as she moved towards Barrington.

'This is Doctor Olaf Jansen,' she announced, eyes twinkling. 'He slapped my bottom when I was born and he's been shouting at me ever since.'

Doctor Jansen shook his head in mock despair. 'She is a hopeless case, this one. I am not at all surprised that she was one of the first casualties of the war.'

Barrington grinned. 'How is she?'

'The wound is clean and through the soft part of the upper arm. She has lost a good deal of blood, but provided she goes to bed and stays in bed for at least three days, there should be no complications.'

'Go to bed,' Barrington told her. 'We are enormously grateful for your help, but you must now do what the doctor tells you.'

'I want to know what is happening,' she said cheerfully. 'Have they agreed?'

'You see,' said the doctor. 'My advice means nothing.'

Tania linked her arm through his and kissed him on the cheek. He gazed up at the sky in mock despair.

Lars turned from a group of men who had been in deep discussion, the Constable clearly not wishing to take part in the decision. 'Colonel, we are in agreement with you that it is necessary to hide the gold until you are sure the route is safe. We will take it down the hill to the log camp and store it beneath the logs until you are ready to move it again.'

'Splendid,' replied Barrington. 'As soon as it is unloaded the convoy will travel back to Valebru and then onto the main Dombas road.'

Lars looked puzzled and translated for the others. They gazed at Barrington with baffled expressions.

'It's necessary that there is no trace of the convoy in this area,' he explained. 'If the trucks move on it will divert attention from your village.'

'But who will be responsible for the gold?' asked Constable Hever with a worried expression.

'I shall,' replied Barrington. 'I will remain with the gold in your village until we have made new arrangements.'

There were nods of approval around the circle of faces, then Tania was smiling up at him from beneath golden eyelashes that caught the afternoon sun like butterfly wings.

'I think it's a wonderful idea, Colonel Barrington. I can show you the mountains and teach you how to speak Norwegian.'

Barrington gave her a wry smile. 'I'm not really planning to stay here that long, Miss Arlberg. And I seem to recall that you have orders to go to bed for at least three days.'

Her eyes twinkled. 'Then you must promise to come and see me.'

He made no reply, going through the crowd to Sergeant-Major Carver who was standing beside the line of trucks surrounded by the NCOs. He looked relieved as Barrington approached, beginning to snap to attention.

'At ease, Sergeant-Major,' Barrington said quickly. 'I want these trucks unloaded in double quick time, then you're to get the convoy out of here back onto the Dombas-Trondheim road from Valebru.'

'So you're leaving it here, sir?'

'It's the safest course. I shall stay and contact London

within the next few days. When you reach Trondheim you'll find one of our destroyers standing by. Inform the Captain that I had to abandon the present plan.'

'Right, sir.' Sergeant-Major Carver cleared his throat, looking at the trucks with a thoughtful expression. 'You think Jerry will still have a go at us?'

Barrington hesitated for a moment, then nodded slowly. 'Yes. I think the chances are that they'll stop you before you reach Trondheim.'

Carver grinned, eyes gleaming beneath bushy brow. 'My feeling too, sir. We'll be expecting them. The lads are itching for a crack at the bastards.'

'Keep it simple, Sergeant-Major. As soon as you see that you're out-gunned, put down your arms and call it a day. When they realize you're not carrying the gold I imagine they'll lose interest.'

The Sergeant-Major looked disappointed. 'We could still make a fight of it, sir.'

Barrington's eyes grew cold and bright, like freshly struck flint, and his voice took on a resonance that straightened the Sergeant-Major's back and put another inch on his height. 'It was not meant as a suggestion, Sergeant-Major. My orders are that you do your utmost to get this convoy safely back to Trondheim. If attacked, you will assess the strength of the enemy and resist only if you have a real chance of success.'

'Sah!' snapped the Sergeant-Major, turning smartly to the NCO's who had been listening to the Colonel's orders with varying shades of relief. 'You heard the Colonel. Let's get the vehicles unloaded and on their way. *I mean now, Barker*!'

Barrington acknowledged his salute, watching him march along the line of trucks, his voice crackling in the brisk air like splintering ice, rising now and then to a shrill crescendo as some unfortunate soldier failed to move at an acceptable speed. There was a hand on his elbow and he turned to find Lars with two young men.

'Colonel, there is a small logging camp about a kilometre north of the village. There are many stacks of timber at this time of year and these would be good places to hide the gold.'

It sounds ideal,' agreed Barrington. 'But that's a long way to carry five tonnes of the stuff.'

Lars grinned. 'We drag them, sir, by horse. The way we haul the timber.'

'Splendid.' Barrington slapped his shoulder, looking relieved. 'You take charge of it. We want them out of sight as soon as possible.'

Lars looked at the lowering sky, sniffed at the air. 'It will snow soon. An hour, perhaps two. We will have it at the camp by then.'

The Norwegian moved away, calling instructions to the groups of men standing in the street. Barrington started towards Constable Hever only to find Tania Arlberg blocking his way. He managed his sternest expression.

'I have a great deal to do, Miss Arlberg.'

'I know. That's why I arranged your accommodation.'

'Well that really wasn't necessary.'

'It's a small village. Someone had to put you up and that meant getting a room ready.'

Barrington forced a polite smile, but his eyes were glinting dangerously. 'Thank you, Miss Arlberg, but kindly trouble yourself no further on my account.'

'All right.' She shrugged, a mischievous smile lurking at the corners of her mouth. 'But don't you want to know where you're staying?'

'If you wouldn't mind.'

She gave him a small white card with an address. He barely had time to glance at it before she said: 'It's the doctor's house at the end of the street. I'm staying there too, so you'll be able to visit me after all.'

She turned and walked away, her blonde hair flowing as she tossed her head with just a hint of triumph. Barrington gazed after her in exasperation, then went to look for

Constable Hever. Beside each truck the cases of gold were piled into neat stacks. It was a formidable task for Lars who was already marshalling groups of men along the line of trucks.

The distant drone of an aircraft had been intruding on his thoughts for more than a minute when he realized that it was not fading away as one would expect. It rose and fell, echoing in the hills, buzzing like some determined mosquito returning again and again to torment the object of its curiosity. And that was what that aircraft was doing, he decided. It was crossing and recrossing the area, searching for something.

He moved quickly to Sergeant-Major Carver who was talking to a group of his men at the head of the convoy. As soon as he saw Barrington he snapped to attention, snarling at the men who were slow to follow his example.

'Sergeant-Major, I want you and your men out of here in double quick time.'

'Sah,' replied Carver, then added hesitantly. 'I-ah, I was just sorting out a meal for the men before we left, sir.'

'An excellent idea,' said Barrington, 'if it wasn't for the aircraft that's been buzzing around for the past few minutes.'

'Aircraft, sir?' Carver cocked his head, looking mildly sceptical, then frowning as he heard the distant drone.

'It could be a German reconnaissance aircraft trying to locate us. If that's the case I don't want you anywhere near this village. Get the trucks moving, make as much speed as you can and try to keep under tree cover until you're back to the main Dombas road.'

'As you say, sir,' said Carver, looking as though he would have liked a debate on the subject.

Barrington was already turning away, moving along the snow-covered pavement towards the uniformed figure of Constable Hever. The Sergeant-Major sighed and turned to his NCOs. 'You heard him, lads. Back on the road.'

'What the 'ell's he frightened of, Sergeant-Major?' asked a

corporal with big ears and butterfly teeth. 'We've done nowt but run since we saw a couple of parachutes.'

'Not for us to question why, Corporal,' Carver replied. 'We're decoys now. A line of Donald Ducks playing tag with Jerry. Something to tell your kids about when you get back to Blighty . . . except they'll never believe you!'

Five minutes later the convoy pulled out of Borgas, heading south towards Annolsetrene where they would take the mountain road down to Valebru. Barrington watched them go with mixed feelings, wondering whether he should have stayed with the men. The closest any of them had been to action was the regimental exercises at Catterick.

He sighed and shook his head as the last truck disappeared into the trees. He wished now that he had stressed the need for caution, that he had explained just how good a German commando unit was likely to be.

7

Wolf Lodtz lay in a shallow snow trench with his white hood pulled low across his forehead, his goggles frosted by the cold, a white scarf across his mouth and tucked into the hood of his parka. A light snow had been falling for the past half hour, effectively obliterating their ski tracks and covering their packs with a feathery down. On either side of the road which passed through the neck of the small valley east of Valebru his three companies were deployed, twin arcs of firepower that would close in a pincer movement on the entire convoy.

Even now, knowing where his men were positioned, it was almost impossible to distinguish them. He looked at his watch, brushing powder snow from the face, astonished to see that it was not yet three o'clock. It seemed an age since they took off from Kiel, yet it was barely nine hours ago.

'Captain!'

He turned, seeing the craggy features of Sergeant Driker poised above his mound of snow, his head tilted in a listening attitude. A moment later he heard the distant murmur of heavy trucks rising steadily as they came out of a fold in the valley and turned towards the steeply rising gradient of the pass.

He removed his mittens, ignoring the numbing bite of the cold, worked the bolt action two or three times before folding down the tubular steel stock. He had taped two 32-round magazines end to end for quick changing and he checked them again before working a 9mm cartridge into the breech. It was a magnificent weapon, superbly engineered at the Erma-Wereke factory under the direction of Hugo

Schmeisser who had developed it from the MP38. The result was a machine pistol producing devastating fire power in the hands of a relatively small force of men. If any one thing was going to win the war, Wolf had frequently been heard to say, it was the Schmeisser machine pistol.

The trucks had begun to bunch together by the time they reached the crest of the hill, changing gear to enter the narrow section of road with steep banks rising up on either side. The thick blanket of snow concealed gullies and ridges, giving the effect of a smooth plain rising up to the skyline on either side where stands of pine trees cut out the light. The driver of the first truck was just turning to Sergeant-Major Carver to suggest a break once they were through the pass, when mortar shells burst in a perfect grouping in front and on either side.

'Good God!' said the Sergeant-Major as the windscreen shattered and blew into the cab. The driver made no reply, slumping forward over the wheel with a hole in his chest the size of a hand. Carver pulled the pistol from his belt and opened the door, dropping down to the snow-covered road as another series of mortar shells exploded further along the convoy.

There seemed to be bullets everywhere, tearing ragged lines across the packed snow, rattling against the side of the trucks like hail. Only as he began to get his bearings did he locate the enemy positions and for the first time he felt a wave of apprehension. They were on both sides, rising up in terraced rows so that every man had a clear line of fire. Yet the soldiers blended perfectly into the snow, their white combat outfits making them a difficult target even if they were standing up. Everywhere he looked stubby muzzles were spitting brilliant shards of light and the air was filled with the crack and whine of bullets.

'You fiendish bastards,' he bellowed, rolling out from his position beside the wheel of the truck and firing a series of shots at the hillside above as he ran along the convoy, crouching down to reload, bellowing for support. Bodies sprawled in ungainly attitudes along the line of trucks, crimson streaks and patches beside them. One or two were moving, but not many. He ran on, rage and despair threatening to choke him as men he had known for years gazed up at him with blind, dead eyes.

The Germans had them in the perfect crossfire, above and angled, so as men tumbled from the rear of the trucks they were mown down without even getting a chance to aim their rifles. The rear truck was in flames, hit by a mortar shell, effectively blocking any attempt to turn back. Heedless of the bullets that searched for him like angry bees, Sergeant-Major Carver reached a point midway along the convoy where a group of four men lay under the trucks beginning to return fire. He sprawled beside them, recognising Corporal James and Private Parker.

'How many more towards the rear?' he snapped.

Parker looked at him with a face so white he thought he was going to vomit. 'Just a couple, Sarge. No more than a couple.'

Carver closed his eyes and took long, deep breaths. He felt on the edge of madness. Three minutes ago he had been in command of forty five men. He tried again, forcing his voice to remain calm. 'Corporal James?'

James lowered his rifle and drew back behind the wheel. 'Yes, Sergeant-Major?'

'We must rally everyone to this point and then attempt to reach the rear of the convoy. Are there many men firing from the trucks?'

Corporal James gave him a despairing look and gestured towards the trucks behind them. 'Anyone alive in those, Sarge, is either bullet proof or Jesus Christ!'

'But . . .' The Sergeant-Major wiped sweat from his brow only to realize it was blood. He felt for the wound, finding a deep groove over his left eyebrow which immediately began to throb. He tried to collect his thoughts, feeding fresh bullets into his pistol until he was calm. There was only an occasional burst of machine gun fire from the hillside. 'There are bound to be more. I only saw ten, perhaps fifteen bodies.'

'There's just as many on this side,' said Parker, his voice shrill. 'And they haven't even used a grenade yet.'

'Jesus Christ!' Said Carver. 'They didn't give us a chance. Not a sodding chance.'

He leaned out, firing in blind rage up the hill. Bullets rattled along the side of the truck, struck the snow an inch from his face. He drew back, his heart thumping in his throat.

'You notice how they're leaving the tyres alone?' said Corporal Parker. 'The crafty bastards want the trucks. That's why they won't use grenades.'

'Right then,' said the Sergeant-Major, 'that gives us a chance. We'll double back to the lead truck and make a break for it. Four hundred yards will have us out of the crossfire and into the pass.'

They gazed at him in disbelief. 'Sarge, even if we got to the truck they wouldn't give us time to put it in gear.'

'He's right,' said Corporal James. 'And don't get me wrong, Sarge, but the Colonel did say to throw it in if we were outnumbered.'

With a bitter curse Carver leaned out from the wheel and bellowed along the line of trucks in a voice that echoed up and down the confines of the valley. 'This is Sergeant-Major Carver. You will cease fire. I repeat. Cease fire.'

There was a single shot from the rear of the convoy, then silence. A moment later a voice spoke with a pronounced German accent. The very sound of it made the Sergeant-Major quiver with rage.

'Sergeant-Major Carver, you will throw out your weapons and stand by the truck with your hands placed on the top of the heads. You have only one minute to obey this order.'

They crawled out and stood facing the truck with their hands flat on their heads. Two privates appeared from beneath a truck further along, then a sergeant and a driver from beneath another. Five men with serious wounds emerged from inside the trucks, but that was it. Almost with disbelief Carver counted and recounted. Only when the Germans had checked every truck did he accept that thirty two men were dead.

'You may turn round, Sergeant-Major.'

He turned to find a slim man of medium build with sharp blue eyes and blond hair cut short. He wore a white combat outfit like the rest of his men, the hood pushed back. The ribbon on his right arm denoted that he was a captain.

'Yes, Captain?' said the Sergeant-Major.

'A pity so many of your men died,' the German said in a sympathetic voice, opening a gold cigarette case and offering it to him. 'Unfortunately this was my men's first engagement and they were somewhat over-enthusiastic.'

'You mean they behaved like bloody murderous animals,' snapped Carver. 'You mean that once they had the smell of blood in their nostrils they couldn't be stopped!'

'Why should they stop?' asked Lodtz. 'As long as you were firing back at us, there was no reason to stop.'

A squat, dark-haired man with a sergeant's stripes on his arm came up to the Captain and shook his head, his mouth small and worried. The officer lit a cigarette, inhaled and exhaled, then gazed at the Sergeant-Major with regret.

'I am afraid that time is of critical importance to this operation, and as a soldier I am sure you appreciate the significance of this attack on your convoy. We have no time for elegant conversations, for subterfuge or deception. I require from you, immediately, the location of the cargo you were carrying.

'Our only cargo was soldiers, most of whom you have brutally murdered.'

Lodtz dropped his cigarette into the snow and ground it beneath his foot. The Sergeant beside him was grim, his eyes small beads of worry. A line of German soldiers faced the prisoners, the machine pistols aimed steadily at them.

'I ask you once more, Sergeant-Major, and repeat that I have no time to argue or interrogate. Where is your cargo?'

'I've told you.'

Lodtz turned to Sergeant Driker and indicated the nearest prisoner, a driver who was untidy and overweight, his trousers damp and sagging from having to scramble in the snow. 'Kill him.'

Driker swallowed nervously, gazing at his Captain with uncertain eyes. Lodtz stared back without a flicker of emotion. The Sergeant cleared his throat and gestured to the nearest guard, a stocky man in his early thirties.

'Carry out the Captain's order, Private Essen.'

The man nodded and tilted the Schmeisser, firing a short burst that ripped through the horrified soldier's chest, slamming him back against the truck where he hung for a moment, blood gurgling in his throat as the last breath left him, before he pitched forward to lie twitching on the ground.

It was a full minute before the Sergeant-Major could speak. His face was suffused with blood, his mouth twisted with disgust. 'You murdering bastard!' he exclaimed.

'I have to locate that gold before dark,' Lodtz said calmly. 'It will take hours to break you with normal methods of interrogation. I repeat, Sergeant-Major, where did you leave the gold?'

Carver looked along the line of shocked men, his mouth drying out with the full horror of the situation. The next man was Private Parker, staring straight ahead with frozen features. Even as the Sergeant-Major gazed at him in despair, the machine pistol fired again and bullets tore into the soldier, hammering him back against the truck where he hung, gasping a curse. A second burst sent him to the ground in a lifeless bundle.

'For Christ's sake, Sarge, it isn't even our gold,' said Corporal James, with trembling lips.

Carver turned back to Lodtz, his face suddenly lined and old. 'We left the cases of bullion in the village of Borgas,' he said in a flat, empty voice. 'What they did with them I do not know.'

'And Lieutenant Colonel Barrington?'

The Sergeant-Major's head came up at the mention of the officer's name. He hesitated, then nodded. 'Yes, he stayed with the gold.' He paused, measuring his words, underlining them with utter contempt. 'But when he learns what has happened here today, Captain, neither Colonel Barrington, nor the British Government, nor the people of Norway will rest until you and your men are hanged for murder.'

Lodtz blinked, his face paling with the full import of the Sergeant-Major's words. He started to turn away, then changed his mind. 'This is a time of war, Sergeant-Major, and I have my orders.'

'I don't believe you have orders to commit cold blooded murder, Captain. And that's what they'll hang you for.'

Lodtz turned and walked away from the trucks, Driker following. They passed Lieutenants Niemens on the way, but he turned his back and put binoculars to his eyes, as though studying the ridges above. When they were clear of the convoy Lodtz stopped and gazed at the ground, rubbing his mouth nervously.

'I did what I had to, Erik,' he said after a moment.

'I know that, sir.'

'You beat them until they are unconscious and then you wait until they come round and beat them again. We have less than an hour of daylight left.'

'You are right, Captain.'

Lodtz pinched the bridge of his nose tightly, closing his eyes, his face suddenly tormented. 'You think it is true, Erik? You think it was murder?'

Driker stirred snow with the toe of his boot. Lodtz opened his eyes and stared at him, a hint of fear showing just for a moment. 'This is war. Total war.'

'Yes, Captain.'

'Then . . .?'

'The British will say it is murder.' Driker cleared his throat, looking at the ground. 'If they live to talk about it.'

Lodtz turned slowly and gazed back along the convoy. Five wounded men and seven others stood in a group beside the road watched by guards. He tried to think clearly, assessing the situation as though it was simply a tactical manoeuvre.

'All the bodies would need to be buried.'

Driker nodded, gesturing to the steep sides of the pass. 'A small avalanche, a few hundred tons of rocks. It would not be difficult.'

'You would take care of it, Erik?'

'It has to be done, Captain.'

Lodtz took a deep breath and nodded his head. 'All right. The rest of us will leave for Borgas. You remain with six men and one of the trucks. If you wish I will give you a signed order?'

'No Captain.' Driker gazed at him sadly. 'There is no need to write anything down.'

Lodtz straightened, nodded, turned to move back towards the convoy. Driker remained where he was, aware of the sky and the trees and the snow, yet totally removed from them. It was as though he was in a separate dimension, observing events without being a part of them. He watched the Captain hesitate and look back, his expression still troubled.

'I appreciate this, Erik.'

Sergeant Driker stepped back into the real world and made a small, dismissive gesture. 'There is no other way.'

Afterwards, when the trucks were pulling away filled with the jubilant ranks of Lodtz's Sky Wolves, Driker tried to analyse his overpowering sense of doom. It was as though part of him knew that he had taken a fateful step which would lead inexorably to disaster, yet knowing it made no difference at all. He was already locked into a new destiny, a new future.

He beckoned to the six men he had chosen and walked slowly across the road to the group of British soldiers sitting on groundsheets smoking cigarettes. The Sergeant-Major saw it in his eyes when they stopped and gave a strangled curse, trying to get to his feet. But the bullets beat them all down, stifling their cries of rage and fear.

When it had been done Driker told the men where to hide the bodies and sat in the truck while they did it. It took an hour and he spent the time trying to understand how the war had brought him to this point in less than a single day.

8

He had been dreaming about India again; about the hill station at Ranikhet with its cool winds and magnificent views over the plains of Ramnager. He had been on the verandah of his bungalow, watching the dying sun set fire to the plains below. Elizabeth had been beside him, reading one of the latest books to arrive from England. The air was heavy with the scent of lotus, and the night chorus of cricket, mosquito and reverberating bull frogs was beginning to rise around them. He stretched, turning towards her to watch the glow of the sun heighten the planes of her cheeks. It was a lovely face, small and finely moulded with the brownest of eyes and a long, graceful neck embraced by folds of chestnut hair. She sensed his gaze and closed the book, lifting her eyes and smiling gravely.

'Yes, Charles?'

The scene splintered and became the dark, empty void of a strange room in Norway.

'Colonel Barrington, wake up, please. Colonel Barrington?'

The voice was vaguely familiar, but in the darkness he could only make out the outline of a face. He sat up, taking a deep breath, his mind clearing as he remembered where he was. The voice was obviously that of Doctor Jansen.

'I'm sorry,' he said. 'Dreaming, I'm afraid.'

'You have two minutes to dress and leave the house, Colonel. Use the back stairs and leave quietly through the kitchen. Lars will be waiting for you outside by an old shed I use as a store room. He will take you to the church.'

Barrington swung his legs off the bed, reaching for the clothes he had placed over a chair. 'I gather there is a reason for this, Doctor?'

'Forgive me, Colonel. The village is full of Germans. They arrived in your trucks about five minutes ago and appear to be searching every house. The Commandant has ordered all men between eighteen and sixty-five to parade in the square in ten minutes.'

'Is there any sign of my men?' asked Barrington, feeling a chill of alarm.

'I don't know, Colonel. I think not.'

Barrington pulled on his trousers, favouring the left leg, feeling for his socks and boots in the dark. The Germans could have left them to march to the nearest town, he decided. All they were concerned with was locating the gold.

'What about Miss Arlberg?' he asked, slipping on his greatcoat. 'If they realize that's a bullet wound?'

'I've already thought of that,' replied the Doctor. 'As soon as you're out of here I'll perform a small miracle with a pillow, ten metres of bandage and my housekeeper's night-dress. As far as the Germans are concerned, Miss Arlberg will be very fat and very pregnant.'

'Fine. I'll get in touch through Lars.'

He found the Doctor's hand in the darkness and shook it, then went out of the door and along the narrow passage towards the rear of the house. In the street outside he could hear shouts and the roaring of truck engines and even as he reached the kitchen there was a knock on the door at the front of the house. He carefully lifted the latch, easing open the door, searching the darkened yard until he could see the outline of the store room. He moved towards it, freezing as a hand caught him by the elbow, the silver topped cane swinging to shoulder height as he turned.

'It's Lars, Colonel,' said the voice.

He grunted, relaxing as the tall Norwegian stepped closer so that he could make out his features. 'Speak before contact next time,' he said shortly. 'That way we don't start hacking each other to pieces.'

'The Germans have men all around the town and at each end of the main street,' he told him as they began to move carefully across the yard to a gate in the fence. 'I'm not sure that we can reach the church.'

'Have to,' replied the Colonel. 'I'm not kitted out for shussing cross-country, and once Jerry gets on top of the situation he'll cover every house and alley. The best chance is now.'

Lars hesitated, listening to the night, then stepped through the gate and motioned for him to follow. They went across some waste ground blanketed by snow, then between the blacksmith's and a white stone cottage that jutted out at the corner of the square. Beyond it, on the other side of the square, was the grey bulk of the church with its lead-covered steeple and blackened oak doors. There were six trucks in the square with their engines running and headlights on, effectively illuminating the entire area. Everywhere they looked there were figures in white with machine pistols and grenades.

'You see, Colonel,' said Lars. 'There are hundreds.'

'Why the church?' asked Barrington, watching the figures as they lined up men from the village who had begun to appear, most of them complaining bitterly at the hour.

'There is a hideaway. An old cellar beneath the altar. They would never find it.'

'Can I get down on my own?'

'Yes. The altar has a cloth hanging down to the floor. Lift it at the rear and you will find a loose slab of stone. It slides to the side and there are steps below. You can slide it back once you are inside.'

'All right. You head out into the square, between the first two trucks, then when the soldiers begin to push you towards the others play drunk and start getting rough.'

Lars grinned. 'Maybe even punch one or two in the mouth?'

'Don't get too carried away. They're likely to lay you out with a gun butt.'

'Take care, Colonel. And don't worry about our gold. There is no man in this village who would talk this side of hell.'

Barrington grinned and slapped his shoulder, watching him step out into the light and begin a shambling walk towards the nearest group of Germans. He edged into the deeper shadows in the doorway of a house, holding his cane tightly, gauging the distance he would have to run.

The Germans turned towards Lars, gesturing towards the growing line of men on the far side of the square. Lars shook his head and spoke loudly in Norwegian, his mouth twisting with contempt as a stocky Sergeant reached for his arm. Within seconds the scene was transformed into chaos. Lars grabbed the Sergeant's arm and swung him round into the two men on the other side. All three slipped and fell in the snow, then with a howl of glee Lars was charging a group of ten soldiers, head down, arms flailing.

Barrington began to run, taking long strides with his stiff left leg swinging beneath him like a pivot. Half way across he was clearly visible in the light of the truck headlamps, but everyone was looking towards Lars who had knocked two soldiers to the ground and was struggling furiously with four more. There was a narrow gap between two buildings and he ran for it, not knowing if there was a fence or some kind of obstacle in his path. In the square every soldier seemed to be running towards Lars until someone clubbed him behind the ear and sent him to the ground where he lay senseless. But Barrington was into the darkness between the buildings, already moving round towards the rear of the grey stone church.

He found a side door open and slipped inside, standing quietly for a moment until he was sure the place was empty. He crossed the flagged floor and turned down the aisle to the altar where he lifted the heavy brocade cloth as Lars had directed. The flagged floor seemed unbroken and he had a moment's doubt as he felt for some handhold, but he found a raised edge with sufficient purchase to exert pressure. In a moment the stone slab had slid aside and he was able to lower himself through the opening onto cold steps. He slid back the stone slab and lit a match, finding with some relief that the room was furnished with a bunk bed, a table, and even a supply of candles.

He lay down on the hard mattress that smelled of decay and pulled the greatcoat around him, pushing his hands deep into the pockets and waiting for the warmth to seep through. The ease and speed with which the Germans had found and taken the village confirmed his earlier view that only a highly efficient commando force would be sent on such a mission. He wondered how the Sergeant-Major had fared, hoping they had not put up too much of a struggle before surrendering.

They were probably walking into Valebru right now, he told himself, cursing Jerry, the weather and fifty tonnes of Norwegian gold. He turned his thoughts to the men in the square above, wondering what the German Commander intended to do. It would take at least a week to interrogate the whole town, so he would probably select a few and subject them to intensive questioning.

Barrington fell asleep wondering what kind of a man the Commander was and just how intensive that questioning would be.

* * *

Outside the church, pacing along the rows of sullen men who had been standing in the snow for almost half an hour, Wolf Lodtz paused in front of Constable Hever and stared at him in icy silence. Hever gazed back, eyes wide and unblinking.

'And so you have never heard of gold bullion carried in a British convoy from Oslo?'

'No, Captain. If there ever was such a convoy it did not

pass through my village. As you can see, we are at the end of the road. Why should a convoy come here?'

Lodtz smiled and gave a mocking bow. 'It is good of you to be so helpful, Constable. It had not occurred to me that such a lonely, inaccessible spot as this would automatically rule it out as a hiding place.'

Hever stared straight ahead, his cheeks flushing as the Captain's voice filled with contempt.

'There is another way we can conduct this interview. I can, for instance, select a number of your women and line them up against the church and begin to shoot them until you tell us. Does that appeal to you, Constable?'

'That would be murder, Captain. Every man in these hills would not rest until he had killed at least ten of you. It would also be in violation of the terms offered by the German Commander in Oslo when he promised on the radio this evening, a peaceful and bloodless occupation of our country. I should think that a mere captain, murdering innocent civilians, would be executed by his own before we had a chance to hang him ourselves.'

It was the longest speech Constable Hever had made since the wedding of his daughter some five years before. The men behind and around him gazed at his ruddy features in astonishment, and then they began to nod their heads, to mutter approval. The murmurs built to a growl of anger, a chorus of determined support. It ceased abruptly as Lodtz struck Hever across the forehead with the barrel of his Luger.

The Constable went to his knees, the blow opening a deep gash that sent blood streaming down his face. A dozen soldiers on either side of the Captain cocked their Schmeissers and aimed at the angry rows of men.

'The next man who challenges my authority will be shot,' he said harshly.

There was silence. More than sixty men ranging from the youngest eighteen-year-old to the grizzled features of Hans Gelder, a man of sixty-four who ran the blacksmith's with his son, stared at the German Commander with varying degrees of contempt. The weight of their anger beat at him like physical contact, causing him to turn away before they recognized the uncertainty in him.

He walked slowly across the square, to the trucks rumbling in the cold night air, the brilliance of their headlights casting long shadows in the snow. There was a tightness in his temples, a sour taste of fear in his mouth. He wanted to try to explain why he had hit the Constable, why it was so important that his first mission was a success. But there was no one he could speak to. There was only a gnawing doubt in his mind, a growing sense of alarm at his own brutality.

There had been a time when it would have repelled him. In the early days, as a junior member of the Berlin *Sturmabteilungen*, he had been horrified by the violence and intimidation of the SA as they roamed the streets demanding allegiance to the Nazi Party. He remembered the great marches of '32, the mass meetings in Berlin, Munich and Frankfurt, when anyone who dared to voice a protest was beaten with the short wooden truncheons until he was a senseless bloody bundle on the ground.

His group leader had been a bullet-headed man with cropped fair hair and eyes like chips of blue Dresden china. His name had been Klaus Heinz and his favourite pastime was baiting intellectuals. Their group consisted of six men, working in pairs, watching for each other's signals and then moving in fast. In the winter of '32 they had been working the university district, looking for professors and lecturers who had refused to join the Nazi Party.

They caught a white-haired old man early one evening and dragged him into a cemetery behind the Museum of German History. He had a number of books under his arm, well-thumbed works by Goethe, Schiller and Brecht, and when Heinz accused him of being an intellectual he shook his head and said in a mild voice that he was merely a student of Germany's greatest philosopher, Immanuel Kant. Heinz knocked him to the ground, tore up his books and screamed abuse at him.

Each time the old man got to his feet and begged them to let him go home to his wife, Heinz demanded to know why he was not a member of the Nazi Party? Why he was not a loyal German? Why he was not reading *Mein Kampf*? The old man replied that he had read *Mein Kampf* in the week of its publication in 1924 and that, as a record of Hitler's struggle against the institutions of the state, it was an interesting work.

'You lie,' screamed Heinz, hitting him across the mouth with his truncheon. 'You are like all the bourgeois intellectuals, full of lies and treachery.'

The old man tried to speak but his mouth was full of blood and his teeth were broken. Lodtz watched the pathetic creature, disgusted by the sadistic pleasure on the faces of his companions. Heinz saw his look and motioned the others away.

'This one is for young Wolf,' he said quietly. 'It is time for him to put his mark on a traitor.'

They stood in a circle and watched him stand over the old man. After a minute he tried to turn away, making an awkward gesture to Heinz. 'He is too old,' he said.

'The older they are more trouble they have caused,' Heinz replied. 'He must pay.'

Wolf gazed at the faces around him, saw the tightening of mouths, the frowns of suspicion. He swung back to the old man and hit him across the head with his truncheon, hoping that he would fall unconscious and that would be an end to it. Instead he stood his ground, blood flowing from a gash above his eyebrow, his arm raised to ward off further blows. Wolf stepped closer, pulled down the man's arm and began to beat him frantically across the face and shoulders, ceasing only when he was slumped on his knees, sobbing, his features dreadfully bruised and bloody.

Hienz beamed and slapped him on the back, congratulating him on his performance. 'Never go in too strong,' he said. 'Work on them. A little here, a little there. As long as they're crying you've got their attention.'

Wolf felt sick when he looked at the bloody features of the man. His white hair was almost entirely crimson and most of his teeth appeared to have gone. He turned away, wanting to get back to his mother and sister, to feel the warmth of a fire, the security of his bed.

'Not yet,' said Heinz softly. 'We must finish him.'

Lodtz could only watch with revulsion as his companions crowded round the old man, kicking savagely with their heavy boots. Long after his choking cries and sobs had ceased the sickening thuds of the boots still sounded in the still, frosty air. Before they left the cemetery they draped his body over a marble cross. The inscription, carved at the turn of the century, read: 'The Lord works in mysterious ways.'

'Captain?'

The quiet voice of Lieutenant Niemens brought him out of his reverie and with a shock he saw that he was sitting on the steps of the church. He stood up quickly, his stomach lurching as he realized that he had no idea how long he had been there. Across the square the prisoners stood together in a sullen group. A cordon of soldiers were around them, others relaxing beside the trucks.

'Yes, Rolf?' he replied.

'The company commanders are waiting for orders, sir. I took the liberty of sending an advance party to the hotel. It could make a useful headquarters.'

'An hotel?' he replied in a surprised voice.

'It's closed for the winter, sir, but quite a useful size. About thirty rooms, positioned on a pine ridge about a quarter of a mile above the village.'

'Excellent, Niemens,' he said. 'I have been considering the best method of breaking these people. It must be done quickly, and, if possible, without serious physical injury.'

The Lieutenant cleared his throat nervously, looking around the square, then bending towards Lodtz with a vaguely apologetic air. 'With respect, my Captain, these people are not yet used to military occupation. In fact, it may be a week or more before our forces are in control of these hills.'

'So?'

'I merely point out, Captain, that any extreme actions by us could lead to retaliation both here and from surrounding villages.'

Lodtz snorted disdainfully. 'What villages? Annolsetrene is ten kilometres away, then it is a further thirty to Valebru. The Norwegian army is two hundred kilometres away, the city of Oslo has surrendered and now they have parades. No one is going to retaliate, Lieutenant. No one is going to do anything except sit by the fire and learn to speak German.'

Niemens mouth tightened and he nodded, beginning to turn away. Lodtz reached out and gripped his shoulder, smiling at the young officer. 'Don't worry, Rolf, there will be no extreme actions as you put it. Take all the men up to this hotel and lock them in the cellar. Make sure they are well guarded and then select four of our best interrogators.'

'And the rest of the villagers?' Niemens asked.

'Leave them alone. Carry out systematic searches every four hours until you find this English Colonel, but do nothing else to antagonise them. There is to be no contact with the prisoners, of course, and no explanation as to why we are holding them.'

Niemens nodded, beginning to look enthusiastic. 'It is a good plan, Captain.'

Lodtz nodded, lifting a finger and gazing at the Lieutenant with grim features. 'But let us make no mistake, Rolf. The men must be broken. The gold has been hidden and we must find it. Pick your men well and tell them to use every means of persuasion.'

Niemens saluted and turned away, moving to the bored groups of commandos huddled round the front of the trucks for warmth. In minutes they were dividing the prisoners between the trucks and starting out of the square up the narrow winding road to the Varennes Hotel. The sky was just beginning to lighten in the east and a fine powder snow was beginning to fall.

9

Barrington awoke to find a young woman of about nineteen gazing down at him with some consternation. Her hair was dark, cut short around the nape of her neck, and her eyes were wide and golden and designed for laughter. The oil lamp she held flickered and drew lines of worry across her face.

'Please, Colonel. Wake up.'

He sat up and stifled a groan as pain lanced through his stiff leg and across the small of his back. He grimaced, swinging his legs off the bed, trying to ignore the orchestrated spasms of pain that seemed to throb from every joint. Beyond the girl he could make out the outline of two other people standing by the stairs. He shielded his eyes against the bright light of the lamp, looking towards them. They moved closer in response to his interest and he began to make out two slim, attractive blondes in ski pants and anoraks. Neither of them appeared to be very pleased with him.

'Ladies,' he said, getting stiffly to his feet and stamping on the paved stone floor. 'It rather looks as though I overslept again.'

'It's seven o'clock, Colonel.'

'Ah,' he gave them a tight smile, 'that late.'

'We have to talk to you,' said the dark haired woman. 'I brought some food. Perhaps if we sit down and introduce ourselves.'

'A splendid idea,' he said, moving towards the table.

There was a basket containing a flask of coffee, some bread, cheese and a small jar of herring. He sat down and began to eat with relish, nodding cheerfully as the woman made the introductions.

'My name is Karen Helrop and this is Olga Morden,' she indicated the girl who had woken him. 'We are both from the village, but this is Michelle Argent from Cherbourg. She has been spending the winter here.'

Barrington drank some coffee, watching their grim faces. 'All right, what can I do for you?'

'Give us permission to hand over the gold.' Said Karen.

He speared a piece of cheese and considered it intently for a moment. When he spoke he tried to make his voice gentle and sympathetic. 'I have a duty both to your government and to mine. I know how difficult it must be, but I cannot grant your request. Not only that, if any one of you should go to the Germans with the location of the gold, you will be guilty of treason and brought to trial eventually.'

'We would not ever do such a thing,' said Olga, the words halting as she struggled with her basic English.

'They took all the men.' Karen said quietly. 'They took them from the square during the night and since then they have searched every house every hour. The only males in the village are eight old men, one almost ninety, and sixteen boys.'

'I'm sorry,' said Barrington. 'Do you know where?'

'The Hotel Varennes above the village. They have been working there all night, putting up barricades, stone platforms for machine guns. They also have some tube things that are in rows on the ridge above us.'

'Mortars,' Barrington explained. 'They fire small bombs. I imagine they have the square covered and the road approaching the village.'

'They will not let us see the men,' said Olga with wide, anxious eyes. 'I ask to see my brother and my father and they just tell me to go away.'

'Will they kill them?' asked Karen in an empty voice.

'I doubt that very much,' replied Barrington, wishing he knew what had happened to his own men.

'But they will torture them until someone tells about the gold.'

Barrington nodded, finishing the last of the cheese and pouring a second cup of coffee. He felt better, the aches subsiding to a dull memory of the pain. He studied the faces of the women, wondering how they would react in a crisis. Michelle seemed to read his mind.

'We want you to tell us what we should do.'

'Is there a telephone?' he asked.

'They cut the wire and took the receiver from the Post Office,' said Olga.

'Can you get to Annolsetrene?'

Karen hesitated for a moment, then shook her head. 'They have men beside the road, and from the hotel they can watch the paths behind the village. Perhaps at night, but with great difficulty.'

'Then there is nothing to be done in that direction for a while at least,' said Barrington. 'We will need information. Get as many of the women as possible to take food, clothing, books to the hotel for the prisoners and the Germans. Play it stupid. You don't know why they are here, but they should be comfortable. Make notes of everything you see. The number of soldiers, the positions of sentries, the kind of weapons they have, where they are placed. Find out the name of the commanding officer, the number of other officers. Every piece of information will be important and help us to decide what to do next.'

They looked at each other with lifting spirits. Olga gave a determined nod and gathered up the remains of the food, replacing them in the basket. There was still coffee in the flask so she left that with him.

'We will arrange for women to go all the morning. Those who speak English can visit the church to pray for their men and spend a few minutes down here with you.'

'It sounds a delightful arrangement,' smiled Barrington. 'I only hope the padre approves.'

'We don't have one,' said Karen. 'The village is too small,

too poor, too uninteresting. In the summer, and on special days, a minister comes from Valebru on a bicycle. He is not happy about the journey.'

'Perhaps it's just as well.'

'You still have not told us what to do about the gold,' said Michelle. 'It is what everyone wants to know.'

'We must protect it,' replied Barrington. 'At all costs.'

Karen's mouth twisted cynically. 'Don't you mean at the cost of our men.'

Barrington shook his head. 'This is a German field unit, they're not going to start shooting civilians without direct orders from Berlin. They'll interrogate, probably use physical methods, but no more than that.'

'Until someone breaks?' Karen pointed out. 'So why wait?'

'Because by the time someone does break I'll have moved the gold to another place.'

Olga gazed at him with huge, astounded eyes, then grimaced and tapped a finger against her forehead. 'You can tell why he is an officer, eh?' she said to her companions in Norwegian. 'All the time he has the answers.'

'So how will you move it?' Karen asked him, looking scornful.

'I'll need forty women with good backs and as many haversacks as you can find.'

'Why should we help?'

'Why shouldn't you?'

Olga gurgled happily and patted Karen on the head. 'He is right again. Come on, Karen, we can find forty women.' She turned to the Colonel. 'And then we go to the place?'

'Tonight, after midnight. We must move five hundred cases, one at a time. That's twelve cases to each woman.'

'Impossible,' snapped Karen. 'I watched the men lifting them. We'd get nowhere.'

'I'll be the judge of that,' Barrington said firmly. 'You find me someone who knows the forest and can tell me where to move the gold. The rest is just hard labour.'

Karen stared at him coldly and nodded her head. 'Very well, Colonel. But I will not carry your gold.'

'You will,' Barrington said confidently. 'You have strong shoulders and a good back. You are independent, so you will work harder than most. You are also proud, so you would not want the others to think you are afraid.'

Olga began to giggle again, getting an angry look from Karen. A moment later they returned to the church, leaving the lamp with Barrington. He lowered the flame to the minimum when they slid the stone aside, then they were gone and the stone slab had slid back into place.

During the next two hours he thought of a dozen things he would need and that he should have asked them to bring. From his pockets he took two pens, three pencils, a small notebook and a compass. He began to make up a list, assuming that he had forty women, of the things he would need to transfer the gold from point A to point B. It soon became clear that it was a formidable task. There were ropes, packs, heavy gloves and torches that would need to be strapped to women's arms, or held in some fashion that did not involve their hands.

After a while he went and lay on the bed, considering his position as objectively as he could. His initial tactic had been proved to be correct. Had the convoy been carrying the gold it would now be in German hands. But his decision to hide the gold in this village could prove to be a grave error. In retrospect he realized that it should have been hidden in the forest by his own men. He stopped, realizing that this would have been no solution either. If the men could be forced to reveal the village, they would inevitably reveal any location.

He thought of the Borgas men held in the hotel. The next few days were not going to be pleasant, but at least the German commandos were civilized human beings with a degree of honour and morality. They were not like some of the animals he had dealt with in Burma. He closed his eyes, the recollection taking him back six years.

He could smell the sweet, pungent odour of the jungle after the morning mist had seeped into the ground, like dissolving layers of cotton wool. He had been commanding a company of The Buffs on detachment to the British High Commissioner who was attempting to establish diplomatic relations with the various Wa tribes. The further east they got towards China the more primitive the natives. The Nan Tau region was jealously guarded by headhunters who were not at all interested in acknowledging the sovereignty of King Edward.

They would come out of the jungle canopy like sleek brown animals, dropping silently amongst them as they marched along the narrow trails. Their faces were streaked with paint and their hair was slicked down with black mud from the river, caked hard into a helmet that was strong enough to withstand the blow of a spear. The Wa headhunters carried short spears and vicious hatchets, some of which could be thrown with considerable accuracy.

It was a spear that had caught Barrington unawares. The warrior had dropped silently from dense vines above him as he shouted orders to the men and began picking off headhunters with his Mauser machine pistol. The man behind struck at his side, but at the last moment Barrington sensed the danger and turned, smashing the spear downwards with the barrel of his gun. It struck him above the knee, piercing into the kneecap in a deep, ugly wound that smashed the cartilage and severed the inner vein. A second later Barrington had tilted the gun and fired into the Wa's chest as he raised a hatchet, but that was the last shot he fired in the skirmish.

They took him by mule to the hospital in Mandalay where he spent two months recovering. As the weeks went by he came to realize that his leg would never be the same. It could no longer bend due to damage to the kneecap and atrophied muscles. So instead he learned to use a cane, to pivot with as much panache as a sergeant-major on parade. Strictly speaking he should have been returned to England and given a pension, but every time the General came to inspect the regiment Barrington was astride a horse.

He smiled wryly at the memory. It had probably been the worst kept secret in the British Army.

There was a grating from above and he sat up quickly on the bed as the stone slab was pulled away. A woman's voice echoed down the stairs, harsh and not at all friendly.

'Relax, Englishman, it is Helga.'

He relaxed, watching a pair of heavy ankles which disappeared into man-sized boots descend the stairs until he was staring at a broad, well-rounded woman in a woollen shawl and voluminous hand-loomed skirt. She dusted herself off, watching him with sharp eyes, sucking on teeth which protruded slightly between thin, pale lips. Her eyes were dark, her hair black and cut short and ragged, as though she did it herself, and when he glanced at her hands he was struck by the strength in them.

'I'm delighted to meet you, Helga,' he said, offering his hand. 'I'm Colonel Barrington

'I know who you are, Englishman.' She gazed deliberately at his stiff leg and the cane he was holding. 'It is a pity you chose to hide in Borgas.'

'It is the gold we are hiding, ma'am.'

'Is it?' She gazed at him coldly. 'Then why are we whispering in the cellar?'

Barrington smiled wryly and shrugged. 'Did you come here to ask questions, or to mock an Englishman?'

She snorted and moved to the table, sitting down. 'There is an old Norwegian saying: "When you piss in the snow make sure you are not wearing skis!"'

'A fascinating thought', Barrington said dryly.

She glared at him. 'And when did you last wear skis, Englishman?'

'When I last saw snow,' replied Barrington coolly. 'Now, ma'am, if we can get on with the reason you are here?'

'As all our men are unwilling guests at the hotel, I have been asked to provide you with information on the forest around the logging camp. I take it you expect the women to move your gold?'

'Your gold, actually,' Barrington reminded her. 'But yes, I hope that forty women using sacks or shoulder packs can manage to carry two cases an hour for six hours. That means finding a new place to hide the gold within fifteen minutes walking distance of the camp.'

Helga leaned back in the chair and clasped gnarled hands around a knee, eyes almost closed as she visualised the area. After a moment she opened them and said firmly. 'It will have to be done quicker, the place I have in mind is some caves about a mile from the camp. It will take thirty to forty minutes along the trails in this snow.'

'Then it can't be done. We must move the gold tonight before the Germans start to break the men.'

'You have a poor opinion of our men, English. Just one night? Is that all they are brave enough to bear?'

Barrington sighed and shook his head. 'No, ma'am. I did not say that. But a mile through the forest in the dark is too much. There must be somewhere closer. A frozen lake, perhaps? A place they could be buried?'

'No. Once in the lake you could not recover them until Spring, and who knows how many Germans may be here by then. The ground is too hard to dig, and the evidence too easy to find. The caves are the answer.'

'But how?'

She took an enormous handkerchief from a pocket in her skirt and blew her nose with a flourish. The sound was so loud that Barrington felt sure the Germans would come charging into the church at any moment. Helga saw his alarm and chuckled, waving the handkerchief like a flag. 'Have no fear, English. We have some of our women permanently on watch in the church. If any of those Bavarian bastards come within a thousand yards we will know.' She paused, frowning, then nodded her head as though endorsing a thought. 'I think it can be done. The cases of gold are small, yes?'

Barrington nodded, holding his hands about two feet apart.

'So we take a pair of skis and rope them together, perhaps a foot apart, and then place two cases on the skis and bind them tightly together. A harness from the cases around the woman's shoulders and she can shuss along the old logging trails without too much difficulty. One woman leaves every five minutes and the whole operation will take about four and a half hours. You agree, Englishman?'

Barrington gave her a baffled look and nodded his head. 'It sounds quite feasible.'

'Except you will be no good on skis, so I think you should stay at the logging camp.'

Barrington smiled coldly and shook his head. 'Thank you for your help, ma'am, but I shall be strolling in the general direction of the caves once the first few are on their way.'

'With a walking stick, I suppose?' She snapped.

'No ma'am, with a ski stick,' he replied equally sharply. 'I'm sure you've seen them. They are used by skiers to stay upright in deep snow.'

Helga gazed at him with bright, angry eyes. The silence grew between them, as cold and brittle as the ice that hung from the eaves of the church above. After a moment she shook her head in disgust, clicked her tongue and rose to her feet, moving towards the stairs. She paused there, looking towards him with a sardonic smile.

'Those who know these things say it will snow tonight. I will bring you snow shoes and ski sticks, but you had better wrap yourself well, English. We would not want you to catch your death of cold.'

After she had gone he paced the small stone room, his stick clicking on the floor, the sound irritating him for the first time in years. He stopped, gripping the head of the cane tightly in both hands, swearing softly as he recalled the contempt in the old woman's face.

'Then why are you hiding here?' she had said.

He moved to the stairs and climbed them slowly, listening

for a full minute before sliding back the stone slab. He climbed out, pushing back the stone, straightening from behind the altar to gaze the length of the church. Two women in the front row gazed back with shattered expressions. He put a finger to his lips and moved to the vestry door behind the pulpit.

Inside light filtered dimly through a narrow, leaded window. A few shelves of dusty books lined one wall, below some stacks of hymn books. Two sagging leather chairs, a scarred oak table and an oil lamp completed the meagre furniture, and for a moment his spirits sank. But in one corner, almost hidden by the bookshelves, was a narrow wardrobe. He crossed to it quickly, grinning with relief when he saw the dusty black cassock and cloak hanging inside. There was also a surplice, two pairs of cracked leather shoes and some vestments that were threadbare, but clearly well looked after.

He removed his cap and greatcoat, slipping the cassock over his head and shrugging it into place. His brown leather boots showed below the hem of the cassock, but fortunately the black shoes fitted and although they were unlikely to be waterproof made him look the part of a struggling rector.

When he emerged from the vestry the two women appeared to display symptoms of cardiac arrest. One of them, clutching her bosom, rushed to the altar and tried to push him back into the vestry, speaking in shrill Norwegian with what was obviously a deep conviction that he was about to get them all shot. The other just sat gripping the rail and looking lost.

He beamed and made the sign of the cross as he limped down the centre aisle, his cane tapping cheerfully beside him. Once out of the church he paused on the steps, looking casually along the street which was almost deserted. There appeared to be two German soldiers on duty at each side of the square, but they seemed more concerned with keeping themselves warm than with questioning the locals.

Barrington adopted his most benevolent smile and walked

down the three steps and out onto the packed snow, placing the stick carefully beside his left foot and checking the grip before swinging forward. Two middle-aged women came out of a house almost opposite the church, freezing in mid step and gazing at him in horror. He nodded and raised his right palm, as though to bless them, and moved on out of the square and along the road towards the doctor's house. The two German soldiers merely glanced at him and continued their conversation.

As he reached the house of Doctor Jansen two Germans appeared from the road leading up to the hotel. One of them had the insignia of a lieutenant, the other was a short, stocky sergeant who was immediately interested in the appearance of a clergyman. Barrington rang the bell and waited, conscious of the approaching Germans, but ignoring them. From the corner of his eye he saw them angle across the street towards him, then the sergeant spoke sharply in German.

The door opened and Olaf Jansen stared at him, his eyes widening with shock. Even as he opened his mouth to speak he saw the approaching Germans. He held out his hand, taking Barrington's firmly and pulling him into the house as he spoke loudly in Norwegian.

'Ah, Reverend Hermannson, what a pleasure to see you. Come in, come in.'

The Sergeant left his companion and hurried forward as the Doctor began to close the door. 'One moment. We were told that there was no priest in the village.'

The Sergeant spoke in German and Barrington turned towards him, replying halting in that language with some relief for his Norwegian was virtually non-existent.

'Then the person obviously meant to protect me, Sergeant. I do not, of course, believe that you would arrest and torture a man of the cloth.'

The Sergeant's face stiffened angrily, the blood rising in his cheeks. 'We do not torture.'

'Indeed,' snapped the Doctor in fluent German. 'Then let

us hope there are no more *accidents* like the one I had to treat an hour ago. The man had a broken jaw and three broken fingers.'

'You know why we are here,' the Sergeant said coldly. 'Tell us what we want to know and we will leave.'

'There is nothing to tell,' replied the Doctor. 'This is a small village full of peaceful, non-violent people who simply want to live their own lives. We have never experienced before this kind of brutal, barbaric treatment, so you will forgive us if we seem to be unresponsive. Until last night we believed that the kind of brutal savages who now infest our town existed only in comics and children's nightmares.'

The Sergeant flushed and stepped back, clicking his heels before turning away. Across the street the lieutenant made a disparaging gesture, grinning at the Sergeant's anger. Doctor Jansen watched them move on towards the square before stepping back into the house and closing the door.

'I hope you have a very good reason for this excursion, Colonel?' he said sternly, leading the way into the small living room.

'I decided it was time to evaluate the occupation of the village,' Barrington said coolly. 'My next stage is to walk up to the German headquarters and take a look at their defences.'

'They're considerable,' said the Doctor, pouring two glasses of aquavit and handing one to the Colonel. 'You wouldn't last two minutes up there once they started speaking to you in Norwegian.'

Barrington sipped the strong liquor, hiding his disappointment at the news. 'I had hoped that they would be limited to German.'

'There is a Captain Lodtz who speaks Norwegian fluently and at least a dozen of his men who can get by. You were just lucky that the Sergeant was not one of them.'

Barrington sat down, stretching out his leg in front of the log fire, staring into the flames. The Doctor watched him sympathetically, wondering where he had come from and how he had been saddled with such a responsibility. The tanned features, lean and lined, suggested many years in the sun. India, he imagined. He looked at the leg which Barrington was massaging absent-mindedly as he gazed into the fire.

'How long have you had it?' he asked quietly.

'Mmmm?' The Colonel glanced up, then saw the Doctor's gaze and stopped massaging the leg with an embarrassed air, as though he had revealed a weakness. 'A few years. Five, actually.'

'I take it nothing can be done?'

'Good God no. Lucky to have it.' He cleared his throat, looking as though he would like to change the subject. Doctor Jansen sat and let him squirm until he said in a clipped voice. 'Native spear in Burma. Smashed the cartilage and made a mess of the tendons. It's no trouble really.'

'No,' said Jansen dryly. 'I'm sure it isn't. But don't you think we should get you out of here? I'm sure we can manage something.'

'Out of the question,' Barrington replied firmly. 'The gold is formally in my possession and I intend to keep it that way as long as I can.'

'They're beating the men up rather badly.'

Muscles knotted along the side of the Colonel's jaw, but when he spoke there was no emotion in his voice. 'I'm sorry about that. I don't think they'll go too far.'

'Don't you?' The Doctor looked at him silently for a moment, then leaned over with the bottle of aquavit and filled the Colonel's glass. 'What happened to your men?'

Barrington stared into the glass, his grey eyes like freshly struck flint. 'I've been thinking about that. Left to walk they should have been in Valebru by now, telephoning a message through to Annolsetrene or at least getting help.'

'My feeling also,' agreed the Doctor. 'There should have been some contact with the village by noon at the latest.' He paused, gazing grimly at Barrington. 'The fact that there has been no alarm suggests the worst.'

B.W.—D

Barrington shook his head, gripping his knee until his knuckles showed white. 'They'll be all right. They may be in a farm under guard. We don't know.'

'It's possible, but you haven't seen the way these men are operating up at the hotel. They're hard, efficient, tough as nails. They don't care how brutally they beat the villagers, or how long it takes.'

'They won't kill,' Barrington said emphatically. 'Your people are civilians and the gold is Norwegian. They have every right to hide it, to remain silent for as long as possible. The German Commander knows that and if he starts executing people he becomes guilty of murder.'

'And my father, Colonel? Will his bones mend more easily because he is a civilian?'

Barrington turned, rising awkwardly to his feet when he saw the young woman at the foot of the stairs. She was tall and slim with rich, reddish brown hair and eyes green enough to match an emerald.

'I beg your pardon,' he said. 'I had no idea there was anyone else in the room, much less the daughter of a prisoner.'

'Sonja has been visiting Tania Arlberg,' the Doctor explained. 'It has been a difficult day for her.'

'Of course,' Barrington replied quickly. 'A day I wish had not happened.'

Sonja gave him a sad smile and moved to the fire, taking the chair that Jansen offered. 'I know. Tania has told me about you. You're a kind man, but a soldier. You brought the gold here because she knew the village and that gave you time.' She sighed, gazing up at him with wide eyes. 'It's not your fault. But what can we do? We can't just sit here, wringing our hands and doing nothing. Why can't we burn them out? . . . Throw rocks at them . . . Just – just do something?'

'You can,' Barrington said softly. 'You can help to move the gold, then we can let the prisoners know that it doesn't matter anymore.'

She gave a sigh of resignation and nodded her mane of chestnut hair. 'I will be there. My father would want me to do that.'

'Splendid,' said Barrington, forcing a smile.

'But before then we must deal with your new role as the village priest,' the Doctor said. 'I suggest you spend the afternoon in the company of Miss Arlberg. She has nothing better to do, so she will teach you as many phrases as you can handle. Then if the Germans do stop you at least you will have something to say.'

Barrington cleared his throat awkwardly and rubbed his knee. 'I-ah . . . I can probably manage with an English-Norwegian phrase book.'

Sonja gazed at him with a wide-eyed innocence he did not believe for a moment. 'But Colonel, she is a perfect linguist and so bored having to stay in bed. It would be foolish not to take advantage of her.'

Barrington coughed, nodded with gritted teeth and dutifully made his way upstairs. He tapped on the bedroom door, hoping she had fallen asleep, but the clear, cheerful voice told him to enter.

When she saw him in the cassock and dog collar she collapsed with mirth. He glared at her.

'I'm sorry,' she gurgled. 'You looked so solemn I thought you'd come to bury me.'

10

The women gathered in the woods beyond the village at midnight. They came in twos and threes, slipping from darkened houses along narrow paths that led over the fields and into the forest. The Germans had placed sentries in the square and at a makeshift road block half a kilometre from the town, but no one had any trouble avoiding them.

Once in the woods Helga Strom took charge, ignoring Barrington who stood in the shadows with Sonja who was handing out the harnesses that would be used to pull the bullion. Most of the women were in their twenties or thirties, relaxed and expert on their skis. All of them carried an extra pair of skis and lengths of rope or leather straps.

'Every fourth person carries a torch,' said Helga, handing out a variety of torches. 'And please remember they must last for the next five hours.'

They set off in single file with Helga leading the way, her powerful thighs sending her along the trail with long, floating strides. She seemed to have a sixth sense which told her when there would be a rocky outcrop, or a fallen tree that meant a detour. Her torch flicked on and off, her voice floating back along the column like a regimental sergeant-major rehearsing the Royal Ballet.

'Come along, ladies, from your toes and thrust – thrust. Slowly, on the bend, but shuss hard along the edges. All together, thrust and glide – thrust and glide.'

Barrington listened to the voice fading away into the darkness. He was moving on foot, wearing snow-shoes and using ski sticks for support. Sonja was with him, carrying the torch which showed the mass of ski tracks running away from them. After ten minutes there was total silence in the forest, as though they had always been alone.

'How far now?' he asked.

'About five minutes to the logging camp,' she replied. 'Why don't you rest?'

'I'm doing fine,' he answered. 'These snow-shoes remind me of swamp mats we tried out in Burma. The idea was to tie our feet to large wooden crosses which were nailed to squares of canvas. By walking over the mud flats and swamps we could save time and make better speed because there were fewer obstructions.'

'What a clever idea,' said Sonja. 'Did it work?'

'Not really. Each time we took a step the sucking noises grew worse. By the time we'd done a hundred yards we seemed to have incensed half the alligator population. They came from everywhere, mad as the devil. Something to do with the noise, I think. Our M.O. was convinced it was part of their mating ritual.'

Sonja giggled. 'How on earth did you get away?'

'Ah, well now,' said Barrington, 'that's where British Army initiative came into play.'

They paused beside the dark bole of a tree that leaned across the trail. She waited, her face a ghostly disc in the gloom. 'So?'

'So we quickly got rid of the swamp mats and waded hip deep for the nearest tree. The alligators attacked the mats until we tossed a couple of grenades to dampen their interest, so to speak. Then one at a time we slid down and waded to high ground. It was all a rather messy business.'

Sonja laughed, flashing her torch ahead. They moved on, following the deeper furrows in the snow, until they could see the cluster of lights around the logging camp.

The first five had left with their cases when they arrived. Helga had put two of the women onto the task of strapping skis together and tying on the cases of bullion. Barrington watched the operation for a while, impressed by the ease with which the loads could slide across the ground. Every few minutes another skier would take off into the darkness pulling six cases of bullion from a crude harness tied across her shoulders. After an hour they paused to rest and pass round flasks of coffee, Helga beaming at the remaining women.

'That's two hundred cases, ladies. And we've still got four hours of darkness.'

There were mock groans from the shadows. Barrington stepped forward, standing beside the stocky figure of Helga. 'You're doing splendidly. All we have to do is keep up this momentum.'

Helga translated, slapping him on the shoulder. There were giggles from the darkness. He glanced at her suspiciously. 'Now why should I wonder if that was an accurate translation?'

Helga chuckled. 'Don't ask, English. I was just giving them an incentive.'

Sonja moved up and whispered. 'She said that as you were the only able bodied man in the village tonight they would draw lots for you when all the gold was moved.'

'Flattered as I am, ma'am,' said Barrington with a perfectly straight face, 'I must remind you that my new role as rector of the parish means I must hold early morning service at seven o'clock.'

'And only one of us will be there, Englishman,' chuckled Helga. 'Perhaps even me!'

'A formidable thought, ma'am,' said Barrington, his eyes twinkling. 'I can see I must pray most fervently.'

Helga laughed the loudest of all, then called everyone back to work. The next consignment left in five minutes and Barrington followed almost immediately on snow shoes. Helga insisted on sending Sonja with him, pointing out that the trail was difficult to negotiate during daylight and for a stranger in the dark it was next to impossible.

'Even without the leg, English, you would be a fool to try it alone. Go with Sonja, but when you take a rest on the way remember – we have not yet drawn lots!'

They left with laughter ringing in their ears, but it was soon lost in a blanket of snow that began to drift down out of the darkness. Sonja led the way, flashing the torch to check the ski trails ahead, but these became increasingly indistinct as the snowfall thickened.

'I hate to admit it,' Barrington told her as they took a rest, 'but Helga was right. We could have left the trail a dozen times.'

'I think we have,' replied Sonja, 'but I know where the caves are.'

Fifteen minutes later they crossed a gully to find ski trails on the other side. Sonja gave a sigh of relief, admitting that she had been worried for some time.

They came out of the forest along the bank of a frozen river with limestone cliffs rising above it. The caves were in the base of the cliffs, but it took five minutes of plodding from one dark opening to the next before they saw the glow of lights. Sonja was about to call out and enter when Barrington caught her arm tightly.

'Shouldn't we have met women returning for their second load?' He whispered. 'There hasn't been anyone on the trail apart from the two who were heading in this direction.'

'That's true,' answered Sonja, frowning. 'Perhaps they're going back in a group.'

'No,' said Barrington. 'And it's too quiet in there.'

He unbuttoned his greatcoat and drew the service revolver from its holster. 'You go in as though everything is normal. I'll wait and see what happens.'

She nodded, her face pale in the gloom, then bent and unfastened her skis, putting them over her shoulder as she walked into the cave.

Barrington slipped off the snow shoes and moved silently to the edge of the cave entrance, the revolver cold in his hand. The harsh command in German that came from the cave was almost an anti climax, every sense had told him that something was wrong. He took slow, measured breaths, feeling the adrenalin begin to flow, the tension come into the muscles across his shoulders. It was years since he had felt the electric awareness that comes with danger, but the responses came as though it was only yesterday. He was no longer conscious of the stiff left leg, of the ache that had been in his muscles minutes ago. He was aware only of the voices from the caves, the shrill protest from Sonja, the sharper voice of a second man speaking German.

He stepped from the blanket of snow like a friendly ghost, taking three measured steps to the deeper shadows against the wall of the cave. Three German soldiers were facing almost a dozen women, the Schmeisser machine pistols covering them steadily. Sonja was arguing fiercely, beginning to lower her skis, her rapid Norwegian clearly baffling the soldiers. Only one of the Germans, a young corporal, sensed the entrance of Barrington. He turned his head, almost a reflex action, his eyes searching the shadows cast by the oil lamp one of the women had brought to the cave.

Barrington raised the gun, watching the shocked realization come into the German's face. Even as he opened his mouth to speak, the Schmeisser swinging round and his body dropping into a crouch, Barrington squeezed the trigger and felt the butt jerk in his hand as a round black hole appeared in the centre of the Corporal's forehead about an inch below the white fabric of his hood.

Barrington stepped to the right, gripping the pistol in both hands, watching the two soldiers spinning round automatically and moving apart to widen his angle of fire. He knew there was little chance of getting them both, even though the corner of his eye was registering the surge of women towards the third German, the vicious arc of Sonja's skis as they took him across the side of the head. He fired, his throat tightening as he watched the bullet hit high up on the soldier's chest, the blood spurting as he staggered back, but it was not going to stop him and the machine pistol continued to swing round, centring on him. Flame licked from the stubby barrel and bullets exploded on the roof of the cave as Barrington fired a third shot that took the man in the left temple, killing him instantly.

The remaining soldier had been knocked backwards by the blow from the skis, but even as he collided awkwardly with the rock wall of the cave he was lining up on the figure in the shadows. One of the women caught at his arm and he clubbed her brutally in the face with the heavy wooden stock of the gun, then aimed and squeezed the trigger.

Barrington's mind was ice cold as he turned towards the last soldier, images slowing down like stop motion frames as he became aware that he was too late. The German was short, stocky with pale eyes and a thin, cruel mouth that was twisted into a lob-sided grin, as though he was about to tell a funny story. But there was nothing funny about the black snout of the gun in his hands.

Barrington stepped to the left, realizing too late that his stiff leg could not cope with the movement. It caught and swung him round with abrupt force, throwing him onto his back. The soldier fired at the same moment, the burst of 9mm bullets screaming off the rocky walls, the staccato roar of the weapon deafening in the confines of the cave. For a brief moment the soldier thought it was his bullets which had thrown Barrington to the floor, and by the time he realized the error of that thought it was far too late. Barrington rolled, raised the revolver and fired three rapid shots that took the soldier in the chest, throat and head.

As the echoes of the shots faded and the blue-grey wreaths of smoke floated out into the night, the women gathered silently around the bodies of the German soldiers. The woman who had been hit in the face with the butt of the Schmeisser was sitting on the floor, watching blood drip from the ugly gash across her cheek with dull, bewildered eyes. Sonja helped Barrington to his feet, the anxiety on her face fading as she saw that he had not been hit.

He stood for a moment, feeling the cold sweat beginning to dry on his face, taking deep breaths until discipline took over and he was calm again.

'All right, who was here when they arrived?' he said sharply, bringing their heads round. He knew that if they looked at the bodies long enough he would have a cave full of hysterical women on his hands. 'Come on, we haven't got all night,' he snapped. 'I want to know precisely what happened.'

Sonja gave him an angry look, then translated for the benefit of those who could not understand English. After a moment, hesitantly at first, three of the women began to speak. They had been flashing their torches back along the trail to help the skiers when they saw a light in a different direction. Thinking that one of their companions had got lost, they shouted and flashed their torches. A few minutes later the soldiers had appeared, holding them at gunpoint.

'Did they leave any other men in the forest?' Barrington asked.

'No,' said one of the women who was no more than eighteen and so pale he felt like advising her to sit down. 'I speak German and they were planning to send a man back to the village when one of our girls arrived with the gold. They decided to wait until we were all here before reporting to the duty sergeant.'

'Did they give you any idea why they were out here?'

'Yes, they were talking about it to each other. They were one of the patrols that are supposed to cover the two roads. The duty sergeant is at the road block with two more men.'

'But isn't that about a mile from here?' Barrington asked with a frown.

The girl nodded. 'They were bored and decided to follow a trail through the forest. They got lost and then saw our lights. I don't think they really knew where they were.'

Barrington went to the entrance of the cave and gazed out into the night. Snow was falling heavily and through the trees, flickering like a dying candle, was the light of another skier. He turned back, facing the circle of women who watched his haunted features.

'There's a good chance that we can get away with this,' he

said quietly. 'We'll keep the bodies here and cover them with snow when we've finished bringing the bullion.'

'There'll be a search?' said Karen Helrop, looking worried.

'From what was said the search will be around the road block, along the road towards Annolsetrene. They can't search an entire forest and this place is so far in the wrong direction they'll never find it.'

'But if they do?' The anxious question came from the French girl, Michelle Argent. 'They might shoot us.'

'Why?' Barrington asked patiently. 'They would know these men were shot by a British service revolver. Why should they suspect women?'

They exchanged worried looks, then as the logic of his words penetrated their fear they began to relax. Sonja had picked up her skis and was examining them to see if they were damaged.

'I haven't had a chance to thank you,' he said warmly. 'That five seconds you gave me was just about enough to save my life.'

Sonja gazed up at him, her eyes the deepest green and almost luminous in the light of the oil lamp which deepened the rich chestnut of her hair. 'You looked fairly capable of killing three German soldiers, Colonel,' she said softly. 'You made it look positively easy.'

'Killing is never easy,' he said, his voice sharper than he had intended.

Her eyes clouded and the luminosity went, as though a shadow had fallen between them. 'I'm sorry, Colonel. I thought that was your trade.'

She left him feeling strangely confused, but almost immediately the next skier arrived and went into a complete panic when she saw the bodies on the floor. Some of the women had bandaged the cheek of the injured girl and decided to leave her at the cave with Barrington until all the gold had been moved. When they had left he sat beside her on a couple of the bullion boxes and tried to cheer her up, but she spoke no English and his Norwegian was limited to 'We shall now pray' and 'Bless you my child.'

The snow continued to fall heavily for the next two hours, making the difficult task of transporting the gold all the more exhausting. By four o'clock in the morning the women were arriving at the cave with their last cases, grey with cold and weariness. And yet, when Helga arrived with the final stack of boxes, there was enough spirit left for jubilation and a round of applause.

Helga spoke briefly in Norwegian, her words soft and proud, and the circle of women around her smiled at each other and gathered their skis and left. Only Sonja remained with Helga, who helped Barrington to drag the bodies of the soldiers to the side of the cave. Each man had a commando knife in his boot, a pistol and Schmeisser, and in the pouches of their white combat blouses were four magazines for each weapon and a canvas bag containing one hundred loose rounds of 9mm ammunition.

'These men were the elite,' said Barrington, hefting the knife in his hand. The blade was the finest steel, honed to a razor sharpness.

'They weren't so hot, English,' replied Helga with a shrug, turning the body of the Corporal onto his face.

'I was lucky,' said Barrington. 'And your girls had courage.'

'My girls!' snorted Helga. 'They are yours, Colonel. They are Barrington's women.'

Barrington flushed and murmured a protest, but Sonja and Michelle had already begun to nod their heads and smile.

'It's your private army, Colonel,' said Sonja with shining eyes. 'Just tell us what you want to do.'

'Provided it is not too complicated and we can draw lots,' added Helga mischievously.

'Ladies, there will be no further operations. You have been splendid, but from now on you will pretend to be quite ordinary women. I say pretend,' Barrington added, 'because quite frankly you've been magnificent and the last word I would use to describe you is ordinary.'

Helga moved closer and gripped his shoulder, beaming up at him. 'Does that mean you fancy me, English, or the pretty one?'

11

The village of Borgas was rudely awakened at seven o'clock by persistent blasts from the horns of a dozen trucks and the banging of gun butts on doors around the square. The elderly couples emerged in dressing gowns and bewildered expressions, and were largely ignored by the Germans. It was the women of Borgas they wanted this time.

'You are behaving in a very stupid fashion,' Captain Lodtz bellowed from the centre of the square, his eyes pale and cold with anger. 'We want only to return the gold stolen by the British to your bank in Oslo. That is all.'

There was a stony silence in the square. Women in dressing gowns, shawls and hastily donned anoraks and pants, stood in groups watched by almost a hundred soldiers with levelled Schmeissers. For the first time since the Germans had come to Borgas there was a clearly defined antagonism in the air. They confronted each other, the oppressor and the oppressed.

'You can save your menfolk hours of unnecessary suffering. All I need from any person in this square is the location of the gold. Give me that and I promise we will be gone from here by noon and your men will be back in their homes.'

He waited, eyes diamond hard, feeling the weight of their hatred like a current of ice cold air. No one stirred. They just stood in silent groups, accusing him with their eyes.

'Then you are fools,' he said slowly, measuring his words with contempt. 'The interrogation will go on and soon enough one of the men will break. But now we come to another matter.' He paused, grinding his teeth, trying hard to control the fury he had felt since being told of the missing men. 'Three of my men have not returned from patrol. If anyone has information about this they should see me or my officers immediately. Should anything have happened to these men I will not hesitate to take action against this village.'

Helga stepped forward, her ample figure incongruous in a voluminous quilted dressing gown. 'What are you suggesting, Herr Haupman? That we have stolen your soldiers?'

Lodtz's cheeks reddened. 'I said they are missing. We are asking for your co-operation in finding them.'

'The chuckles began as a whisper of sound on the fringes of the crowd and then it grew, spreading from group to group until the women and old people of Borgas were shaking with laughter. The soldiers facing them gazed stiffly ahead, their cheeks burning with humiliation.

Sonja called out to Captain Lodtz as the laughter finally died. 'We don't have your soldiers, Captain. Perhaps they have run away to Annolsetrene, or Valebru? If you give us back our telephone we can call and find out for you?'

'German soldiers do not run away,' snapped Lodtz.

'Maybe they found the gold,' said Helga Strom, her eyes gleaming with mischief. 'Maybe they were searching the forest and found it in the middle of the night. So much gold, so much temptation. They just couldn't resist it.'

There was more laughter. Karen Helrop suggested that the soldiers had fallen asleep in the woods and forgotten what time it was. There were other suggestions, including being eaten by bears and dying from exposure.

As the comments and laughter continued, Lodtz called over Sergeant Driker and spoke quickly, the muscles knotting along his jaw. The Sergeant hesitated, looking uncertain, but Lodtz sent him off with an angry gesture and turned back to the assembled villagers.

'It is good to know that you laugh so easily,' he said with chilling menace. 'But let me assure you all that if harm has befallen my men then you will pay the penalty, irrespective of age or sex.'

There was silence around the square, then a growing murmur of horror as Sergeant Driker appeared from one of the trucks leading a slim, stumbling figure who only the previous day had been a nineteen-year-old youth whose infectious grin had made him one of the most likeable people in the village. As he drew closer to the groups of women the murmurs turned to moans of shock. The eyes that swung from side to side were lost and vacant. The tousled hair was matted with blood, most of his front teeth were missing and from the slackness of his mouth the jaw was broken. The arm that Sergeant Driker held had rough blood-stained bandages around the wrist and hand, the other arm was in a sling and splinted with two pieces of wood.

With a scream of agony Olga Morden broke away from the women who were gripping her arms and ran towards her brother, the ugly bruises and gashes across his face and head becoming all the more horrifying as she reached him. But the worst thing was his eyes. They gazed at her without comprehension, like a helpless child.

'You Nazi bastard!' she screamed, swinging a small fist at Driker's face.

The Sergeant caught it easily and turned her round, pushing her back towards the crowd. 'Look after your brother, or we might take you up the hill instead.'

She ran towards Captain Lodtz who was gazing ahead without expression. 'You pig!' she spat. 'You Nazi pig! You stand there in your fine uniform with your clean face and straight back and you pretend that you are a human being. You pretend that you have feelings like me and my people. But you have not. You have only the feelings of a pig. You should be down in the mud, grunting and grovelling with the rest of your family!'

She paused, breathless, her eyes flashing. Lodtz's face was pale with fury. He lifted a finger, aiming it at her like the barrel of a pistol. 'One more word and I will have your brother shot where he stands. Just one word.'

Olga gazed at him for a moment, then turned and went to

her brother, gently taking his arm and walking him away into the crowd. The Captain's threat had silenced the growing murmur of anger, but the soldiers were still keeping their fingers on the triggers of the Schmeissers.

'That man refused to co-operate. Other men will do so, are doing so. If any of you mothers and sisters have a sense of compassion, a source of pity for these men, then it takes only a word in my ear.' He stared at the stony features facing him. 'What happens to these men is the fault of every one of you who refuses to reveal the location of the gold.'

Lodtz turned away and began to walk across the square towards the road leading up the hill. Sergeant Driker fell in beside him, both staring straight ahead. They were almost across the square before the Captain saw the figure in a black cassock standing at the doorway to the church. He was leaning on a black cane, as though he was lame.

'Is there a priest here?' he asked Driker.

'A Reverend Hermannson. No one says much about him, except that he lives in rooms behind the church.'

Lodtz was about to ask further questions when Lieutenant Niemens stepped in front of him, saluting formally and standing stiffly to attention.

'Yes, Rolf?'

'Captain, it is necessary to inform you that the men of my company are concerned about the conduct which is being required of them on this mission.'

Lodtz stared at the Lieutenant until his cheeks reddened and his gaze dropped. When he spoke his voice was a chilling whisper. 'I note your protest, Lieutenant, and your disloyalty.'

'I have always been a loyal admirer of your brilliance, Captain,' replied Niemens stiffly. 'But we are soldiers with a pride in our achievements. We should not be torturing civilians, shooting women, or even . . .' he paused, his eyes glassy. 'Or even murdering prisoners of war.'

'I see. And you wish this complaint to be formally entered into the company records?'

'Yes, sir.'

Lodtz smiled thinly and glanced to the side of the street, noting that the lieutenant of Green Company was within earshot and two of Niemen's NCOs. 'I will make a full report and give you an opportunity to sign it,' he said smoothly. Then bending forward, with a smile, added softly. 'But you are finished, Rolf. I promise you that.'

Niemens stepped back and saluted, remaining at attention until Lodtz and Driker had walked briskly away up the hill. He took a deep breath and felt for his cigarettes, looking gratefully at Lieutenant Dobermann who held one out to him already lit.

'Jesus!' he said.

'It had to be said.'

Niemens nodded, drawing deeply on the cigarette, trying to still the trembling of his hands. 'I know, but when he looked at me just then there was murder in his eyes. It's gone to his head, Franz. He's over the top.'

'It doesn't matter, we'll be out of it soon enough. I'll give it six more hours, then they'll crack and we'll have the gold.'

'But then he's a hero,' pointed out Niemens with a worried frown. 'And they say this mission was planned in Berlin.'

'It doesn't matter. When we make our reports about his methods Oberkommando will never accept them. They won't even believe they were necessary.'

Lieutenant Niemens was uncertain of Dobermann's logic, but signalled to his sergeant to dismiss the men and began moving up the hill with his companion. Across the square the women were filing silently into the church. He felt a sense of pity. Praying would not stop Wolf Lodtz.

12

'So show me how to kill him!'

Olga Morden stood in the aisle of the small church, facing Barrington in front of the altar. More than fifty women had filed into the pews, watching with grim features as Olga confronted the Colonel.

'Killing is not that easy,' Barrington replied quietly. 'I told you that much last night.'

'But you did it. Three of them. All I want is one. Show me how to use the guns we have at the cave. Just tell me the rules and then I will walk up to that pig of a Captain and kill him.'

'And his men will kill you.'

'I don't care about that.'

'I do,' said Barrington. 'So does your brother. If they kill you he will find a gun and kill some of them. The same for your friends. If their brothers or husbands are maimed then they too have the right to take a Schmeisser and shoot Germans. And they too will be killed. At the end nothing is accomplished, except a lot of dead bodies.'

There was silence for a moment in the church, then Helga Strom stirred restlessly and stepped out into the aisle beside Olga, taking her arm gently.

'I understand what you say, Englishman, but it is of no help to Olga. This morning, on the radio from Oslo, the Germans were talking about a peaceful occupation of our country. But there is already a free radio station and it said that only Oslo has been taken. The army is fighting along the border with Denmark, and the British Navy is blockading the west coast. These pigs have no support. They came by parachute and they are just as isolated as we are.'

Barrington considered her thoughtfully, then moved to the front pew and sat down. 'If that's the situation it will take weeks before they occupy areas like this. They'll have to land forces along the coast, and they can't do that until they have control of the sea.' He looked at them, smiling for the first time. 'Eventually Germany must take Norway, but it seems as though they have been over optimistic. I'd say we have the rest of April at least.'

'So?' asked Helga.

'If I could contact the Navy they would send a detachment up the road from Trondheim.'

'If that happens there will be a battle and maybe the Germans will kill our men?' pointed out a dour-faced woman in her late thirties.

Helga pulled a face. 'You've seen that road, English. The Germans could hold it at a dozen points, and behind us there is nothing except dense forest and mountains until you reach the old road which takes you to Glamos. In the summer there are trails and rivers to follow, but now, in the winter, we are the end of the line. The . . .' She frowned, searching for the word.

'Cul de sac,' supplied Barrington, beginning to wish he had never heard of Borgas. 'It does rather look as though we have presented the Germans with an impregnable position.'

'Only on the outside,' said Sonja quietly. 'On the inside they're vulnerable.'

Barrington nodded, accepting the point. 'True, but in this case it doesn't help. All the men who could fight are up in the Varennes. In any event it's out of the question, we'd still be outnumbered.'

'But with the element of surprise,' insisted Sonja.

'She's right, English,' said Helga. 'They won't be expecting the women to fight or the men to be freed. They're watching the roads, patrolling the forest, looking for people from outside Borgas.'

'If we could free our men,' said a woman who was wearing

baggy cord trousers and two sweaters. 'If we could just stop the torture and get them out of the Varenne.'

'I know,' Barrington said sympathetically, 'but I'm afraid it's a good deal more complicated than that. These are crack German commandos. You don't take them by surprise.'

'They're not supermen,' said Karen Helrop, her eyes glinting angrily. 'They don't frighten me.'

'If I can get help I will,' Barrington promised.

'And while you wait they torture and maim and turn our men into . . . into . . .' Olga began to sob brokenly. Some of the women did their best to comfort her.

'It is a matter for the village,' said Helga firmly. 'They are our men and we cannot sit around and wait and hope for a miracle. If anything is to be done, we must do it.'

Barrington gazed at them in exasperation. 'Ladies, believe me, there is nothing that can be done against a highly trained, well armed force of paratroop commandos.'

'We can kill them,' said Olga in a shrill voice.

'Kill them and free our men,' said the woman in baggy cords.

'And why not?' asked Sonja with growing excitement. 'We are on the inside. They don't consider us to be a threat. And we already have some weapons.'

Michelle jumped to her feet, eyes shining. 'I am with you. If each of us killed two men with surprise, it would be enough.'

'Nonsense,' snapped Barrington. 'If it were possible, you would still be left with half the German force, your element of surprise gone and in its place a ruthless determination to wipe out your village.'

'But we would have freed the men,' pointed out Sonja. 'There would be almost a hundred of us.'

Barrington gazed up at the ceiling, counting up to ten. 'Ladies,' he said, 'there is no way it can be done. You would have no chance.'

'The way I had no chance of reaching you?'

Barrington swung round at the sound of Tania's voice.

She stood half way along the aisle wearing blue ski pants and a red anorak. Her left arm hung a little stiffly by her side, but apart from that and the paleness of her features it was impossible to tell that she was still recovering from a bullet wound.

'What are you doing out of bed?' Barrington demanded.

'The Doctor is busy with Olga's brother. After seeing him I decided I have had enough of beds.'

Barrington glared at her and turned back to the women. Sonja smiled sweetly, almost purring. 'Is it really true that Tania saved the entire convoy and all the gold, Colonel? Even after she had been shot?'

Barrington cleared his throat, his eyes glinting. 'That may be an exaggeration.'

'But didn't I hear you tell the doctor?' asked Sonja, her smile positively angelic. 'And if Tania could win against all those well-trained German soldiers, surely we can manage something?'

A dozen heads nodded and the murmur of agreement held a note of anger. Barrington sighed and held up his hands. 'Look, ladies, you're over-wrought and I can't blame you, but what you're suggesting is impossible. It would take weeks, months, and at the end of it you would not have the strength or the will to win.'

'And last night, English,' snapped Helga. 'Was there no strength to haul your gold? No will to succeed?'

'Yes, yes,' Barrington said wearily. 'You were magnificent.'

'Then teach us?' demanded Tania, her eyes flashing. 'Tell us what to do, how to do it, when to do it. Then if it's possible we will succeed.'

Barrington gazed at them in exasperation and rose to his feet, moving towards the altar with his cane tapping rhythmically on the stone floor. Beneath the large wooden cross and the carved figure of Christ, his eyes gazing blindly at the strangest congregation the church had ever seen, Barrington turned back to face them. He still believed the idea was ridiculous, a total miscalculation by women who had never seen anything more violent than a stag hunt, but convincing them of that would need more than words.

'Very well,' he said, 'You want to attack the Germans and free your men. I can devise a plan, show you how to carry it out. But first I need some information from all of you.' He waited until Helga had translated. 'I must first know how many of you are prepared to die.'

There was silence for a moment, then Helga snorted with disgust and waved a fist at him. 'Cheap tactics, English.'

'No,' said Barrington. 'When planning any attack you have to know how many men you are prepared to lose. I mean it seriously. How many of you can we lose?'

They gazed at him with pale, forlorn features, like young girls who were being asked to give up their tickets to the ball. One by one they nodded, mouths tightening, and stepped out into the aisle. Helga was the last, gazing over their heads with pride. There were ten women left in the seats.

'They have young children,' explained Helga. 'They will help, but not fight.'

'Very well,' he said with resignation. 'We will make a start, but only on the understanding that you do exactly as I say. If there is anything you cannot do, or are not prepared to do, then you drop out.'

He waited. They stared back with unanimous commitment. He sighed and turned to the women in the pews. 'You ladies can set up a system of watches and alarms. One in a house at each side of the square, another directly facing the church. The moment Germans approach us you will give some kind of alarm. Split yourselves into shifts, one hour only so they don't get used to your faces, and change your overcoats and anoraks for each shift. Now off you go.'

The group of ten mothers left with smiles of enthusiasm, delighted with the importance of their task. Barrington turned back to the others, studying them intently. Some of them he knew by name, such as Olga Morden, Karen Helrop, Helga and Sonja. Others he knew only by sight, meeting them briefly in the darkness of the forest. There were thirty-one in all, a dozen in their late teens or early twenties, and about ten in their thirties. The remainder were stocky or thin, their faces tanned and lined, their hair showing touches of grey. He considered them with open scepticism until Helga stepped forward and nudged him in the ribs.

'Don't worry about the older hens, English. It's the chickens you're going to have to work on.' She pointed to Mrs Tollinson, a bluff, heavy featured woman who was beginning to consider the Colonel with open dislike. 'And don't get on the wrong side of Ma Tollinson. She owns half of the only bar in the village, cooks like an angel and won the local skeet shooting championship two years running.'

She beamed at his confusion, then indicated a tall, thin, weary looking woman who wore rubber boots up to her nightdress and somebody else's overcoat. She looked like a refugee with nowhere better to go.

'And that's Korina Mattel. She's the wife of our butcher, Johan Mattel, and apart from having the sharpest knives in the village, she can gut and bleed a pig in less time than you can cut a slice of pork.'

'Thank you, Helga,' Barrington said dryly. 'I do begin to get the message. I think we'll start by sorting everyone into their respective groups. There will be three. We'll give them code names now so that we always refer to them that way. Suggestions?'

He looked at the circle of faces. Tania was already opening her mouth. He gave her his brittlest smile, but she went on regardless. Her choice of code names was simplicity itself. Group One was to be called Lillie, because it was to deliver the hammer blow at the German headquarters. Group Two would be Michelle, because she would be in that group and the French interest should be noted. And the third group would be Tania. She stopped for breath and beamed proudly at Barrington.

'I take it you intend to be in Group Three,' said Barrington.

She nodded.

'And is there any other significance?'

'Of course,' she said, delighted that it had escaped him. 'It's for Britannia.'

Barrington cleared his throat sternly and growled: 'Very well, Lillie, Tania and Michelle. Now I need to know about special skills with anything resembling a weapon?'

'I can handle any kind of shotgun,' said Mrs Tollinson, 'and I'm pretty handy with light rifles.'

'She can light your cigarette at two hundred yards, English,' murmured Helga.

'All right, Mrs Tollinson. You go into Lillie Group and take on the role of marksman. I'd also like you to saw down a double-barrelled shotgun and get a sack of shells.'

'How short?' she asked in a matter-of-fact voice.

'I'll be working close quarters. Give me twelve inches of barrel.'

The woman clucked her tongue, smiling happily at the thought. 'I give you my best gun, Colonel. Over and under. Rubber soled butt.'

'If I ever get back I'll have my gunsmith replace it in London.'

Helga gestured to a slim young girl sitting at the rear of the group. She had short brown hair and freckled features, a small woollen cap making her look no more than fifteen. 'That's Heidi. She's good with a bow and arrow. Her father taught her since she was ten.'

'She doesn't look much more than that now,' muttered Barrington, adding in a louder voice: 'Just how good are you, Heidi?'

The girl blushed and twisted a leather purse between her hands, blurting out finally, 'I can kill a deer.'

'How close?' asked Barrington.

'Twenty-five metres, once.' She paused nervously. 'But if I use target arrows I can be accurate to thirty metres.'

He worked it out, studying the girl. She looked too frail to pull a bow, much less place one on target ninety feet away.

'Suppose you had to hit a man and stop him in his tracks. Could you do it?'

She blushed and shook her head. Barrington gave her a comforting smile and started to turn away. 'But I would not think of the Germans as men,' she explained. 'We know they are pigs. I would place the arrow in the chest or the throat. Either place would stop them.' She smiled her nervous smile. 'Permanently.'

'All right, Heidi. You join Michelle Group. And I want four topnotch skiers in that group. People who can move fast in and out of trees, day or night.'

Helga made the decision, calling out the names of four women who went to stand with Michelle and Heidi.

'Anyone else with talents?' asked Barrington, half expecting someone to hold a black belt in judo.

* * *

The church proved to be an ideal centre for training the groups in spite of the proximity of the German soldiers in the square. During the day none of them ventured into the church, much to the disappointment of Christine Peterson who had devised an elaborate system of signals guaranteed, she claimed, to give a full minute's warning. Not only did the Germans avoid the church, but they seemed to accept without question the frequent groups of devout women who spent so much of the day in prayer.

During the summer, when the village shared a minister with Annolsetrene, the church was also used for gymnastics and folk dancing. Barrington quickly made use of the equipment, clearing one side of the church of pews and laying down mats and a jumping horse with some old, but serviceable, climbing ropes which they hung from the oak beams. By mid-afternoon he had most of the women close to total exhaustion and, he hoped, beginning to regret their eagerness to enlist.

'The general fitness of you all will be critical,' he told the perspiring circle of women, 'and I expect you to do the maximum of exercises when you are in your own homes. Each morning we'll have a session here, working through the climbing and crawling routine for about two hours.'

There were groans as Helga translated for the ones who did not understand.

'I thought we were going to use guns,' complained Sonja. 'Not drop on them from the ceiling or crawl under their beds.'

'A gun is only as good as the person using it. No matter how hard we train, or how fast I speak, I can't turn you into better gunmen than those German commandos. Your only hope is surprise, and that ends the moment someones fires a gun.'

'All right, English,' said Helga with a sharp look at Sonja. 'We do what you say.'

Barrington rose from his seat and walked out onto the mat, facing the semi-circle of women. He beckoned to a girl called Magda Peters, who was barely eighteen. She was small and slim and very pretty.

'Your assignment starts this evening, Magda. I want you to go up to the hotel and ask to see your uncle. Take your time, hang around the guards and find one that is interested.'

She looked at him nervously. 'Interested?'

Barrington grimaced. 'Attracted to you.'

'Oh,' her face cleared and she beamed at him. 'That is no problem. I can get any of them interested!'

'Splendid,' said Barrington with some relief. 'Find a young sentry at the hotel and get talking to him, then arrange to meet when he is off duty. During the next few days get to know him, do all you can to make him keen on you, and try to find out the shifts the guards have and the times they change during the night.'

She nodded happily. 'I will do that, Colonel.'

'She's a bit young,' said Sonja sourly.

'She's old enough to kill,' replied Barrington, turning to Michelle Group. 'I want the skiers in this group to start doing some trail skiing. If the Germans try to send you back, or ask question, argue with them. Say you're doing cross-country for the winter sports. Tell them anything, but insist on the right to use some of the trails around the village.'

'How hard do they insist?' asked Helga.

'Don't run any risks and make them suspicious, but up to that point as hard as they like,' replied Barrington. 'I don't expect you to win, but if you do manage to get approval there may be a chance for one of you to head for Annolsetrene.'

'I could do that at night, anyway,' insisted Helga.

Barrington shook his head. 'I need you to lead the groups, Helga. Anyway, getting to Annolsetrene won't accomplish that much. We can't bring them into it, not without telling them about the gold, and can we trust them that far?'

They looked at each other. Sonja and Tania pulled faces. Helga smacked a fist into the palm of her hand. 'No. There is no love lost between the villages.'

'All right, then,' said Barrington. 'We'll forget about it. But we're going to need explosives at some point. Where could that be obtained?'

'The logging camps always have some,' said Karen. 'They use it for breaking up log jams on the river. But I don't know where they keep it.'

'Who would know?'

Helga swore softly in Norwegian. 'Everyone who knows is up in the Varennes.'

'Not everyone,' said Tania. 'Some of the old men must have seen it used in the camps.'

'Find out,' said Barrington. 'Talk to all of them. If there are explosives in the area we can use them.' He turned to Lillie Group. 'As soon as you leave here I want you to start gathering information about the hotel. I want floor plans, entrances, information about walls, ceilings, the roof, any cellars. Everything that is known about that hotel I want on paper as soon as possible.'

They began to get to their feet, stiffly, their sweaters and blouses damp with perspiration. Some smiled wanly as they left, others gave uncertain nods. Tania hung back with Sonja, searching for an excuse. She found it as her cheeks began to flush.

'What about the mats?' She said. 'Don't you want us to put those back?'

'No. If the Germans come in whoever is around can say they are used by the Keep Fit class.'

'You're the only one who is going to be around,' pointed out Sonja. 'We'd better teach you the words.'

'Oh I can do that,' offered Tania quickly. 'You must have a lot to do, Sonja.'

Sonja gave her a tight smile and left, waving to Helga who was talking to two of the members of Lillie Group. Barrington considered Tania with a cool smile. 'I've got a great deal to do,' he said. 'I'm not sure I'll have time to learn any Norwegian.'

'It's the first priority,' she said firmly. 'If we lose you we lose everything. So far you've been lucky, but if that German officer decides to see what is going on in here . . .'

Barrington grunted and reluctantly nodded his head. Helga came over to them, smiling wearily at the Colonel. 'So we are on the way, English. How soon do you think?'

Barrington frowned. 'We can't wait more than a week, and if the Captain steps up his methods of interrogation we may only have a day or two. It's Monday, so I suggest you think in terms of Saturday night.'

Helga considered him grimly. 'You think it can be done, English?'

Barrington shrugged. 'We'll know Wednesday night,' he said.

'Wednesday?' asked Tania.

'That's when Tania Group breaks into the Varennes so that I can use their radio. If we can do that and escape detection we have a chance.'

'And if you don't?' asked Helga.

'I shall be their prisoner,' said Barrington, 'and you can decide whether or not to hand over the gold.'

'It's a stupid idea,' said Tania. 'You can't risk everything to use their radio. Just tell me the message and I'll get it through.'

'You,' said Barrington firmly, 'are not even going on Wednesday.'

She glared at him. 'It's my group.'

'Miss Arlberg, I wouldn't put you in charge of the Ladies Sewing Circle, never mind a saboteur squad.'

Red spots burned in the paleness of her cheeks. 'Let me ski to Annolsetrene? I can use a telephone.'

'And then what? Call England through the Oslo exchange? Contact the harbour master at Trondheim and ask him if he'd mind bringing the Captain of an English warship to the phone?' He softened his words, trying to take the sting out of them. 'Tania, we'll do it my way and then if things go wrong there'll only be one person to blame.'

'But why is it so important to use their radio?'

'It's the only one in town, and if I can just get five minutes on it then this entire operation becomes worthwhile.'

Tania's mouth tightened, but she nodded reluctantly. Helga ruffled her hair affectionately and left, promising to be back for the evening service.

They talked aimlessly for a while, Tania coaching him with a few more Norwegian sentences. Although he could memorise them easily enough, the accent was a problem, particularly the *ö* vowels. Privately he believed that his only hope lay in switching to poor German after the opening sentence and hoping they appreciated his attempt to co-operate.

He crossed to the mats and began to pull them against the wall, trying to ignore the savage aching of his leg. It had been acting up all day since the trek through the snow the previous night, but the exertion of showing his pupils the rudiments of self defence had twisted muscles already badly strained. He paused, leaning against the wall, feeling waves of pain flow up from his knee, knotting his stomach and bringing a cold sheen of perspiration to his face. Tania, who had been helping him, glanced up and was immediately concerned.

'It's your leg, isn't it?' she asked.

He said nothing, taking deep breaths until the nausea had passed, then turning to limp slowly down the aisle towards the vestry. 'If you'd be good enough to finish putting the mats against the wall,' he said.

She watched him go into the vestry, worried by the paleness of his features. 'What a pair we are,' she thought dismally. 'I can't use my left arm and he can't use his left leg.'

When she had awkwardly dragged the last of the mats against the wall she went to the door of the vestry and tapped gently. The second time she knocked Barrington told her to enter. She went in, feeling the tightness in her throat that came so often when she saw him. It made her want to blurt out words, quite meaningless words, so that she didn't have to feel his eyes on her and hear the gentle timbre of his voice.

He was lying on the narrow bed against the wall, a patchwork quilt over his legs. There was a notebook beside him and a pencil, but she doubted that he had been working.

'I'm all right, Tania,' he said with a brief smile. 'Just leave me to get some rest.'

'Why are you such a solitary man?' she asked him helplessly. 'Why can't you just hold out a hand?'

He cleared his throat forcefully and sat up, starting to swing his bad leg off the bed until she ran forward and stopped him. He gave her an exasperated look.

'Miss Arlberg,' he began, firmly.

'Tania,' she corrected, with equal firmness. 'And if you don't let me see that leg of yours and get Doctor Jansen if necessary, I promise you I'll be back with Helga, Mrs Tollinson and Korina Mattel. Between the four of us we'll examine the leg whether you like it or not.'

'That's taking unfair advantage, in fact I'd say it was verging on blackmail.'

She waited. After a moment he sighed and pulled up the black skirt of his cassock. Beneath it he was wearing his service trousers, rolled up below the knee. When he pulled the left trouser leg clear of the knee her breath caught in her throat and she gazed at him with concern. The ragged scar that ran along the side of his knee, ending in a pitted hollow below the joint, was badly inflamed and the kneecap itself had swollen to almost twice its size.

'The doctor will have to see this,' she said. 'It's terribly inflamed.'

He grimaced, shaking his head. 'Doctor Jansen has got better things to do. Anyway, the leg often acts up like this. By tomorrow morning the fluid will have gone and it'll be normal.'

'That won't be normal for a week unless you do something,' she said sternly. 'We need you, Colonel. If you keep working on that leg you'll be on your back by Wednesday.'

He glared at her. 'Ma'am, I think that most unlikely.'

'Sir,' she snapped, 'I think you must be delirious!'

He grunted angrily and leaned back against the cushions, folding his arms. She reached out and touched the knee, noting his wince of pain with some satisfaction.

'I'm going to see the doctor. It needs a poultice of some sort, probably hot and unpleasant, and you're not going to argue.'

'I don't want the doctor near this church,' declared Barrington. 'If the Germans should find me out, and they know he's been here, then the one man you may need desperately will be a prisoner or worse.'

'All right,' she said, accepting his decision grudgingly. 'But I can still get the poultice from him and treat you myself.'

'For a lonely skier, Miss Arlberg,' Barrington said sarcastically, 'you appear to have enormous reserves of knowledge.'

'Just practical experience,' she replied waspishly. 'I spent most of my childhood at Doctor Jansen's. My mother was his nurse for almost ten years.'

'I knew there was a Nightingale look about you,' he murmured.

'Kindly remove your trousers, that ridiculous cassock and whatever else you're wearing by the time I get back,' she told him in an icy voice. 'I shouldn't be more than ten minutes.'

After she had gone Barrington sat up and swore loudly and with feeling for a full three minutes. He then removed his clothes and lay back on the bed, covering himself with the quilt and a sheet that was so threadbare even the moths were too ashamed to whet their appetite.

Tania was true to her word, returning in slightly under ten minutes with a basket of food and a suitcase containing a blanket, sheet, and the hot poultice mixture. Barrington gazed at the suitcase with alarm.

'Didn't the Germans question you?' He asked.

'It's snowing a blizzard outside and they're only stopping people coming and going from the square. Relax, even if they come into the church I'll tell them you sprained your knee skiing.'

He smiled dryly. 'Well that's obvious. One only has to look at it!'

She had taken a piece of muslin off a bowl that was filled with a steaming grey mud that gave off a pungent odour. 'They won't get a look at it once this is on.'

'It smells like jellied embalming fluid.'

'Doctor Jansen said it would hurt like hell.'

She smiled at him and spread the first layer over his knee. He went very quiet for some minutes, at first trying to lift himself above the waves of pain, then trying to recall how bad it had been when they got him back to Mandalay.

The medical post had been a single brick bungalow with a clay tiled roof and narrow windows that kept out the sun and trapped the smells of flesh losing the final battle. Around him were various soldiers, some Indian, others British. Most had suffered accidents or succumbed to disease, but at the end the cause did not matter, only the battle and its outcome. As the weeks went by he watched men no longer aware of their identity, of their body, of God, King or Country, give up and drift away in the still hours before the new day began.

They died of gangrene, of beri-beri and typhus, and often they were glad to go. The sister was a nun, lined and grey before her time, and she nursed him through the nights when he writhed and moaned in the grip of pain-racked dreams. He passed the crisis when he dreamt that he had got up from his bed and unfastened the sandbags from around his foot, carrying them out onto the verandah. Somehow he knew that if he walked away with the sandbags all the pain would be gone – for ever. Yet he found the will to walk back into his room, to place the sandbags back on his foot and get into the bed again.

'It will go hard after a while,' Tania told him in a subdued voice. 'And the pain will go then.'

'It's easing already,' replied Barrington, managing a smile.

She bathed his face and his chest, ignoring his protests, then covered him with the clean sheet and woollen blanket. She had brought herrings in madeira and in sweet dill pickles, and cheese and fresh bread which they ate as darkness cloaked the softly falling snow.

When the poultice was hard she showed him how to cut it away in sections with a knife, wincing each time he pulled a piece from the knee. The swelling had gone down noticeably, but he was still flushed and feverish. When all the poultice had been cut away she bathed the knee and wrapped it in the muslin, placing a cushion beside it before covering it with the bedclothes.

'I take it all back,' he told her, holding up his hands. 'I couldn't have wished for a better nurse.'

She blushed. 'Someone had to do it.'

'And you did.'

He gazed at her until the blood burned high in her cheeks and she rose from beside the bed, gathering things aimlessly and putting them in the suitcase. There was a small bottle of schnapps and she offered it to him, but he shook his head already feeling drowsy.

She finished putting things into the suitcase and closed it turning to him with the tightness in her throat, not sure how she would say goodbye. He was asleep, his breathing shallow and sometimes strained. She hesitated, not wanting to leave. The decision to stay was the easiest she had ever taken.

He awoke in the early hours of the morning and found her asleep on the bed beside him. Her eyes opened instantly, briefly bewildered, then quickly warm as she became aware of him once more.

'You idiot,' he said softly. 'You shouldn't be here.'

'Why not?' she asked quickly, defensively. 'You're not a prude, are you?'

'I'm old enough to be your father, so go home Tania Arlberg.'

She opened her mouth to make an angry comment, then snapped it shut. He was watching her, thinking he had won. She smiled, slipped her good arm round his neck and kissed him firmly on the mouth. At least it showed she was not afraid of him, she told herself.

The thought had barely surfaced when she realized that things were beginning to happen. For one thing, his arms had gone around her and were starting to exert a very considerable degree of pressure. And for another, the kiss was going on for a very long time.

'Er, Colonel?' she said nervously, coming up for air.

'Charles,' he murmured, and kissed her again.

Tania had always regarded kissing as a fairly harmless pursuit that was good for a giggle when regaled to girl friends the following day. There had been a student three summers ago who took it all very seriously and ending up taking her virginity on a hot summer's night when she had only really intended to go for a walk. But it all paled into insignificance when compared with Barrington.

She was vaguely aware that her legs had become numb and trembly, whilst her heart was going too fast to count. At some point the blanket and quilt rose and engulfed her, and sometime later she realized that she was as naked as Barrington.

There was a moment when they both paused, staring deeply into each other as though searching for confirmation, and Tania remembered later that the only fear she felt was that Barrington would remember he was a gentleman and change his mind.

For Barrington it was a strange, almost mystical union. Images of his dead wife floated behind his eyes, her pale features and gentle smile opening doors in forgotten corners of his mind. The warm, scented woman who twisted and turned beneath his hands was like the essence of forgotten summers, the very spirit of youth. And only when he plunged into her, crying out, feeling her arch and cling to him, did he open his eyes and see the face of Tania Arlberg.

13

Gustav Mesner broke at eleven fifteen the following morning after Sergeant Goff had immersed his head in a bucket of water for the third time.

The water torture had been the idea of Private Pohl who had been subjected to it as a child by two bullies who regularly found victims along the banks of the Isar River in Munich. The terrifying memory of being held under water until the lungs seemed to be on fire had stayed with him over the years, surfacing the previous day when he had proudly suggested it to Sergeant Goff.

They had tried it in a bath at first, but there seemed to be something incongruous in taking a dishevelled prisoner up the stairs to one of the elegant bathrooms on the first floor. There was also the inescapable fact that the bathrooms were badly designed for torturing the occupants and after thrashing about on two or three occasions, usually getting as wet as the victim, Sergeant Goff went back to working in the hotel cellar and came up with the bucket variation.

The interrogation team was made up of Sergeant Goff, two corporals who boxed for the regiment, and four privates who tended to overdo things if left too long on their own. Sergeant Goff had once read a book on the subject and repeatedly told them that breaking arms and fingers was no use at all. The pain was quickly anaesthetised by shock, the broken bone had to be splinted before complications set in which would cause the doctor to be called, and the entire effort was wasted because pain and shock easily transcended fear.

'What we need,' said Goff, 'is a condition which will derange the mind, dissolve courage, destroy resolve and create a state of total subjugation through fear. No more boxing practice. No more work with the vice, or the hammer, and definitely no more beatings with the rubber hose. It's bloody hard work and all you've got at the end of it is a semi-conscious moron who spits in your face.'

The bucket leaked and was barely large enough to take a size 7 head so Goff ordered his interrogators to look around surreptitiously for a size $6\frac{1}{2}$, maximum. The closest they found was $6\frac{2}{3}$ and the head in question belonged to Gustav Mesner.

Mesner was a relatively recent resident of Borgas, arriving the previous year to take over the bakery from old Harald Kortik who passed away quietly from coronary thrombosis shortly after putting his last batch of bread in the oven. Nobody really took to Gustav's bread, always insisting that it was inferior to Kortik's and was too moist, or too dry, depending on the day.

Although Gustav Mesner always laughed his staccato laugh that sounded more like the broken exhaust of Tollinson's van, and always explained that he used the same flour, the same recipe, the same mixers and the same oven, they still insisted that his bread was the worst bread they had ever eaten in Borgas and in summer they would walk down to Annolsetrene and bring back loaves for all their friends. The effect of this was to nurture a germ of bitterness in Gustav's soul; to produce such venom, such bile, that some nights he lay in his small room above the bakery and wished for famine across the land; wished that all the grain was sold and gone . . . except his. And then he would bake his bread and every loaf would be bought with a plea, an abject appeal for his mercy. They would heap the most lavish praise upon him, make declarations to the perfection of his bread and beg him for just one small loaf.

In this frame of mind Mesner was blind-folded and forced to his knees, his head then pushed into a size 7 bucket filled with ice cold water. The first time was not so bad, although he thrashed around and moaned and when they unplugged him from the bucket went through an impressive display of contortions and retchings which had Sergeant Goff quite worried. The second time he knew what to expect and took a huge breath, thrashed mightily after barely thirty seconds, and after one and a half minutes took a mouthful of water. They were convinced he had succumbed and turned him over onto his back, pumping him out and slapping his face.

Corporal Biermann suggested a glass of brandy to bring him round, but the Sergeant's acid reply instantly killed all feelings of compassion. As it was they left Mesner alone for half an hour before blind-folding him again. He trembled and moaned, then as the water touched his face screamed loudly, begging them to let him talk. And as he talked, deep down inside, he was filled with a sense of elation. He had got even with Borgas at last.

The village knew that someone had talked when Captain Lodtz paraded Red Company in the square at noon dressed in their white combat uniforms and carrying skis. Mrs Tollinson was about to cross the square to the church with the Colonel's lunch when the German company began to form up. She stopped to watch, curious. Other women appeared in the doorways of houses, others came from the church in ones and twos, wrapping shawls around their heads to hide the sheen of perspiration.

When Sergeant Driker had called the men to attention Lodtz turned and considered the villagers, his eyes gleaming with triumph. Mrs Tollinson was the nearest person to him and she gazed back with just the right measure of contempt to take his attention from the women still drifting away from the church.

'No doubt you are wondering what we are doing,' he said after crossing to her, slapping a short, leather-bound cane into the palm of his hand.

'I can guess,' she said in a bored voice.

'And what would that guess be?' Lodtz asked, smiling tightly.

Mrs Tollinson gazed past him at the waiting soldiers, then said in a bored tone, 'I suppose someone has talked.'

'Exactly,' replied Lodtz, turning to encompass the other spectators and raising his voice to carry across the square. 'We now know that the gold has been concealed in your logging camp.'

'That's very good news,' said Mrs Tollinson. 'I was beginning to think it was all a figment of your imagination, Captain.'

He favoured her with a wafer-thin smile. 'I'm sure you were in this very square when the British trucks were being unloaded. I'm sure your husband was one of the men who took it to the logging camp and told you proudly of what he had done. But your little game is over, now.'

'Oh I'm sure you're right,' said Mrs Tollinson. 'Except that I'm not married, not interested in any gold, and the last time a British soldier came to this town was two years ago . . . on holiday.' She started to move past him. 'But if you want to make a fool of yourself, Captain, I'm sure you don't need any help from me.'

Lodtz's mouth tightened angrily and he reached out, gripping her arm and pulling her round. The cloth slipped from the basket she was carrying, revealing a casserole, some bread and cheese and a bottle of beer. Lodtz poked at them with his cane. She ignored him until he raised the cane and tapped her arm.

'And where might you be going?'

'To church,' she said calmly. 'It is my day to cook the priest's meal.'

'Indeed,' said Lodtz. 'He's very fortunate. I must meet him.'

'Sunday is a good day,' she said icily. 'Now if you don't mind . . . ?'

She waited until he released her arm, then walked away across the square. Lodtz controlled his anger with an effort, wishing he had time to follow her into the church. Instead he turned to Driker and signalled him to move the company out.

The women around the square watched the Germans march down the street with flat, empty faces. No one spoke or displayed any kind of emotion until the crump of boots on snow had faded. Two guards remained in the square, leaning idly against the trucks. Helga moved casually among the women, dropping a word in an occasional ear. Some of them strolled up the road towards the hotel, others entered the church by the front and side entrances.

In less than five minutes the square was empty again while the unsuspecting guards still leaned against the truck, occasionally glancing at the sky which was darkening, bemoaning the fact that it looked as though more snow was on the way.

In the church they were also discussing the weather, only Barrington was welcoming the fact that snow was due.

'When Lodtz fails to find the gold at the logging camp he's going to get mad,' said Barrington. 'And when he's mad he's not thinking straight.'

Facing him was Lillie Group, nine women in a semi circle around the edge of the mats where they had spent the morning learning the brutal art of unarmed combat. It had not been pleasant.

'The most important ingredient in the make-up of a killer is the desire and the need to kill,' the Colonel had told them. 'If you can unlock that beast inside you, then you have won half the battle. We are then only concerned with method.'

He picked up a piece of wire tied at each end to short pieces of wood. He gripped the handpieces, pulling the wire tight, then flipping it into a loop. 'This is the garrotte, still the most efficient means of killing a man since the days of Pontius Pilate. The trick is to flip the wire over the victim's head and cross it fast, then pull tight and hang on. The average man can survive for no more than two minutes, but a trained commando can do a lot in that time. He can kick, use elbows, bend and try to throw over either shoulder, or even go for the knife in his boot. But if you hang on, keep up the pressure, he'll never get at you with a knife and all the other things are just bruises.'

He moved to one of the pews and flipped the wire over the carved post at the end of the bench. Even as he threw the wire he was crossing it, changing the hand grips and yanking hard. The thin steel scored the solid oak and more than one of the women went pale.

'Next you have the knife.' He lifted one of the wide-bladed hunting knifes used by the Germans. It had a serrated edge close to the handle and a convex blade honed to a razor sharp edge.

'You hold this with the cutting edge on top and strike up, never down. Bring it up from either hip, staring the man in the face, and once you strike keep bringing it up, using all your strength, ripping up through the soft part of his belly into the diaphram and under his rib cage into the heart. Don't hesitate, don't lose your nerve. Once you start you go all the way or he'll tear the knife from your hand and slice it across your throat while you're still trying to apologise for being there.'

He stabbed the knife into the pew, letting it quiver there while they thought about it.

'We'll be taking them from behind as often as we can, won't we?' asked Mrs Mattel.

'True,' agreed Barrington, 'but Lodtz's men won't be that easy to surprise. I'm assuming that in most cases they will have turned and will hesitate because they find themselves looking at a woman.'

'But if he does have his back to us,' persisted the butcher's wife. 'Do we go for the throat over his shoulder, or try for the kidney?'

'Kidney,' said Barrington firmly, 'Strike hard, either the left or right side, then as he staggers back step aside and go for the throat the moment he turns. The shock and pain of the kidney wound will make him vulnerable for at least one minute. That's when you go for the throat.'

'What about the chest?' asked one girl, her freckles standing out like buckshot against the paleness of her features. 'They all seem so big. Why not a hard stab in the chest?'

'Not that easy,' said Barrington. 'In the first place he can see it coming and counter the blow. In the second there's a one in three chance that you'll hit a rib and cause nothing more than a flesh wound. And thirdly,' he smiled at her sympathetically, 'if you miss anywhere in the chest region he's not fatally wounded. That means you're dead.'

He faced the group, taking the knife from the ledge and turning it in his hands. 'I could teach you how to swing a piece of weighted hose, a stocking full of sand, an iron bar or a piece of chain. It's a waste of time. You will only stand a chance if you can get close enough to the German without him knowing. And, if you're that close it's the garrotte or the knife.'

For the next hour they had trained on the mats in the church, using weak string and pieces of wood so they could circle other members of the team and rise silently behind them, flipping the string over the head and pulling it tight in one fluid movement. Although one or two members of the group remained clumsy and unconvincing, Barrington could not help but be impressed by the dexterity of the others. Karen Helrop was by far the swiftest member, her athleticism enabling her to move with the speed and agility of a panther. Taking long, loping strides she would flit silently from behind one of the church pillars to flip the cord around Helga's throat before she had the slightest warning.

Later, when the rest of the group were leaving, Barrington took Karen and Helga aside. Although the women were in complete contrast, Helga short and stocky, Karen very tall and slim, they were both strong and well co-ordinated.

'I'd like you to spend a couple of hours each day working together on unarmed combat,' he told them. 'The groups will be using knives and garrottes, or even guns, but I will need at least two of you who can work without any kind of weapon.'

'Does that mean we'll be with you tomorrow night?' Karen asked eagerly.

'If you want to be.'

The girl's eyes gleamed and she nodded, twisting the cord in her hand as though already tightening it around someone's throat. Barrington felt a moment's caution, wondering whether the emotions he was creating in these women were worth the goal he was seeking. Yet he knew there was no other way, that even if he held back the initiative had already been taken. Hiding his reservations he began to teach them the finer points of unarmed combat.

'You have a maximum of two blows to disable your opponent,' he told them. 'They must be delivered accurately and with all the force you can muster.'

He began with the head, showing how the flat blade of a hand could strike beneath the nose, crushing the mucous membrane and soft bone into the antrim, breaking or seriously damaging the inferior dental nerve. Executed correctly the blow was fatal, but at worst the opponent would lose consciousness.

'Your problem with Lodtz's commandos is that they will be trained to counter that blow and will drop their head, making it difficult unless you have them completely by surprise. Easier blows are beneath the left and right ears. Again your target is the inferior dental nerve and by striking into the depression behind the jaw you can sever the nerve, or crush it so effectively that the brain blacks out under the shock.'

'Suppose they're wearing helmets?' Helga asked.

'Then forget about the head and go for the body,' Barrington told them. 'Use a fist, straight arm, and strike with full force into the kidney or the groin.' He glared at Karen, daring her to smile. 'The groin is the most vulnerable spot. Strike a man there with your fist, knee or foot and you can be sure of at least one minute. In that time take your own knife, or his, and end it.'

'What's the best way?' Karen asked, her eyes gleaming with interest.

Barrington hesitated, then stepped up to her and pulled her head back by the hair. As her throat became exposed he held the knife against it. 'It takes seconds, and it's foolproof.'

He released her and she smiled, her eyes glowing with a hunger that sent a chill of alarm through him.

'I can't wait to see if it all works,' she said softly.

Helga gave her a sharp look. 'We do it only when we have to,' she said coldly in Norwegian.

Karen looked at her and smiled, taking the knife from Barrington and running her finger along the blade. 'Of course, Helga,' she murmured. 'But isn't that why we're here?'

Later in the day, when Lodtz had left for the logging camp with his men, Barrington faced the women of Lillie Group. A plan had been forming in his mind since he had watched the German Captain leave, knowing that the man's triumph would soon turn to rage. His reluctance to voice the plan lay in his deep-seated belief that war was a man's domain. In spite of the enthusiasm with which the women had undergone the training so far, he suspected that they were still unaware of the brutal reality they would need to face in combat.

Helga, as though reading his mind, stirred restlessly and took the steel wire of a garrotte from the pocket of her anorak. 'What is it, English? You think we do not know how to kill the enemy?'

'You have a vague idea,' the Colonel replied. 'The reality is something I cannot show you.'

'Is that why you called us here?' asked Magda, sounding impatient. 'To tell us we are too weak for war.'

Barrington sighed and shook his head. 'No.'

'What then?' snapped Karen, a knife suddenly gleaming in her hand. 'What is it you want?'

Barrington's head came up at her tone and his eyes glinted dangerously. 'Very well,' he said quietly. 'We'll make a start tonight. When Lodtz gets back from the camp he is going to be very angry indeed. He'll probably run a house-to-house search, make a few threats, but he'll have no proof that any of you were involved. His only course is to put out patrols after dark and hope to pick up any of you moving about.'

'Perhaps he'll take us all up to the Varennes as well?' suggested Korina Mattel. 'It would be safer.'

'He doesn't know that you're dangerous,' Barrington pointed out, then added with a grim smile: 'Even I don't know if you're dangerous. Lodtz thinks of you as housewives, fairly docile village women who will accept whatever he tells you because he has your men. It's not in Lodtz's character to think that any of you are responsible for his missing men. At the moment he's putting it down to an accident, or at the worst to some of my men left here with the gold. It's time we confused him.'

The women waited, some pale and tense, others calm and expectant.

'Tonight you work in three groups,' he continued. 'Get into the trees around the village and wait for Lodtz's patrols. They'll probably move around in pairs. Follow them and when you're in position, kill.'

'How many?' asked Helga calmly.

'Three patrols of two or three. Don't take anything bigger than that, and remember it must be silent. Get the bodies to a frozen lake or deep snow drift and hide them, letting the heavy snow cover your tracks.'

'And if the snow stops?' Magda asked, her voice thin and tense.

'Come back,' said Barrington. 'The object of this exercise is to get Lodtz worried. Take out six of his men, hide the bodies, and tomorrow night he'll have half his strength patrolling the town and the forest.'

Helga chuckled softly. 'And tomorrow you go for his radio?'

Barrington nodded. 'The last place he'll expect to find us.'

'You'll have your six, Colonel,' said Karen with a chilling smile, turning the knife as though it was already buried in someone's stomach. 'It's the very least we can do.'

Before leaving, Mrs Tollinson laid out his meal of beef casserole, boiled potatoes and bread she had baked herself that morning. She made Barrington sit at the table in the vestry, opening a bottle of lager and half filling a glass which she handed to him.

'You must not worry about us, Colonel,' she told him. 'There are some who will become afraid, who may not have it in them to strike a man down even if he is the enemy. But when they see that it is our lives as well as their own, they will do what must be done.'

'You should not have to do it,' he said bitterly. 'I am a soldier and things like the garrotte and the knife can be reconciled as expediency, the demands of modern warfare. But you are not soldiers.'

He considered her with a worried expression. She clucked softly and patted his head, like a warm-hearted nanny with a bewildered child. 'The world is changing, Colonel Barrington, and the role of women is changing with it. If you had men with which to fight, then we would probably stay at home and wait and worry. But you have not. All you have is the women of Borgas at your side, weak as we are, and we will fight for our gold and our men. Now eat and forget about the rest of it.'

It was not an easy thing to do. Long after she had gone he was still wrestling with the morality of what he was doing. How many Borgas women would die in the next few days, he asked himself repeatedly? How many would be haunted for years by the acts he was demanding of them?

Michelle Group were due to arrive for training at two o'clock, but Tania arrived first with the detailed plan of the hotel he had asked for. Her cheeks grew pink when she gazed at him, her eyes searching his as though she was not sure of the welcome.

'Are you all right?' she asked.

'The leg's improving,' he replied. 'How about you?'

'Oh,' she shrugged, trying to be casual, 'the arm has almost healed.'

'So you're back to normal?'

'Not quite.' Her eyes were very bright and she took a deep breath before adding. 'Not after last night.'

'I'm sorry about that. I can only assume it was due to the fever and . . .' he cleared his throat forcefully. 'To the proximity of a most attractive woman.'

'You make it sound like contamination!' she snapped. 'Like foot and mouth or rabies!'

'I'm sorry,' he said sharply. 'It was more of an aberration, a flight of idiocy by a man old enough to be your father.'

'I don't care if you're old enough to be my grandfather,' she flared. 'I want to know what you're going to do about it?'

'Do about it?' He look puzzled.

She stepped closer and he was uncomfortably aware that the brightness of her eyes was caused by what looked very much like tears. He gritted his teeth. Women in tears filled him with terror.

'Well you can't just pretend it didn't happen.'

'I've apologised,' said Barrington, beginning to flounder. 'Apart from cutting my throat or offering my hand in marriage, I can't think of anything else.'

'You don't have to,' she said. 'I accept.'

'Which?' he asked in a desperate voice. 'The knife or the ring?'

'The ring, idiot,' she replied, and put her arms around his neck.

He gazed down the church, wishing desperately that the door would open and someone would enter. He would cheerfully have settled for Captain Lodtz. The door remained closed, however, and after a moment he disentangled her arms and pushed her gently away.

'You're quite alarmingly mad,' he said. 'Beautiful girls like you do not go around getting hitched to old crocks like me.'

'That wasn't your line last night,' she said wickedly.

He cleared his throat a couple of times and searched for an answer. 'I can't really say I was myself last night,' he managed. 'It must have been something in the poultice.'

'I don't believe you,' she said, kissing him on the cheek. 'But as I'll be putting another one on tonight we can see if it has the same effect.'

Before he could think of a suitably cutting rejoinder, the members of Michelle Group began to enter the church. The French girl who had given her name to the group was one of the first to arrive and after one glance at Tania gave a knowing smile and arched an eyebrow high enough to make any further comment superfluous. The others stood around, nodding to each other and grinning slyly at him.

He gazed at them in exasperation, wondering how he could have travelled so far in life without realizing that women were the most devious and devilish creatures on earth.

14

When Wolf Lodtz arrived back at his headquarters his anger had subsided to a dull throbbing behind the eyes; a burning sensation in the throat every time he thought of the British colonel called Barrington. Somehow the man had managed to stay at large, to move the gold whilst Lodtz and his men were less than half a mile away.

'It's impossible,' he snarled, slamming his fist onto the highly polished oak table that dominated the hotel dining room. 'Barrington could not have stayed with more than three or four men. Our information on the strength of his convoy could not have been so inaccurate.'

The officers and NCOs of Lodtz's Sky Wolves had been summoned to the dining room which served as operations room and staff office, standing uneasily around the long table. Lieutenant Niemens was the only one of the officers who made no effort to conceal his indifference, gazing pointedly at the panelled ceiling as Lodtz glared at the men.

'Fifty tonnes. Fifty!' he snarled. 'How many can one man carry?'

'He must have had help,' said Niemens in a bored voice. 'Perhaps some of the women.'

'You're a fool, Niemens,' replied Lodtz, his lip curling contemptuously. 'There were five hundred cases of gold, each weighing a hundred kilos. There are not that many women, either here or in the surrounding district.'

'Sir, can we be certain that the prisoner told the truth?' asked Lieutenant Dobermann.

'There were signs,' replied Sergeant Driker wearily. 'Hundred of cases, brought by horses, make quite a mess of the ground. The problem is there were no signs of it leaving, apart from ski trails that were soon lost beneath the falls of snow we've been having.'

'Five hundred cases!' A sergeant from Blue Company shook his head in bewilderment. 'What kind of a man is this Barrington?'

'A fool!' snapped Lodtz. 'An imbecile if he expects me to believe that he has taken the gold away. It is still in the forest, probably close to the logging camp. He has simply found a fresh hiding place.'

'It would account for our missing men,' Niemens pointed out. 'They probably stumbled on him and got killed for their trouble.'

'We are not here to indulge ourselves in speculation,' snapped Lodtz. 'I want a maximum effort from each company. House to house search, just in case they're hiding cases in the village, and a full sweep of the area around that logging camp. I want at least a hundred men out this afternoon, and tonight we're going to patrol this village and the forest around it. If anything moves I want to know. Do I make myself clear?'

The officers and NCOs nodded, moving restlessly as though eager to be away.

'Half our strength would leave us vulnerable up here, sir,' Lieutenant Niemens pointed out with bland features. 'May I suggest a dozen or so two-man patrols circling east and west. If there were any signs of movement they would surely find it?'

Lodtz stared at him coldly for a moment, then waved a hand to dismiss them. 'That will be all.'

The men snapped to attention and left, murmuring to each other beneath their breath. Sergeant Driker waited until the last man had closed the door, then moved up to Captain Lodtz who was staring moodily out of the window.

'We'll have to get the message off to Berlin, Captain?' said Driker.

Lodtz said nothing for a moment, watching a teenage girl

talking to Private Wilner who was on guard duty at the entrance to the hotel. The girl was fair haired with a pretty face and a slim, attractive figure. Wilner was clearly impressed.

'Why is Wilner talking to a civilian girl?' asked Lodtz.

Driker stepped up to the window, glancing towards the soldier. 'The girls have been getting curious, Captain. It is natural.'

'Of course. But not for Wilner. If it had not been for that bastard Wilner we would not even be here. We would be in Oslo, with the gold, waiting for an Iron Cross!'

Lodtz turned, his eyes blazing. Driker swallowed and nodded quickly. 'I will reprimand him and move him from the main entrance, Captain.'

'Yes, move him. Put him at the back, by the mortars, and double his duties.'

Driker nodded, mentally kicking himself for putting the private in such a prominent position. 'And Berlin, sir?' he asked hesitantly.

Lodtz grimaced and went to the table, sitting down and pulling a message pad in front of him. He took out his pen, staring at the pad for a moment. 'Do you believe the prisoner Mesner told the truth, Erik?'

'He gained nothing by lying, Captain. And there were clear signs that heavy cases had been stacked at the camp.'

'Then where are they?' asked Lodtz in a helpless voice. 'Where is the Englishman? We have searched the village, the forest, the roads. Why have we not found him?'

'We will, Captain.' Driker said quickly. 'If he is still here.'

Lodtz gazed at the message pad and doodled on it with his pen. 'We are being made to look like fools, Erik. A simple operation in which we had superior strength and the element of surprise. The gold was beneath us. We flew over it, Erik.'

He gazed at the Sergeant, his expression baffled. 'Yet we lost it through a slip of a girl and an English Colonel. Fifty tonnes of gold. Vanished into thin air as though the man is a magician. Where, Erik? In God's name where is it?'

Lodtz slammed the table and sat hunched over his fist, glaring at the wall. The Sergeant moved round the table to face him, his expression carefully neutral.

'We are still in control of the area, sir. As you say, the gold cannot have moved any great distance. May I suggest you inform Berlin that you now know the area in which the gold has been hidden and that you expect to recover it within the next forty-eight hours?'

'They will laugh, Erik. They will hold their sides and shake with laughter. And then they will pass the message to the Führer.' Lodtz shuddered and put his head in his hands. 'We must find it. Quickly.'

'We will, Captain,' replied Driker confidently. 'I know we will.'

Lodtz wrote quickly on the pad and handed it to the Sergeant. He read it, his mouth tightening. 'Are you sure this is wise, Captain?' Driker asked. 'You are saying that the gold is secure, which suggests it is in our possession?'

'I know what I'm saying, Erik,' snapped Lodtz. 'I'm saying we know approximately where it is and we have the area under our control so there is no likelihood of it being moved. That is what *secure* means.' He paused, stabbing a finger at the Sergeant. 'But you find that gold for me, Erik. Find it before that bastard Niemens gets a chance to file anything over my head.'

Driker nodded, tearing off the message sheet and putting it in his tunic pocket. 'I have already taken the liberty of starting a file on Lieutenant Niemens, sir. It contains certain incidents in which he has shown disloyalty to you and to his men.'

Lodtz's head came up and he beamed at the Sergeant, slapping the table with his hand. 'Excellent. That's exactly what we need. The man's untrustworthy, questions the most innocent order. You've heard him. Write them up, Erik. I'll sign them. I'll teach him to criticise my decisions.'

The Sergeant nodded and moved to the door, pausing there to glance back. 'Just leave it to me, sir.'

'We had to kill them, Erik.' Lodtz said suddenly. 'The operation just didn't have room for prisoners.' Driker said nothing, 'Berlin will understand. Even if Niemens opens his mouth, Berlin will be with us on that, Erik.'

'Yes, Captain, replied Driker, feeling a chill of apprehension as he read the naked doubt in Lodtz's eyes. 'You had your orders.'

Lodtz continued to sit at the empty table long after Sergeant Driker had left, turning the words over and over in his mind. *Of course he was right*, he told himself. He had specific orders to stop the gold at all costs. *At all costs*. He repeated it aloud, the words somehow easing his tension. '*At all costs. No matter what. The gold takes precedence*.'

He felt better, rising from the table and moving to the window. Private Wilner was still talking to the girl. He ground his teeth, remembering the ski girl and the way his shots had thrown up little fountains of snow ahead of her, behind her, on either side. If only one of those shots had been on target . . .? He seethed, the tension returning as he thought of how close they had been to success.

The thought inevitably made him consider the possibility that they would not succeed. He gripped the window sill, staring across the snow at the young private and the girl, but seeing instead the bodies of the British soldiers. He had to succeed. It was the only way he could justify those bodies!

* * *

Magda Peters was beginning to enjoy her meetings with Herman Wilner. He was young and freckle-faced and often tongue-tied, but he was also witty and full of fun. She found herself forgetting that the meeting was Colonel Barrington's idea, simply enjoying the company.

'If your German was as good as my Norwegian,' he was telling her, 'we would be completely compatible.'

'But there is nothing wrong with my German,' she said in German, her eyes wide and innocent.

'So there you are,' he said in Norwegian. 'We make the perfect couple. I'm off duty at three o'clock. We could go for a walk.'

'It will probably snow,' she said, pulling a face. 'And anyway I said I would help my mother. She is very worried about my father.'

Herman Wilner grimaced and glanced instinctively towards the pine-clad walls of the hotel that loomed above them. 'I am sorry. Our Captain is determined to get the gold.'

'So let him,' she said sharply. 'We don't have it. Go to some other village.'

Wilner looked down at the snow, his freckled cheeks flushing with embarrassment. 'You promised we would not talk of that, Magda. I can do nothing about it.'

'You could let me see my father?'

'It is impossible. The cellar is guarded all the time.'

'You're just saying that.' She pouted, sensing a chance to gain useful information. 'I'll bet you've not even been down there.'

'I have. I was there this morning, standing in for a friend. All the men are in the main wine cellar. There are two guards by the door all the time and a Sergeant and four privates in the small room at the top of the cellar stairs. They are always there.'

'Even at midnight?' She looked sceptical.

'Well, the Sergeant and his men finish about eleven. But the two guards at the door are always on duty. They change at midnight and at noon.'

She seemed to relent, giving him a small smile. 'I suppose you're right. Tell me about your home in Dusseldorf?'

'It is very like this,' he said, brightening. 'We live in a small village called Lanrop which is in a valley surrounded by trees, just like Borgas. In the winter we would ski and in the summer my sister and I would take our canoe across the lake. We have other friends with canoes and at weekends we would camp and cook on wood fires. The summers at Lanrop are wonderful.'

'I wish it was summer.'

He stared at her, his cheeks flaming, his mouth opening and closing twice before he managed to blurt: 'You are the most beautiful girl I have ever seen. I wish you would come to Lanrop with me in the summer.'

Her eyes sparkled and she began to nod, then stopped, her face clouding. 'We are at war. I will still be a prisoner in the summer.'

'Oh no, Magda. It will all be over by then. This invasion is only to make our borders secure against the British and French. And we are only here to stop the British from taking away your gold reserves. By summer it will all be sorted out and there will be a treaty between our countries and everything will be fine.'

He stared at her earnestly, his blue eyes wide and sincere. Magda sighed and looked bewildered. 'I don't know. You are doing such terrible things.'

'It is our Captain,' Herman said desperately, dropping his voice to a whisper. 'He ordered me to shoot a skier. A girl. Of course I didn't. At least I shot at her, but missed.'

Magda concealed her interest with an effort. 'The man is a monster.'

'We are just soldiers. We do what we are told.'

'Then you are as bad as he is.'

'I would be shot if I refused,' he said miserably. 'I don't like what we are doing here, but neither does Lieutenant Niemens and he can do nothing about it either.'

'You mean most of you don't like it?' She looked surprised.

'I don't know about that. Some of the men . . . they are specially picked. They came out of the Sturmabteilungen, the Brown Shirts. They seem to enjoy it.'

She looked back towards the village, pulling the fur-lined collar of her anorak around her throat. 'I will have to go.'

'You'll come again, though?' he asked quickly. 'I'm back on duty at eight o'clock.'

'That's late,' she said dubiously.

'Please. It will be quieter tonight. They say a lot of the men are going out on patrol.'

'Oh? What time?'

He shrugged, looking uncertain. 'I'm not sure. They'll be night patrols, though. Until after midnight at least. Please say you'll come.'

She hesitated, then gave him a radiant smile and nodded. 'All right, Herman. I'll come about nine o'clock.'

He watched her walk away down the narrow road until she went out of sight around the bend. When he turned back to look at the hotel he found Sergeant Driker staring at him coldly. He snapped to attention.

'Fraternising, Private Wilner?'

'No Sergeant. She is just a . . . a girl from the village. We talked.'

'I'll bet you did.' Driker's lip curled contemptuously. 'I'll bet you told her everything she wanted to know.'

'Oh no, Sergeant,' he said quickly, alarmed by the implication. 'She is not like that. We just talked about . . . about our homes and summer and . . . just family things.'

Driker stared at him coldly until his cheeks went red. 'Tonight, Wilner, you will be on guard duty at the rear of the hotel. You will patrol the mortar positions from midnight until noon tomorrow.' The Sergeant paused, then added maliciously, 'and don't worry about the girl. We will take care of her when she comes around again. We'll teach her one or two tricks they wouldn't know in Borgas.'

Wilner paled, his freckles standing out alarmingly. 'I would ask you to leave her alone, Sergeant.'

'Go to hell,' replied Driker, turning away.

Wilner took a deep breath and spoke rapidly in a thin, nervous voice. 'Is that really why we are called the Sky Wolves, Sergeant Driker? Because we hunt in packs and kill and rape defenceless people.'

Driker stopped and came back, his eyes ugly. 'Watch your mouth, Wilner, or you'll wish you'd never heard of the Sky Wolves.'

'I wish that already, Sergeant. I thought we were supposed to be efficient soldiers, a highly trained force of commandos who would fight the enemy.'

'And what are we?' Driker asked softly.

'Torturers,' replied Wilner. 'Torturers of civilians, perhaps worse if what they say about the British soldiers is true. And whatever you are threatening to do to Magda.'

Driker controlled his rage with an effort, his blazing eyes boring into the young private. 'We are the elite,' he said finally, icily calm. 'And if any of us forget that, try to destroy what we stand for, then I will see that man in hell, Private Wilner. I'll see him in hell!'

Driker turned and walked back towards the hotel. Wilner took a deep breath and wished his knees would stop shaking. He marched briskly along the perimeter of the hotel grounds, stopping finally to gaze up at the lighted windows. He wished it really was a hotel and that he was not the enemy. He understood now why his mother had cried when he left Lanrop last Autumn, and why his father had warned him that the German war machine was fuelled with hate. 'This is not a visionary's war, a conflict of ideals, of territorial dispute. I believe you will find only hate and destruction – and ultimately that will corrupt you all.'

15

'If any woman has any doubts about her ability to kill, either through lack of conviction or physical weakness, you must speak now.'

Barrington stood in the pulpit wearing the richly embroidered vestments of the church, a prayer book clasped in his hands as he addressed the congregation below. The fact that it consisted of a dozen hard-eyed women in ski pants, anoraks and woollen caps, and each of them had concealed in their pockets at least one knife and a home-made garrotte, was only slightly bizarre.

'Very well,' said the Colonel when no one spoke, 'you will move in squads of four and take up positions along prominent ski trails in the forest. The Germans are operating three-man patrols with instructions to bring in anyone found in the forest after dark. The fact that you are unarmed will tend to allay their suspicions, but you will still need a reason for being in the forest after dark.'

He pointed to the squad which would be led by Korina Mattel. 'Your squad will pretend that one of your members has a broken ankle. Take a hunting rifle but make sure it's unloaded, and tell them you went out after deer. After all you run the butcher's.' The other squads came up with similar covers.

'How long before we attack them?' Asked Korina Mattel.

Barrington shrugged. 'It's very much up to you. The important thing is to make them believe that you are just an innocent party. They'll still have to take you in for questioning, but they'll be off guard once you get moving along the trail.'

There was a sudden rattle on the roof and Barrington made a quick gesture, bringing the women to their feet, prayer books in their hands. 'Let us pray,' he said loudly in Norwegian.

The door opened and Sergeant Driker stepped into the church, a pistol in his hand. He glanced at the small congregation, then moved aside to allow Captain Lodtz to enter. Together, eyes fixed on Barrington, they moved down the aisle until they were level with the front pews. Barrington continued to stand with hands clasped, his features adopting what he earnestly hoped was a reverent expression.

'You are the priest?' asked Captain Lodtz.

Mrs Tollinson, who was nearest, turned and spoke to him.

'We are in the middle of evening service. Can you not leave us alone even here?'

Lodtz gave her the bleakest of smiles and turned to look up at Barrington. 'Come down here, priest.'

Barrington considered him with a calm, almost benevolent expression, then closed the prayer book and descended the steps from the pulpit, placing his stiff leg carefully on each step and using the walking stick to take his weight. Lodtz watched with narrowed eyes until Barrington turned to face him.

'Now then, Captain?' asked Barrington in halting German. 'What is it that must interrupt my service?'

'We will speak Norwegian,' snapped Lodtz.

Barrington shrugged. 'If you wish,' he replied in Norwegian, watching Helga wince as he failed to get the correct accent on *ønsk*. He made a polite, apologetic gesture and continued in German. 'But if you would permit me to practise my German I would be obliged. Now that my country is being occupied by your Army I shall soon have to speak it as much as Norwegian.'

Lodtz frowned, accepting the logic of his argument. 'Very well,' he answered in German. 'It will also help my Sergeant. They tell me your name is Hermannson?'

'Yes, Captain. The Reverend Josef Hermannson.'

'And how long have you been here?'

'Since last autumn. I spend the summer months at Annolsetrene and cycle up here on Sundays for the services.'

'With that leg?' Lodtz was immediately suspicious.

Barrington nodded, mentally cursing his stupidity. 'It was cycling up here that was responsible for the injury,' he said smoothly. 'I was knocked into a ditch by a car, badly damaging the kneecap.'

'Let me see it,' snapped Lodtz.

Barrington hesitated, glancing beyond Lodtz to the women. He could see from the faces of some of them that they thought he was still wearing his service trousers beneath his cassock. Karen had risen from her seat and was moving casually towards Lodtz, her right hand in the pocket of her anorak. He tried to tell himself that she really wasn't crazy enough to try to take Lodtz in the church, but as she nudged Olga who immediately rose to her feet and began to follow, he knew that she was. Clenched in that right hand in her pocket was the garrotte, all ready to flip around Lodtz's throat.

'Very well, Captain,' he said quickly, raising his cassock to reveal the inflamed scars around his knee.

Lodtz stared intently at the leg for a moment, frowning. 'You say it was done last year?'

'In July. That is why I came to live in Borgas.'

'Some of the scars seem older. And the inflamation is fresh.'

Barrington shrugged, letting his cassock fall. 'It still acts up, once a month at least. I use poultices to ease the inflamation.'

'I see.' Lodtz seemed disappointed, exchanging looks with the Sergeant before nodding to the women and starting back towards the door. Karen stepped around him as he walked past and to Barrington's horror began to take the garrotte from her pocket.

'Karen!' said Barrington sharply.

Karen turned towards him, her mouth pinched and angry. Lodtz and Driker reached the door, leaving the church without a backward glance.

'That was damned stupid, young woman,' Barrington said in a voice that reminded them of cold steel. 'It was also against my orders. Disobey me again and you will leave the village.'

'And if I refuse?' said Karen.

'I shall shoot you,' Barrington told her calmly. 'I shall shoot anyone who jeopardises the operation and the lives of those who will be taking part.'

Karen stared at him with eyes like amber beads. Olga nudged her, whispering softly. Karen ignored her, the clenched hand still in the pocket of her anorak, still clutching the steel wire she was longing to use. He waited, not sure which way she would go. After a while, as the other women began to move restlessly out of the pews, she suddenly chuckled like the gurgle of water in a rocky brook.

'I am too eager, eh Colonel? Too quick for you.'

'Too hungry,' said Barrington. 'Women who are hungry for things like that worry me.'

Karen stepped towards him, placing her lips quickly and softly against his, stepping back before he could turn his head away. 'There are all kinds of hunger, Colonel. You should know that. But mine will work for you, for Borgas.' She smiled a *death's head* smile. 'The next man I kiss tonight will be the man I kill.'

After they had gone Barrington sat in the front pew, looking up at the tragic figure nailed to the cross suspended above the altar. But he found no help there and the pangs of conscience merged with anxiety and doubt to fill him with more confusion than he had ever known in his years as a soldier. The presence of the women was difficult enough to rationalize, but to use them, to transform them into killers for the sake of bars of gold filled him with revulsion. Yet the alternative was equally abhorrent to him. If he surrendered the gold to Lodtz it would certainly buy freedom for the men of Borgas, and perhaps innocence for the women already slipping through the night with their knives and garrottes, but how many bombs and bullets and Messerschmitts would it buy for Hitler . . . and how many lives would be lost as a direct result? All to be laid at his door.

He did not know how long he sat before the altar, his head bowed as though in prayer, searching for other solutions which were not as extreme. The candles they had lit at the start of the briefing burned down and sizzled out, the light dying with the flame. When Barrington raised his head and stretched aching shoulders, he found Tania sitting at the end of the pew, watching him with dark, unreadable eyes.

'How long have you been here?'

'I don't know. I thought you were praying.'

Barrington gave her a crooked grin and rose stiffly to his feet. 'Don't let the cassock fool you.'

He crossed the darkened church to the small vestry and switched on the light, drawing the curtains as she followed him into the room. He saw that she had a basket and suddenly realized how hungry he was.

'So what were you doing?' she said, placing a jar of herring, a smoked sausage and some bread on the table. 'You looked pretty grim to me.'

'It's a grim business,' he said, sitting down to eat.

Tania sat facing him, shaking her head when he offered her the herring. 'You still haven't come to terms with the fact that we choose to do this. You are only the catalyst, the instrument.'

'Without me you would not try.'

'Without you it would not be necessary, the men would be home, the gold would still be in the Bank of Norway.'

'Without Hitler Germany would be brewing beer and eating sausages and having a jolly good time.'

'Not quite,' said Tania with a sad smile, 'but I take your point. All I want to say is please stop blaming yourself, feeling that whatever happens will be your fault. It isn't like that. We want help, not a bleeding heart.'

'I'm giving you all I can,' replied Barrington tersely. 'It's your bad luck that you got landed with an invalid.'

Tania gazed at him angrily. 'I never meant that. You know I didn't.'

'It's a fact of life, Miss Arlberg.'

'Don't you dare call me Miss Arlberg,' she said furiously.

He grimaced. 'That's something else we have to talk about. I don't know what I was thinking of last night.'

'Don't change the subject. We are talking about the operation and just how vital you are. You don't seem to realize that without you we would be completely lost.'

She gave him a wide-eyed look. He glared back, feeling the sense of exasperation that was becoming a familiar part of their relationship. 'We still have to talk about it,' he said stubbornly.

'All right.' She managed a smile. 'But later, when you've eaten and I've put a fresh poultice on your knee. How is it, by the way?' she asked as he opened his mouth to argue. 'I heard that the obnoxious Captain had a look at it.'

'He was full of sympathy.'

'I'll bet.'

Tania sat back and let him finish the meal, her eyes moving back to him frequently as he ate the bread and sausage. He drank the beer she had brought, but left the aquavit, knowing he would need a clear head for the rest of the night.

'Was it ever like this in India?' Tania asked after a while.

'India is a different world,' he said. 'People live their lives in a different way and for different reasons. There is violence, but it is swift and cruel, like the tiger that comes down from the hills to kill because it knows no better. And the tribesmen, riding mules and running barefoot up hillsides into cannon and musket volleys because they are ruled by hate and despair and that can only be measured in violence. And the people, so many millions of people, gentle and full of hope in spite of the squalor and disease.

'India is a kaleidoscope of life with all the colour and magic you could wish. It smells different, sounds different, assaults your senses when you see it for the first time so that you are never quite the same again. It is a love affair with a hundred women who all have the same name.'

'Oh how sad you are,' she said.

He cleared his throat gruffly and drank some beer. 'I spent the best part of my life there. I met and married my late wife in India.' He looked at her, his grey eyes piercing in their honesty. 'I should have told you about her. About how much I felt for her.'

'You didn't have to,' Tania said quietly. 'I knew. I knew last night.'

'I'm sorry.'

'Don't be.' She eached out and touched his hand. 'But I would like to know about her.'

He stared into his glass, hesitating as though reluctant to go back. 'Her name was Elizabeth. Elizabeth Grant. We met on the bank of the Ganges when I was escorting Prince Jawardi and some British diplomats. There were two million people in and beside the river. Two million. And I saw her immediately, sitting on the back of an open car. It was a Cord. An American car, all silver and white, as though it had just rolled out of the workshop. And she had a blue and white parasol to keep the sun off her face, and a blue dress.'

He looked apologetic. 'I'm sorry. We were married three months later. Married for fifteen years. Then one day she caught cholera. It was all over in a week. Just the funeral and the flowers. We never had time for children. Never had time to buy the house in England, or even think of it. We both loved India.'

'How long ago did it happen?' Tania asked, her voice no more than a whisper.

He smiled a sad smile. 'Oh, three summers ago. You are

the first woman I have looked at with anything more than idle curiosity.'

She rose from her seat at the table and came round to him, the tears wet on her cheeks. She knelt beside him, her arms around his neck. 'Kiss me. For God's sake kiss me.'

16

Above the pine-covered slopes that rose in gentle waves towards the ridges in the north, the shifting curtains of light from a spectacular aurora borealis were casting a silver radiance over the snow. Although the aurora was primarily a silver blue, a giant iris directly overhead pulsed and quivered, throwing waves of purple and red and gold across the night sky, like the surf from some cosmic ocean.

In the clearing the four women crouched beside the massive bole of a Scots Pine that soared high above them, its needles sifting the changing light so that kaleidoscopic patterns moved across the clearing, turning the snow into breath-taking mosaics of colour.

'Do you think it's some kind of omen?' asked Maria Kesselrig, the youngest member of the squad. She was nineteen with golden hair plaited and wound around her head beneath the woollen ski cap.

'Sure it is,' replied Mrs Tollinson, her stocky figure deep in the shadows. 'It means that Spring will be late this year, that there will be more snow and the geese will honk when they pass over Borgas. That's what the Northern Lights mean. That's why we get them every year at this time.'

Sonja laughed softly and patted the embarrassed girl on the shoulder. 'My mother used to tell me they were having a fantastic party in the ice palace at the North Pole and one day, if I was very good, I would get an invitation.'

'The only invitation I ever got was from Larg Hansen,' said Anna Rekvarik. 'He told me that if I lost my virginity when the Northern Lights were in the sky I would have good luck for the rest of my life.'

'And did you believe him?' Mrs Tollinson asked curiously.

'No,' replied Anna, who was tall and fair in her late twenties. 'I just pretended to.'

They laughed softly, stopping when a voice called out in German.

'Positions,' snapped Mrs Tollinson. 'Anna, you move last. Remember.'

Anna swallowed and nodded, lying back in the snow. Sonja glanced at Mrs Tollinson who nodded grimly. The girl turned, cupping her hands around her mouth, and called out. The German voices came back almost immediately, echoing among the trees.

'At least three,' said Mrs Tollinson, her voice no more than a whisper.

'Suppose it's more?' asked Maria.

Mrs Tollinson thought about it, her head sunk low in her shoulders, staring into the shifting patterns of coloured light. When she raised her head her eyes gleamed coldly in the dark. 'If it's four we still go.'

The men came off the trail beside the clearing, their white combat uniforms giving them a ghostly appearance in the eerie light. They were wary of the women at first until they saw the figure of Anna on the ground with Sonja kneeling beside her. There were only three, two young privates and a corporal who cocked his Schmeisser and unclipped his skis, moving carefully across the clearing until he was looking down at the prostrate girl.

'You have trouble?' he asked, his Norwegian mispronounced and barely intelligible.

Mrs Tollinson moved casually to stand beside him, speaking in German. 'It's very fortunate for us that you came, Corporal. Anna had a bad fall four hours ago and we think her leg is broken.'

'You were told to stay in the village,' grunted the German, laying his gun on the ground and kneeling beside Anna.

Sonja pulled off her woollen cap and shook out her

chestnut hair, smiling at the soldiers who had kept on their skis, edging into the clearing. Maria Kesselrig strolled to them, looking worried and tense.

'We thought we were going to be here all night,' she said.

The soldiers did not understand Norwegian and gave expressive shrugs, looking apologetic. The girls moved closer, one on either side of them. Sonja put her hand in the pocket of her anorak gripping the wooden pegs of the garrotte, her eyes on Maria who had unfastened the waist buttons of her anorak and had obviously decided on the knife.

The Corporal was gently feeling Anna's knee, beginning to frown as he found no swelling. Anna cried out, grasping his wrist as though to push his hand away. Mrs Tollinson stepped behind him, dropping the garrotte over his head, slamming her knee into his back and pulling it tight. The Corporal's eyes bulged and he tried to reach for it, but Anna was gripping both of his hands, her face white and terrified as he gurgled and desperately tried to heave the stocky woman over his head. But the steel wire was already slicing into his throat, through the trachea and the jugular. Blood began to spray outwards over Anna who gave a terrified cry and let go of his hands.

Mrs Tollinson increased the pressure, feeling the life going out of the man beneath her. She felt no fear or revulsion. She felt no different from when she killed the Christmas goose, twisting its neck until it stopped jerking in her hands. The Corporal was like that. One moment he was straining against the garrotte, the next he was just a heavy weight in her hands. She took a deep breath and released the handle of the garrotte, letting him fall forward into the snow.

As Mrs Tollinson stepped behind the Corporal and flipped the steel wire around his throat the soldier beside Sonja took a full two seconds to comprehend what he was seeing. He glanced at his partner, reaching for the gun on its sling across his chest, and to his horror saw the pretty girl with the golden hair plunge a commando knife into his friend's stomach. Even as he was trying to come to terms with the horrific images, a steel wire bit into his throat and he felt the slim hard body of the girl against his back.

He reached for the wire that was like a searing band of fire around his throat, but there was no way he could grip it. A wave of terror went through him as he felt the strength of the girl, but seconds later his training took over and he let himself go loose, falling back against her. All the air had gone from his lungs and there was a heavy thumping in his head, and from the numbness of his throat the wire had already cut deep and severed nerves, perhaps the arteries. He pushed the thoughts out of his mind, concentrating on the knife in his boot. The girl could not hold his weight and was staggering back, the pressure easing briefly on his throat. He felt the shaft of the knife against his fingers, slid it out of the scabbard in his boot and reversed it, ready to strike up behind him.

Sonja gripped the garrotte more firmly in her hands, turning with the falling body, ready to sink her knees into his back. At the last moment she saw the knife in his hand, striking up towards her stomach. She rolled away from it, releasing the garrotte, the gleaming blade hissing past her throat. She kept on rolling, coming up on one knee, plucking her own knife from inside her anorak. The German was on his knees, pulling the wire away, his white smock red with blood, his face almost purple. He was sucking in deep, gurgling breaths, trying to get to his feet.

From the corner of her eye she saw Mrs Tollinson turning from the Corporal, and on the other side Maria was behind the soldier who clutched his stomach with bloody hands, her knife already poised over his throat. She gathered herself and lunged towards the German, knowing that each second gave him more strength. He turned towards her sensing the danger, a gurgle of protest in his torn throat. She held the knife in front of her, plunging it into his stomach just above the white webbing belt, then ducking beneath his arm as he tried to strike at her with his knife. She moved ten feet away and sat down in the snow, gasping for breath as fear and exertion took the last of her strength. He went slowly to his knees, his face going very pale, contorting with a new agony until consciousness left him and he fell forward into the snow.

Sonja wanted to cry, but Maria was already doing that beside the still body of the other private. Slowly she got to her feet and went over to the girl, pulling her away from him, taking the knife from her hand and plunging it into the snow until it was clean.

Afterwards, when they had dragged the bodies to a nearby lake and slid them down through the hole they had earlier chopped in the ice, they counted up their gains. Three Schmeissers with four magazines each, three Mausers with spare magazines, and three wide-bladed knives.

But the most important gain was the knowledge that they could take on a highly trained German commando and, given the element of surprise, beat him at his own trade.

* * *

Tania had stretched out on the bed beside Barrington, lying beneath the coverlet with him in the dark. The room smelled of the pungent odour of the kaolin poultice which she had smeared over his knee an hour before, and which was now hardening into the ugly grey compound that would have to be cut away from the knee when it was cold.

'How does it feel?' she asked.

'Not bad at all,' he replied. 'You're getting quite good at it.'

'I used to help the doctor on holidays until my parents moved to Tretten.'

'Is that where they are now?'

'Yes. My mother will be worried. She would expect me to have telephoned or visited them by now.'

Barrington was silent for a while, then said: 'I never asked you what you were doing in the valley?'

'I was going back to Vinstra where I teach English. I'd been staying with a girl friend. We spent the night and morning listening to the radio and the reports about the battle in Oslo Fjord. We could not believe it was happening.'

'I imagine there were a few generals in London who felt the same way.'

'How long will this war last?'

'Yours? About a month or two. I suppose there'll be some sea battles and perhaps a landing by British and French troops, but Jerry has got clear supply lines back to Germany and ultimately he'll take you over.'

'And the rest of it?'

'I think that will depend on Russia and France. If they both put the pressure on and the British Expeditionary Force gets full support, we could be into Germany by Christmas and the whole thing should be over by this time next year.'

She turned her head, trying to see his face in the darkness. 'You don't sound as though you believe that.'

'There's a problem or two that needs to be ironed out. A few lessons we haven't learned.'

'Such as?'

'We're as old fashioned as the French. We still think in terms of trenches and fixed firing lines. The Germans are into modern warfare. That's why they're here in Borgas and walking the streets of Oslo. They move fast, go for superiority in the air and speed on the ground. If they do it well enough they could take Europe and move against Moscow before we've even thought about a winter campaign.'

'And then it would be a long war.'

'I'm afraid so,' said Barrington. 'I'm afraid it could be a very long business indeed.'

'So winning here is even more important.'

He smiled at her in the darkness and squeezed her hand.

'That's exactly it, my dear. We have no real idea of how important that gold might be.'

'I wish I knew how they were going on,' she said fervently.

Barrington nodded, feeling the hollowness in his stomach every time he thought of the women out in the forest. 'At least there's been no alarm,' he said. 'We can be thankful for that.'

* * *

Gunther Pabst and Walter Lear were enjoying the night ski through the forest. They were both expert cross-country skiers and until they joined the army had spent most weekends on the forest-covered slopes of Bavaria. They had been assigned to do a long outward sweep from the road block to the Imso River, skirting the two largest lakes to the north before coming back towards Borgas. It had been a great ski, the brilliant aurora in the sky filling the slopes and valleys with shifting schisms of light.

Gunther was in the lead, negotiating a narrow twisting trail between tall pines that leaned together and the spruce with their snow-laden boughs sagging across the paths. He ducked beneath one such branch, straightening and pushing himself on with his ski poles. He paused, avoiding an outcrop of icy rock, and glanced back to see how Walter had negotiated the spruce.

What he saw filled him with horrified disbelief. Two girls in tight ski-pants and light anoraks had him on the ground and one of the girls seemed to have a wire around his neck with her knees in his back. Even as he watched the second girl plunged a knife deep into his side. With a choking cry of rage Gunther unslung the Schmeisser and worked the bolt action. He was starting to aim the gun when he felt the searing pain in his side that almost immediately turned to a spreading numbness in his back. He tried to swing round, gripping the moulded stock of the gun, but unaccountably he stumbled and the gun began to sag in his hands.

He saw a woman rise up from the snow beside him, her face devoid of all emotion, her eyes dead in their sockets as though she was incapable of any feelings. She was heavily built with greying hair beneath a bobbed woollen hat and her hands were gnarled, older than her face, as though her life had been hard and testing. In her right hand was a long, thin knife that glittered in the pale light. There was another thump in his back and a pain that went right through him, taking all sensation from his left side. The gun fell from his hands and he swayed on his feet, watching the woman who faced him, wondering if it was also a woman who was behind him stabbing him in the back.

He tried very hard to speak. To explain that this was all unnecessary. That she had no right to hate him like this. But the words would not come and from a long way away he saw the gleaming knife rise up and disappear into his stomach. Then the blackness swooped in and he knew no more.

* * *

Barrington gingerly cut away the last piece of the clay-like poultice and sank back on the bed with a sigh of relief. Tania examined the knee, then poured him a glass of aquavit.

'You can have the drink now. It looks good. Really healthy.'

'You should try it from this end,' he answered.

She laughed, gathering the pieces of poultice in the muslin which had bound the knee and putting them in a paper bag. She crossed to the jug of water and poured some into a bowl, washing her hands.

'It really needs a week of complete rest.'

'You mean like your arm? The one you use constantly!'

She smiled. 'It's almost healed. I'll be fit for tomorrow's raid.'

Barrington sat up quickly, glaring at her. 'You can forget that, Miss Arlberg. You are not part of the team.'

'I'm as fit as you,' she flared.

'You're superfluous. I'm the only one who can transmit the message.'

'You're not going without me!' She came back and sat on the edge of the bed, her cheeks red and angry.

'You're not going and that's final.'

'Then we're through,' she snapped. 'If you jettison me just because of a scratch on my arm I'll never speak to you again.' She hesitated, searching for some greater threat. 'And further more, our engagement is off.'

Barrington gave her an amused look. 'I didn't know we were engaged.'

'Pig!' she said.

'I only recall making a tentative suggestion which you took very literally.'

'Liar!'

'Obviously we were unsuited for each other. My age, your youth and impetuosity, your refusal to accept my decisions, would have made it quite unworkable.'

'That's not true,' she exclaimed. 'I was only thinking of you.'

Barrington adopted a sceptical expression. 'I find that hard to believe, Miss Arlberg.'

'Don't call me Miss Arlberg! You sound like my headmaster.'

'I beg your pardon.'

Barrington lay back with his hands behind his head. She sat and fumed for a few minutes, then poured two glasses of aquavit and held one out to him. He raised himself up on an elbow and took it from her.

'What's this for?'

'I don't like to argue.'

'Neither do I.' He raised the glass with a smile and drank it. 'Although it has certainly taken a weight off my mind.'

'Why do you say that?'

He leaned back on his pillow, yawning. 'All that talk of

marriage. Quite ridiculous really. Can't have that sort of thing.'

Two bright red spots appeared on her cheeks and she stood up, drinking the glass of aquavit in one gulp. 'Really Colonel?' she said in a voice that sounded like breaking glass.

Barrington turned his head, giving her a worried look. She was slipping the woollen sweater over her head and placing it on the plain wooden chair beside the bed. He frowned, glancing surreptitiously at his watch. She was unbuttoning her blouse and slipping out of it.

'Just what are you doing?' he asked, his mouth suddenly very dry.

She unzipped her tweed skirt and let it fall to the floor, stepping out of it and gazing down at him with perfectly calm features. 'I am getting into bed,' she said coolly. 'There is a curfew in the village and I see no reason why I should get shot just to preserve your precious dignity.'

'That's neither accurate, fair, or even true,' he said, adding tautly: 'You could at least turn out the light?'

She took off her bra and slip, then sat on the edge of the bed to remove her stockings. When she rose to face him she was wearing only a pair of white briefs and a distinctly pink complexion. With her eyes fixed on his she slid out of the briefs and under the coverlet, lying with her back to him.

'If you want the light out,' she said, 'you'd better turn it off yourself.'

He grunted and reached for her. 'I don't know where you learn these dreadful tricks,' he said, taking her in his arms, 'but they're having a devil of an effect on my peace of mind!'

* * *

The only warning that Korina Mattel's squad had was the sudden slither of skis on snow, the sliding crunch of skiers going into a christie, and the harsh command in German for them to put their hands in the air.

Korina Mattel lifted the hunting rifle over her head, glancing across at Karen Helrop and Olga Morden who were sitting on a fallen tree. Gerda Lanrig, the woman who was supposed to have a broken ankle, was still leaning against a tree as the German patrol swept across the clearing. She started to slide towards the ground when the leading soldier, a Sergeant, aimed his machine pistol and snarled a command. She straightened, going pale, her arms lifting above her head.

The Sergeant was Hans Giestner, a barrel-chested bull of a man with cropped fair hair and small blue eyes that had an opaque quality about them, as though they needed a polish. With him was Private Osterich, a heavily built man with dark, saturnine features and eyes as black as ebony beads. He and Giestner had entered the commandos together, had served Lodtz with both pride and pleasure. It was Sergeant Giestner who had been put in charge of the execution squad on the Valebru road. And Osterich had been the first man he had chosen.

'So what have we here?' said the Sergeant, moving to Karen and Olga. 'A couple of little rabbits out in the woods.'

The men laughed. The two younger privates were not too sure of what was happening, but they could tell from the Sergeant's voice that this was going to be no ordinary detail. Osterich stepped out of his skis and crossed to Mrs Mattel, taking the gun from her hands and opening the breech. He relaxed when he saw it was empty. She patted her pocket and spoke to him in German.

'I keep the cartridges in my pocket. We are out hunting for deer.'

'Why should you leave the village at night for deer? You know the Captain's orders. No one must leave their homes after dark.'

'My husband is the butcher,' replied Korina. 'We have little meat left and you will not allow me to go to the market at Valebru. What else could I do?'

'You could stay at home, in bed, obeying orders,' snarled Osterich and gestured to the two privates. 'Watch these two. They make me itch.'

The Sergeant removed Karen's woollen hat and ran his hand through her hair, seizing a handful and jerking her head back as she tried to pull away. 'Not so fast, little rabbit,' he said. 'There are questions to be answered.'

'She doesn't understand German,' called Korina Mattel.

'Everybody understands Sergeant Giestner,' he replied and jerked Karen to her feet by her hair.

She cried out in pain, then stood stiffly before him as he unfastened her anorak and began a deliberately clumsy search. He took the long, thin knife from the waistband of her slacks and held it up, turning it in the eerie light that filtered through the trees. Red, gold and silver burned on the blade.

'So she has a weapon,' said the Sergeant. 'The little rabbit wants to be a lion.'

'It is to skin the deer,' called Mrs Mattel. 'We all have them.'

'Shut your mouth,' snarled the Sergeant. 'Next time you open it one of my men will put something unpleasant in it.'

He looked at Osterich and laughed. The soldier came up beside him, sniggering as he looked at Karen. The Sergeant had stepped in front of Olga, taking off her hat, pulling her hair free. She started to get up off the log but he smiled and shook his head. 'No, you are fine there, little rabbit. I think it is time you performed some small service for Germany. Eh, Herman?'

Osterich nodded, laughing softly, his black eyes gleaming as Olga gazed at them with a bewildered expression. The Sergeant stepped closer to her and unbuttoned his trousers, taking his time, his laughter growing as her bewilderment changed to shocked revulsion. She started to pull away, shaking her head, but his laughter stopped abruptly and he took a fistful of hair and pulled her towards him. In his right hand he held a luger, placing the barrel between her eyes. She went very still, then as he moved his hips, opened her lips and took him into her mouth.

Osterich sniggered and gazed at Karen, his thick tongue moving across his lips as she stared back defiantly. He stepped closer to her, placing his hand lewdly between her legs. She ignored him completely and turned to glance at Korina.

Olga felt she would choke. The Sergeant was now holding her head with both hands, moving with increasing urgency, pushing himself into her throat so that she could only moan and gag and try to ward off the waves of nausea that swept through her. Her hands hung by her sides and as his boot brushed against her right hand she felt the cold handle of the commando knife projecting from its scabbard. Tentatively she pulled at it, surprised at how smoothly it came free. Almost with disbelief she hefted it in her hand, felt the sharpness of the blade on her thumb.

With the knife in her hand she was no longer a mindless animal being taken and humiliated by another kind of animal. It gave her strength and in seconds it gave her both rage and courage. She pulled back as his movements became more violent, gripping him in her left hand and swinging the knife up between them. It cut through cleanly, with only a slight resistance, and then she was staggering to her feet, the penis in her hand, spurting a fountain of blood towards him.

The Sergeant's scream did not even sound human. It screeched up into the night, making the blood run cold, and went on and on as he sank to his knees, clutching himself, the blood spurting between his fingers with each frightened beat of his heart. Olga watched him for a moment without pity, then the knife flashed out and laid open his throat from ear to ear.

Osterich still had his hand between Karen's legs when the Sergeant screamed. The sound was so horrifying that he wasted valuable seconds taking in the scene before fumbling for the safety catch of the Schmeisser. It was all the time Karen needed to scoop up the butcher's knife that the

Sergeant had so carelessly dropped beside the log. Even as Osterich was swinging his gun towards Olga, she was slipping it between his ribs at a precise angle for the heart. His entire body shook, as though with palsy, and he fired a brief burst of shots into the snow at his feet. And then he was dead.

Korina Mattel had her favourite boning knife deep in the German soldier's back within two seconds of him turning to see what was happening. He died instantly and then she ran to the second German who was struggling to free himself from the garrotte which Gerda had got around his neck. The wire had fallen too low, partially around the neckband of his combat jacket. Even as Korina reached them he had his hand on Gerda's wrist and was pulling her over his shoulder. The butcher's knife took him below the left breast bone, slipping efficiently into the heart.

They dragged the bodies to a nearby ravine and spent half an hour covering them with drifts of snow they swept up with branches of spruce. Olga was very quiet, keeping to herself, and when they had finished she seemed relieved at Mrs Mattel's suggestion that she and Gerda would take the weapons into the village while Karen and Olga made a wide detour and approached the village from the east. They stayed in the clearing after the two women had left, sitting beside each other on the log.

'You were fantastic, Olga,' said Karen. 'I've never seen anything so fantastic.'

Olga shook her head, trying to speak. Her shoulders began to shake. Karen put her arms around her, pulling her down into the snow beside the log. 'Don't cry,' she said. 'That spoils it all.'

'What do you mean?' Asked Olga. 'Spoils what?'

'Oh, Olga,' said Karen in a strangely breathless voice. 'You were so exciting, so fantastic. I can't tell you how you made me feel. Like now. I feel it now.'

She kissed Olga on the mouth, forcing her lips wide, slipping her tongue between her teeth and flicking it backwards and forwards. Olga tried to pull away but the girl was strong, her hands moving over her body, pulling open her anorak and blouse, teasing her nipples with trembling fingers.

'No,' gasped Olga, her eyes wide with shock. 'I'm not like that. Please stop.'

But Karen had no intention of stopping. Her mouth moved down the girl's neck, across her shoulder and down to her breast. Her hands pulled at the waistband of her slacks, slipped between her legs to caress her. Olga tried to struggle, but there was no more strength in her. She lay passively in the snow, unable to prevent the raw emotions that rose within her. After a while she cried out and clutched the woman to her.

17

Wolf Lodtz was awakened at seven o'clock when it became obvious that no less than three patrols were missing. He stormed into the operations room where the various squad leaders were grouped around a map of the district laid out on the table. Most of them had been on patrol for most of the night, then out again at dawn in an attempt to locate the missing men.

'How many?' asked Lodtz furiously. 'How many fools are lost this morning?'

'Nine,' Driker replied quietly.

Lodtz's eyes bulged. 'What are you telling me, Sergeant? That we can lose nine highly trained commandos, the elite of the Germany Army, within a mile of this headquarters without so much as a shot fired in warning?'

One of the corporals stepped forward and indicated an area to the west of the village. 'I was in this region, sir, shortly after midnight when I heard a brief burst from a Schmeisser. There was no further shooting and I assumed that one of the men had fired at a deer or something.'

'I see. A patrol fires a warning burst and you interpret that as a late night hunting spree?' He stared coldly at the man. 'What is your name?'

'Corporal Schmidt, sir.'

'It's now Private Schmidt!' Lodtz glared at the others around the table. 'Did anyone else see anything?'

Various heads were shaken. A Sergeant Melcher glanced at his companions, then shrugged and suggested that so many men could only be taken in ambush situations. It was the view of many of the men that this had been carried out by the village of Annolsetrene, some ten miles away, and that they had been organised by the English Colonel.

'We think they set ambushes after dark and waited for our patrols, sir.' He paused, beginning to get nods of support. 'The only way our men would have given in without a fight is if they were completely out-numbered.'

'And not even then,' snapped Lodtz. 'Was all the training a waste of time? How many enemy ambushes do we walk into?'

Lieutenant Niemens had entered with Doberman while the sergeant was speaking. 'That doesn't sound like a Norwegian village to me, Captain. They're not likely to travel ten miles through the woods to start murdering German soldiers.'

Lodtz turned on him furiously. 'Somebody is murdering German soldiers, Niemens. Someone who does not appear to have your distaste for acts of war.'

Lieutenant Niemens stiffened, his cheeks flushing. 'I have no distaste for war, Captain Lodtz. Only murder.'

'Then who do you suggest is out in those woods? The English Colonel with some of his men? A few villagers perhaps? Or the fairies of the forest who just wave their little wands to cast a spell on Osterich or Sergeant Giestner?'

Some of the men smiled grimly at the suggestion. Driker frowned thoughtfully at the map and shook his head. 'There has to be something here that we missed, sir,' he said quietly. 'Our men may walk into an ambush, but they would not surrender without a fight. There would be considerable gunfire, and the squad leaders had flares to use in an emergency.'

'Just the point I was trying to make, sir,' said Niemens stubbornly. 'Our men were taken off guard. To me that suggests it was caused by people from this village, not outsiders. In any event,' he added logically, 'I don't see how skiers could reach us from Annolsetrene at night. Even the fittest of men, travelling across country in the dark. Impossible.'

'What people are you talking about, lieutenant,' snapped Lodtz. 'A few old men? Some children?'

'I'm talking about the women of this village,' the Lieutenant said quietly. 'We take their presence for granted, but suppose they have decided to fight.'

Lodtz snorted with laughter, gazing around the table where sergeants and corporals joined in with chuckles of derision. When the Captain finally spoke he made no attempt to conceal his contempt for the Lieutenant. 'Women do not fight, Lieutenant. Women sit at home by the fire and weep a little. They do not go out in the middle of the night and tackle highly trained German soldiers with a kitchen knife. Only an imbecile would waste our time and his own with such a ridiculous suggestion.'

Niemens' face was red, but he persisted stubbornly: 'I still suggest that tonight we place all available men in the forest around the village. Each patrol should be within hearing distance of the next, the full complement forming a net around the village. In my opinion, Captain, such a move would catch those responsible for our missing patrols. A group of women!'

'Very well, Niemens,' said Lodtz, smiling condescendingly. 'You can organise the operation for tonight. You will go out there with all available men and by this time tomorrow I expect you to have some prisoners.' He paused, staring at him coldly. 'In the meantime I shall test your theory. These women you imbue with such strength and courage will be told that if they have not recovered the gold within twenty-four hours I shall begin to execute the men of Borgas at the rate of one an hour.'

There was silence in the room until Sergeant Driker cleared his throat and asked nervously. 'At what time will the ultimatum begin, sir?'

Lodtz thought about it for a moment, then glanced at his watch. 'We'll say from dawn tomorrow. That will give them time to think about it.'

18

It was a crisp, sunny day and the smoke curled up in still columns from the wood framed houses around the square in Borgas. Everyone seemed to be out, crossing the square, pausing to talk to the women who were cleaning the windows of the church and sweeping out the porch. The trucks lining one side of the square were being guarded by a single young soldier called Johann Klaus.

Johann guarded the trucks every day from nine o'clock in the morning until darkness fell at six thirty. He was a tall, gangling youth of nineteen who had been chosen as one of Lodtz's Sky Wolves because of his height and his abilities as an athlete at high school. Apart from being an exceptional long distance runner, he was also a first class skier and held the junior cross country championship for Bavaria. In training he had shown considerable aptitude for weapons, particularly the throwing of grenades which had earned him the company trophy at the training camp at Kiel.

His interest in the war was minimal, consisting of a vague picture of German movements in Poland and its ambitions in Europe. As far as Norway was concerned he fully believed the propaganda that the occupation of Norway and Denmark was vital to protect them from invasion by Britain and France. Beyond that young Johann's curiosity did not extend, nor did he have any particular views on the state of the world in general. He was, however, distinctly interested in Michelle Argent.

'And what does that badge mean on your sleeve?' asked the French girl, looking terribly impressed.

'Grenade throwing,' replied Johann. 'I specialise in throwing grenades.'

'Good heavens,' said Michelle, her eyes round. 'Are you terribly good at it?'

He nodded, smiling at her expression. 'We have to be. A grenade must be put within six feet of its target or you might as well not bother.'

'It sounds very dangerous. Perhaps I shouldn't stand so close,' she murmured. 'In case one of them goes off.'

He laughed. 'I don't have them with me now.'

'Oh,' she looked relieved. 'Do you keep them in a safe place?'

'Yes, we've made an armoury in one of the store rooms at the hotel. I keep them in there.'

'You must feel very important having all those grenades?'

He smiled modestly. 'Well they're not all mine. In action most of the men would draw two. It's just that I would have as many as I need.'

'Good heavens,' said Michelle, round eyed. 'If you all have two and you get as many as you need, you must have tonnes and tonnes of grenades.'

'Not tonnes. We dropped special ammunition pods from the aircraft and one of them carried the grenades.'

'And others?'

'Oh, spare ammunition for our Schmeissers and mortar bombs.' He grimaced. 'I shouldn't really be telling you all of this.'

'Why on earth not?' she asked. 'You don't think I'm a spy or something, do you?'

'No, of course not.' He laughed at the very idea.

'There you are then. I'd better go to church now, but I'll see you later.' She gave him a smile that made his knees go weak.

'You go to church a lot, don't you?' he said as she turned away. 'I mean, in the middle of the day.'

She glanced over her shoulder, trying hard to look

reverent. 'We're praying all the time. It's for the menfolk, you know. We're asking God to take care of them.'

'Oh,' he winced. 'I'm sorry. Especially now.'

She paused, looking curious. 'Why especially now?'

He stood awkwardly, scuffing his feet in the snow, wishing his cheeks would stop changing colour. 'It's our Commander, Captain Lodtz. He's issuing a special demand for the gold at noon.'

'And?'

He hesitated, then said in a rush. 'He's going to start executing your men in twenty-four hours.'

She looked at him like a bewildered child. 'Executing them? But . . .? But they haven't done anything?'

He bit his lip, his cheeks flaming. She turned and ran towards the church, a sob floating back to him. He gazed at his feet, wishing he was in the infantry instead of the paratroops. He was sure that life would be simpler and he wouldn't feel quite so . . . so responsible.

When Michelle entered the church she went straight to the altar which was being dressed with early snowdrops and primroses by two of the *Watcher* squad. She paused beside the partially concealed entrance to the cellar.

'Who's down there, Maggie?' She asked.

'The Colonel's with Michelle Group doing weapon training,' replied Maggie, who was grey-haired and wrinkled. 'They're due to finish in half an hour.'

'I'd better hurry,' said Michelle and slid the slab aside. Maggie shrugged and crossed to help her, pushing the slab closed and placing the basket of flowers upon it.

Barrington was demonstrating the firing mechanism of the Schmeisser to ten attentive members of Michelle when the French girl descended the steps, pausing in the shadows at the foot of the stairs. The small, stone-walled room was lit by an oil lamp on each wall, but the ventilation was bad and the air was heavy with fumes from the lamps. The Colonel glanced towards her, but she made a small gesture and settled back to wait until he had finished.

'It's really very good of the Germans to bring this particular weapon to Borgas,' said Barrington, holding the Schmeisser by its skeleton steel stock. 'It's still very new, developed from the 38 model by a gentleman called Hugo Schmeisser. It's light, accurate, is held easily by the foreward magazine and the pistol grip, and is ideal for you ladies to blast away to your heart's content.'

He held it in both hands, demonstrating the grip with the steel stock folded forward. 'You've got thirty-two rounds of 9mm ammunition in the magazine and when you're firing the gas from the exploding cartridge automatically drives the carriage back and reloads, tripping the firing hammer as long as you're holding back the trigger. In simple terms that means you are firing bullets at the rate of five hundred a minute. Any questions?'

Michelle Argent quickly raised her hand, her forehead creased in a perplexed frown. 'How can we fire so many bullets in a minute if the box under the barrel only holds thirty-two?'

Barrington forced a patient smile. 'That's the speed the bullets are fired, Michelle. It's not how many you fire. These are machine pistols so you do not vary the rate of fire. You aim, squeeze the trigger, and for a few seconds you are the ultimate in fire power.'

'And then while we fumble to change the magazine the enemy wipes us out?' suggested Anna Rekvarik.

'You'll be spending the rest of the afternoon practising just that,' replied Barrington. 'And when you're using them for real I want just short bursts. A quick pressure should loose off six shots. Do that five times, then duck behind a wall or a tree, unclip the magazine and clip a new one in. You can do the whole operation in two seconds. One and a half if you're really trying.'

Barrington took the magazine off, then clipped it back in. Maria Kesselrigg, on the front row, indicated the bolt on the side of the breech. 'Do we cock the gun every time?' She asked in halting English.

'Just the first time you fire. It's fully primed every time after that until you change the magazine. You must re-cock the weapon each time you reload.'

He looked around the group, hefting the machine pistol in one hand. 'This group will be my first assault team. So far we have twelve Schmeissers and as soon as the attack commences I expect a further six. But for the moment six of you in this group will have a machine pistol, a knife and a garrotte. Two of you will operate with explosive charges working with Helga and Heidi, who will be using her bow and arrow to place charges and to remove the guards at the main entrance. Helga and I will be using shot-guns, so I suggest you all keep well clear as we go in.

'What you must work at for the rest of today and tonight is speed. Those of you with Schmeissers must practise again and again and again. I want you to be able to roll and come up on a knee. Spin out from behind a tree, or out of a doorway and crouch, gun ready to fire. I want you diving left or right as you start to change that magazine. And all the time you're moving, all the time you're firing, I want you to keep cool and look for grenades and ammunition. As you pass the body of a soldier pause, crouch beside him, remove his spare magazines and any grenades he has in his belt.'

He swung the barrel of the Schmeisser in a steady arc that encompassed them all. 'Run out of ammunition and you are dead. Fire wildly and you waste ammunition. I want you cold and steady as a rock, firing a quick burst, moving on and covering so that your partner can clean the ammo from your kill. Do it that way and we'll get into their headquarters . . . and once we're in we have a chance.'

He nodded to Helga who rose and began to brief the group on various ways to conceal the Schmeissers in their bags or clothing for the walk across the square. She and Barrington had discussed it before the session and felt that the Germans would have no reason to search women in the middle of the day, but nevertheless most of the women would be carrying the Schmeissers under their clothes, strapped either to their backs or beneath voluminous skirts.

'I thought this was my group?' said Michelle when he reached her by the stairs. 'I didn't even know about the meeting.'

'I want you in Tania Group,' Barrington told her. 'I'm going in with this group and Helga. Tania will hit the back of the hotel and grab four of the mortars, pulling back to that raised mound. From there you can dominate the road into the village and the road out of the square up to the hotel.'

'You mean we use the mortars.'

'Right. Tania is a teacher and you're a student. I hope that means you're both good at maths because you will have to try to set the elevation, the rest of the squad giving you cover and supplying you with mortar shells.'

'Sounds fascinating,' Michelle said dryly. 'What does Tania have to say about it?'

Barrington cleared his throat a couple of times, trying to look severe. The French girl grinned at him. He grimaced. 'She doesn't know yet. I-ah . . . I thought you-ah . . . might mention it?'

'I'll mention it, Colonel, but if I know Tania she's quite likely to aim her first mortar at you!'

Barrington nodded, grinning ruefully. 'She does have something of a temper. But what brought you here?'

'Oh heavens!' exclaimed Michelle. 'It's about Lodtz's latest plan. Apparently we're to get an ultimatum. Unless we hand over the gold and, I suppose, stop shooting his soldiers, he's going to start executing the men at noon tomorrow.'

'That's a pity,' said Barrington. 'I was hoping he'd wait a week before getting that drastic.'

'You expected him to execute the hostages?' asked Michelle in astonishment.

Barrington nodded grimly. 'Since yesterday I've been forced to accept the fact that my own men are no longer alive. If they were we would have had reconnaissance planes over, some attempt to reach us from Valebru or Annolsetrene. If Lodtz is capable of shooting prisoners, as he must have done, then he is also capable of shooting civilians as well as torturing them. I'm afraid we have a rather nasty specimen of Nazi Germany. A man who cannot be reasoned with.'

'Then what can we do?' Michelle asked.

Barrington thought about it for a moment, then shrugged. 'We will have to see what happens tonight.'

* * *

By late afternoon the entire village had read the notices posted around the square and in the Post Office. Barrington's advice to everyone was that they should appear to be more anxious than antagonistic, despairing rather than desperate. He found time for a brief rest in the vestry as the sun sank behind the snow-covered hills, having spent two hours with each of the groups, rehearsing them in every method of killing, from the steel of a knife to the bloody blast of a sawn-off shotgun. There had been many pale faces, but the mouths had been firm and the hands that followed his were quick and without a tremble.

He lay on his bed, wondering at the strength of the women. They seemed to have such reserves so that each time you thought you had found them out, struck the bottom of their resolve, they would come back, eyes like diamond splinters, hands chopping, knee searching for the groin and a scream of rage in their throat. He knew there was courage in them, knew that somehow he had captured the spirit of freedom in the women of Borgas.

It was no longer the gold, though that in itself meant a great deal to their pride. It was no longer the men, though the women were all prepared to give their lives to save them. No, he told himself. Something else had happened in Borgas. The women had stepped out of the shadow of their men and from that moment they had seen new horizons, a new life with or without German occupation. What they were looking at was a life in which they knew, would always know, that freedom meant far more than raising children and going to church on Sundays. It meant freedom of choice, of the spirit, of their sex. It meant that no decision could be rejected, no question remain unasked, no duty withheld.

It meant that they were free to fight for what they believed, for their men, their homes, their birthright. But having fought and won things would never be the same again, for it had always been the man's right to fight for his king, his country, and his family. Now it was a woman's too.

Barrington sighed and wondered what he had done to Norway.

His reverie was disturbed by a tentative tap on the door of the vestry. He swung his leg awkwardly off the bed and gripped his cane, pushing himself to his feet.

'Come in,' he called in Norwegian.

The door opened and Olga Morden entered, her eyes downcast. 'I would like to talk to you, please,' she said.

'Of course, Olga.' He gave her an encouraging smile.

'I have a confession to make,' she said in a voice that was little more than a whisper. 'And you are the only one I can make it to.'

Barrington cleared his throat awkwardly. 'You appreciate that I am only wearing the cloth,' he said. 'Confessions really aren't my line.'

'I know, but there is no one else. Anyway,' she straightened and stared at him fiercely. 'I must tell you because I cannot be part of Lillie Group any more.'

'I see. Well, of course, that's your privilege,' he said, hiding his disappointment. 'I suppose last night was quite a shock for you?'

She looked at him in astonishment. 'You know about last night?'

'Of course. I had a full report from Helga this morning. The results were everything I could have wished for, but naturally it was a brutal realization for you. I can't expect all of you to be prepared to go on.'

'Oh it's not that, Colonel,' said Olga with some relief. 'After what they did to my brother I hate all Germans. Not just hate. I want to kill them. Really want to.'

Barrington looked bewildered. 'Then why can't you stay in the group?'

Olga went red and she bit her lip, staring at the floor. Barrington waited, unable to imagine what could be on her mind. After a moment she looked up, her eyes very bright. 'It's Karen,' she said.

'Karen?'

'She raped me last night.'

Barrington blinked and gazed down at his cane to hide the sudden rush of blood to his cheeks. He cleared his throat at least three times before glancing up at the girl. 'I'm not quite sure I understand, Olga?'

'Karen Helrop stayed with me after we had killed the Germans and when we were alone . . . she raped me.'

Barrington was silent for a full minute, wishing he was anywhere else. There was no doubt that Olga was serious. Her mouth was trembling and there were tears in her eyes. 'But how?' he said finally, feeling a complete idiot.

'With her fingers,' Olga said miserably. 'In the woods, getting inside my clothes, using her fingers.'

'Good God!' said Barrington, finally beginning to understand.

Olga began to sob, stumbling towards the bed. Barrington moved with her, taking her in his arms, sitting on the bed with her so that he could cradle her head on his shoulders.

'Don't worry about it,' he said gently. 'You will go into Tania Group and we'll see that Karen stays away from you.'

Olga began to shake with deep racking sobs. He patted her head, still dazed by her revelation. 'I'm not a lesbian,' the girl said. 'I don't want to be a lesbian.'

'Of course you're not,' murmured Barrington, resisting

an urge to clear his throat. 'I'm sure there's absolutely no question of that.'

She lifted her head, looking at him through tears. 'You're sure?'

'Positive. A thing like that, dreadful I know, but not a . . . not . . . a state of mind,' he finished weakly.

She began to sob again and he held her against his shoulder, awkwardly patting her on the head. He wondered if there was anything he could do and had immediate visions of Karen Helrop screaming denials and attacking him with her favourite garrotte.

'We'll do something about it,' he said, patting the girl's head and wondering what. 'We can't have that sort of thing happening. Good God no.'

Olga lifted her head, smiling through tear stains and kissed him impulsively on the cheek. 'You're such a good man, such a leader. I know if you tell her to leave me alone, she will.'

'Then I shall do that,' said Barrington, smiling at her.

There was a sharp, pointed cough from the doorway and he glanced up to see Tania standing there, her mouth a thin line of seething indignation. 'I just called by,' she said in a voice that clinked like ice cubes in an empty glass. 'But perhaps you'd rather I came back later?'

Olga got quickly to her feet, stepping away from the bed with an apologetic look at Barrington. 'I'd better go.'

'There's no reason to,' replied Barrington, reaching for his cane and pulling himself off the bed. 'I'm always glad to be of help.'

'I know, and thank you.'

Olga ducked her head, blushing beneath his gaze, and hurried out of the room, avoiding Tania's glance. Barrington went to the small spirit stove in the corner of the room and lit the burner, putting on the coffee percolator. Tania walked stiffly to the table and slammed down the basket she was carrying with a clatter of dishes and a bottle or two. Barrington glanced over his shoulder, beaming at her.

'Oh, you decided to stay.'

'Against my better judgement.'

'Don't you mean your baser instincts?'

'I consider that an insulting remark.'

'And I consider your comments in front of that girl in the worst possible taste.'

'You're suddenly very concerned about Olga Morden.'

'I'm concerned about them all. And for your information Olga was one of the women who quietly and efficiently reduced the German fighting strength by nine last night, and gained that many machine pistols into the bargain.'

Tania glared at him furiously. 'Was that why she was here? Getting her merit badge pinned on!'

Barrington took a deep breath, about to make an angry retort, when the percolator began to boil. He brought it to the table with two mugs and began to pour the coffee. Tania watched, quietly seething at his lack of response.

'Sugar?' he asked.

'Black,' she replied.

Barrington sat down and stirred his coffee, leaning forward to forage in her basket, feeling the warmth of the casserole. He lifted it out, found a spoon in the basket and tapped it on the heavy clay lid. 'This for me?'

Tania banged her mug on the table. 'Just what were the two of you doing in here?'

'To answer that question fully would require a breach of confidence and I'm afraid I don't feel inclined to make that concession to you. Do I get the casserole or do you want to take it back with you?'

'Eat it,' she snapped.

'Charming.'

Barrington removed the lid, wincing at the heat, and began to eat. After a moment Tania took out a bottle of beer, a bottle of schnapps and glasses. She poured beer and aquavit for them both. He raised his glass, drank, and resumed eating the casserole which was beef and carrots and quite delicious. Tania began to look increasingly miserable.

'I suppose Olga is going with you tonight,' she said bitchily.

'No,' said Barrington. 'I'm using Lillie Group. It's Mrs Tollinson, Magda, Sonja, Heidi and Karen.'

'I'm coming,' said Tania.

'You're too emotional,' replied Barrington.

'I am ice cold!' she snapped.

'I was sitting in my room having a perfectly normal conversation with a girl of what . . . ? Nineteen? And you are accusing me of lechery before you're through the door.'

'I did not accuse you of lechery. I asked what you were doing.'

'Whatever it was it was my business.'

'I see. You expect me to look the other way every time I find you with your arms around another woman.'

'I expect you to behave responsibly,' Barrington answered stiffly. 'I expect you to behave like a soldier, like the rest of the women in our groups. And as for coming on tonight's operation, if you venture within one thousand yards of the Varennes I will instruct Helga to arrest you.'

Tania rose to her feet, her eyes glistening, and deliberately threw the glass of aquavit into his face. He gazed up at her, unblinking, until she gave a sob and ran from the room. He wiped his face on a napkin she had thoughtfully provided with the meal and finished the casserole, depressed by her anger, but soon reconciled to the view that it was probably for the better.

19

The Hotel Varennes was an L-shaped building constructed of quarried stone and pine, the roof clad in pine shingles. It had three floors, the uppermost built entirely of pine and oak with windows jutting out at twenty-foot intervals. There were fifteen windows on the upper floor, ten of them on the long arm of the L. The middle floor was half clad in pine, the remainder in solid blocks of stone, whilst the ground floor consisted of granite blocks with an Italian tiled floor.

Its chalet design and pine facing was typical of many Scandinavian hotels and from the tree-covered slopes to the north side of the hotel Barrington was able to relate the three floor plans provided by Helga's team with the reality of wood and stone that confronted him. From their position, some twenty feet above the hotel, he could see how the main entrance gave way to a large open room with a log fireplace which was the main source of heating in the hotel. Beyond that was the dining room, now used as Lodtz's Operations Room, and around it the kitchens, administration offices and a gallery running along the rear of the hotel which was south facing and acted as a sun lounge during the summer.

He turned to the dark figures lying beside him in the snow. They had gathered beyond the square on the deeply shadowed slopes along the road to the hotel. It had taken almost an hour to reach their present position and the time was five past one. Two lights burned in windows on the second floor, but the upper floor where the bulk of Lodtz's Commandos would be sleeping was in darkness. Barrington was fairly sure that one of the lighted windows was the office being used as a radio room.

'What do you make of the lighted windows?' he whispered to Sonja.

'The second one is the Radio Room. I'm sure of that,' she said. 'But the other . . . I suppose it could be a guard room.'

'Not on the second floor,' replied Barrington. He turned to Heidi and called her forward. 'I gather you worked at the hotel in the summer.'

'For the season,' she agreed.

'How about that first lighted room? What would it be?'

She frowned at the yellow square glowing in the night. 'I think it is used as the Housekeeper's Office,' she said. 'It opens into the main corridor and into a small kitchen to the side.'

'Then they're probably using it as an orderly room. I suppose there is a phone connecting to the main switchboard in the hall?'

'Yes, I'm sure there is,' replied Heidi.

Barrington spread his floor plan of the second storey and made a mark where the room ought to be. He looked back at the hotel and pointed to the gallery that ran along the rear. That's the way we go in, but we'll come out from the end of the second floor wing, so bring about forty feet of rope.'

She nodded and slipped away to the bag of equipment they had carried up the hillside. Barrington beckoned to Magda who crawled up beside him.

'There's a guard patrolling the rear of the hotel beside the mortars,' he said, pointing out the sentry. 'Can you tell if he's the man you've been seeing?'

'I've been trying to get a look at him,' she replied, staring towards the distant figure. 'He could be. Anyway, Herman said that his sergeant had it in for him and he would be on all night every night.'

'Suppose you appeared in those shadows? How do you think he would react?'

'I don't know,' she said warily. 'It is very late.'

'Do you think he would be suspicious?'

'Herman?' She smiled and shook her head. 'Oh, no. He would think that I had changed my mind.'

Barrington looked puzzled. She blushed.

'He wanted me to stay all night before.'

'Ah, splendid,' said Barrington, then added quickly, 'not that I would wish to commit you in any way ah . . .' He tailed off awkwardly.

'Yes, Colonel, I know. What do you want me to do?'

Barrington cleared his throat quietly, then indicated the rear slope beyond the mortar battery. 'If you can get him into this area for one hour, we should be well gone by then. If that's impossible, then at least keep his back to the gallery as we go in.'

She nodded, smiling quickly. 'I can do that. Bye.'

She slid away into the darkness between the trees, all sound of her lost in seconds. Mrs Tollinson came down from the ridge above, gesturing at the clear night sky. 'We could have done with snow.'

'Can't have everything,' said Barrington. 'I want you and Sonja in first, checking doors, corridors, all the way along that gallery to the service stairs.'

'No problem.'

'If we're spotted and there's no chance of going on, we use the lugers.'

She nodded. 'Otherwise it's wire or knife.'

'Precisely, Mrs Tollinson. Good luck.'

She grinned, her teeth gleaming in the moonlight and slapped his shoulder. 'And you, Colonel.'

They slid down the slope to the last line of trees, then took turns to make crouching runs for the rear of the hotel. Barrington was the last to run, leaning heavily on his cane and taking long, loping strides so that his left leg swung incongruously, like a determined contestant in a three-legged race. When he reached the rear wall of the hotel Sonja and Mrs Tollinson had already checked out both sides of the rear block. Heidi was peering cautiously round the corner, looking towards the gallery.

'Two guards at the main entrance, another two inside,' reported Sonja breathlessly.

'Just one at the rear, but Magda hasn't made contact yet,' said Mrs Tollinson.

Barrington moved to the corner, flattening himself against the wall before looking round. The guard was at the far end of the grounds beyond the mortars and as he watched the man moved forward into the shadows, reacting to something. A moment later he could pick out the slim figure of Magda standing beside a tree.

'We'll give her five minutes,' said Barrington, swinging back behind the corner of the hotel.

'If Magda needs five minutes she's losing her touch,' said Karen waspishly.

'Well she is rather a shy girl,' remarked Barrington tersely.

Karen leaned against the wall and shook with silent laughter until Mrs Tollinson whispered sharply in her ear. Barrington noted that Karen had the luger on the outside of her dark anorak, its butt never too far from her hand. He lifted his walking cane and tapped the gun lightly, his eyes boring coldly into hers as she reluctantly gave him her attention.

'That gun is not to be used before a German weapon has been fired and the alarm given. Clear, Miss Helrop?'

'Perfectly,' she replied. 'But I still like to know its close.'

'Just as long as we understand each other,' he said crisply.

The guard was still talking to Magda, glancing back towards the hotel a couple of times as though reluctant to reach a decision. Suddenly the girl spoke sharply, loud enough for them to hear. 'Then let's just forget the whole idea,' she said and turned away into the woods. The soldier ran after her, following her into the trees. Neither of them returned.

'Time to go,' announced Barrington. 'Karen and Heidi will bring up the rear.'

They edged round the corner of the hotel, crouching low, watching the area of woods into which the soldier had followed Magda. They ran along the side of the gallery, its glass-framed walls mildewed and streaked with the stains of winter. Beyond they could make out the deserted interior, light gleaming from occasional doors into the hotel. They reached the entrance to the gallery and quietly forced the catch, letting themselves in and relocking the doors before crossing the tiled floor, latticed by deeper shadows from the window frames, until they reached the inner stone wall and began to edge along it towards the door which led to the service stairs.

The sound of Barrington's cane clicked loudly on the tiles and he froze, cursing softly. Mrs Tollinson stepped up beside him, producing a pair of scissors and gesturing for his glove. He took it off, grimacing as she cut off one of the fingers and beamed at him. He gave her a grudging nod of thanks and slipped the leather finger-piece over the end of his cane. It fitted snugly enough and no longer clicked on the tiles when he went forward.

The door to the service stairs was stiff, creaking loudly as they eased it open. They froze, hearing distant voices which Barrington identified as the German guards in the main hall. He stepped into the corridor, glancing towards the lights some two hundred yards further along. If any of the soldiers looked towards them they would see nothing for their eyes would be blinded by the lighted room they were in. He turned, gesturing sharply, and the women ran swiftly up the stairs.

They moved quickly and efficiently now, Mrs Tollinson in the lead with Sonja beside her. At the second floor they dropped to hands and knees and crawled silently into the corridor, remaining flat on the floor until they were certain there was no guard. Barrington followed next, gesturing silently for Karen and Heidi to remain by the stairs.

The corridor seemed interminably long, the lighted

doorway of the Radio Room two thirds of the way down. They began to walk, pausing beside each darkened door, listening for movement within before stepping quickly past and moving on to the next room. By the time they had covered half the distance, Barrington's face glistened with perspiration and Sonja's hands were trembling uncontrollably. The air itself seemed charged with tension, like static building to the point where it must arc from wall to wall. As though to prove the point they began to hear the sound of static, a hiss and crackle echoing eerily along the corridor.

Mrs Tollinson was the only one who seemed unaffected, slipping from shadow to shadow without a sound, pausing in an alcove and becoming part of the woodwork so that Barrington, almost close enough to touch her, had to look twice before he could pick her out.

They reached the last doorway before the Radio Room where the echoing static translated itself into the radio receiver, occasionally crackling with interference. Barrington's mouth was dry, every nerve stretched impossibly tight as he edged forward. If the operator was on duty the entire operation would have been a waste of time. He glanced round the door jamb, ready to pull back the instant he saw a German. The room was empty. On a table against the far wall was the portable radio pack where the receiver hissed softly to itself.

He beckoned to Mrs Tollinson who flitted through the shadows and stopped beside him. 'Find the operator,' he whispered. 'He will be asleep near enough to hear the receiver in case any message comes through.'

She nodded and moved silently away. He turned to find Sonja beside him, a question on her face. He leaned towards her, gesturing at the room. 'Tricky. The operator is keeping a listening watch.'

Mrs Tollinson clucked her tongue softly, drawing him to her on the other side of the doorway. She was beside a partially open door. Inside was a small, darkened room, with the vague outline of a man on the bed. He was breathing deeply, an occasional snore grating in his throat.

'Close the door,' whispered Barrington.

She did it very slowly, an inch at a time, until she could carefully slip the catch. They waited a full two minutes in case the lack of receiver sound awoke the operator, but there was silence. Quickly Barrington went into the radio room, closing the door and crossing to the high-powered transmitter which occupied two thirds of the pack, the receiver at the top. Putting on ear phones he tuned it to the frequency he had been given in London and spoke softly into the microphone. Behind him Mrs Tollinson and Sonja stood on either side of the doorway, knives in their hands.

'This is Mother Goose for Blue Lady. Mother Goose for Blue Lady, come in?'

He waited, wiping perspiration off his forehead as it dripped onto the message pad. The receiver hissed and gurgled, but yielded no English voices. He finely tuned the frequency and switched on the microphone again.

'This is Mother Goose for Blue Lady, come in. This is Mother Goose calling Blue Lady, come in.'

He switched off, clamping the earphones against his head. Very faintly he heard a voice in English. He turned up the volume, switched on and gave the call sign. This time the reply was louder.

'Hello Mother Goose, where have you been?'

'I'm sitting on the eggs in a village called Borgas and need assistance, urgently. What is the position at Trondheim? Over.'

'We are the last ship. Orders are to pull out in two days if you have not arrived by then. Can you give reasons for the delay? Over.'

'About two hundred of them. German paratroop commandos led by a Captain Lodtz who tried to cut us off and have now occupied the village, holding all the local men as hostages. I remained here and sent the convoy on without the gold, but the Germans ambushed it and returned with the trucks. I suspect that they wiped out the entire detachment. Over.'

There was a long pause, then a different voice that sounded shocked. 'Hello Mother Goose, will you confirm that you are the last member of the convoy? Over.'

'Hello, Blue Lady. That's about the scheme of things I'm afraid. The gold is well hidden, but I shall need help to get it out. Can you lay on Marine Commando in an air drop, or ski assault of the village? The German companies are crack units with mortars, grenades, machine guns and Schmeisser machine pistols. We must move fast. Over.'

'Negative, Mother Goose. We have no available force and can see no possibility of forming one within the next week or two. Suggest you leave gold hidden and get down to us at Trondheim. Over.'

Barrington grimaced and looked towards the two women at the door. They were watching him, mouths tight, eyes empty of emotion, but he could feel the tension in them. He turned back to the transmitter.

'Hello, Blue Lady. I'm afraid I cannot do that. I'll try to pull something off and, if I'm successful, I'll see you in forty-eight hours. Over.'

'If you're on your own, Mother Goose, it is hard to see what you can pull off. Can you be more explicit? Over.'

'I'm afraid I can't, Blue Lady. The situation here is rather tricky. Over.'

'I can imagine,' the voice replied dryly. 'Would you mind explaining where you managed to get the long-range transmitter? Over.'

Barrington grinned. 'I'm using German equipment they've got in their headquarters. Quite useful, but doesn't give much time for chat. Must go. Mother Goose out.'

He switched off and reached for the transmitter tuner, cursing under his breath as he realized he had not made a note of the last frequency. He spun the dial and hoped that the operator was sloppy and would not become suspicious.

He got to his feet, collecting his cane, and made for the door.

'I hope they thought it was worth it,' muttered Mrs Tollinson as he passed her.

'I had to make the try,' he said and opened the door.

The Radio Operator stood gazing at him in bleary confusion, wearing only a shirt and trousers, but he reacted quickly, lunging at the Colonel, who stepped aside and slammed the cane across the side of his head. The man staggered forward, crashing into the table and over-turning a tray with a coffee pot and mug on it. They hit the floor with a clatter, but Barrington was more concerned with the man. He slammed the head of the cane into his kidneys, then rapped him hard behind the ear. He slumped to the floor, unconscious.

Karen and Heidi arrived in the doorway, tense and alarmed.

'The guards in the main hall just called up the stairs,' said Heidi quickly. 'They're bound to come up.'

'Into the next office. Fast,' snapped Barrington. 'Get that rope out of the window and start sliding.'

They ran along the corridor towards the Housekeeper's Office which was being used as an orderly room. The light was on and a German was sprawled in a chair at the desk, fast asleep. Karen beamed and pulled out her garrotte, stepping behind him. Mrs Tollinson elbowed her roughly out of the way and slapped the butt of her luger behind the German's ear.

'No time for that,' she said, and opened the window. 'Out onto the balcony and drop the rope. Move!'

Karen gave her an ugly look and stepped through, followed by Heidi.

In the Radio Room Barrington was systematically smashing the transmitter and receiver with the butt of his revolver. Sonja was by the door, her face white and strained. 'They're coming up the stairs,' she whispered.

'On your way,' he said. 'Get out and warn everyone in the village to hide the weapons. There's bound to be a big search. Get out and warn them.'

'I'm not leaving without you,' she said stubbornly as he picked up his cane from the floor and started limping towards the door.

'Ye Gods!' he said savagely. 'Won't any of you women obey orders?'

She gave him a hurt look and ran out of the door. Barrington glanced quickly round the office, then followed her into the corridor. There were shouts from the stairs, a sense of urgency in the clatter of boots. He tried to run, swinging his leg awkwardly, the cane slipping on the tiled floor because of its leather cover. Before he could recover he had sprawled full length in the corridor, his cane spinning away from him. There was a shout. He turned and propelled himself into the orderly room by his hands. Sonja was hesitating at the window.

'Out,' he snapped.

She disappeared as he pulled himself awkwardly to his feet. There was the sound of boots in the corridor, urgent voices. He knew there was no chance of getting back his cane. He lurched across the room, threw himself through the window onto the balcony. He paused, gulping the ice cold air. All the women had gone, a fact which gave him a small measure of relief. He climbed over the rail, gripped the rope between his gloved hands and dropped, letting the rope slide fast until it began to burn through the gloves. But then he was in snow at the corner of the building and ducking quickly round it.

There were dim figures in the darkness ahead of him, but he waved them angrily on and began to make his own stumbling way towards the nearest trees. He reached them and fell flat as guards appeared at the corner of the building, flashing powerful torches across the snow. He buried his face in the icy carpet and held his breath. After a while he pulled back deeper into the trees and got to his feet, using branches for support as he made his way with difficulty along the side of the road.

He checked the time, surprised to find that it was almost two o'clock. He could hear no clamour of German guards from the village, a fact which surprised him for he had expected an immediate reaction to the broken radio equipment. There was no sign of any women, either, which also puzzled him. Sliding and stumbling he finally climbed down to the road and walked painfully into the square, heading for the church.

He was half way across when the truck headlights came on, filling the entire square with blinding light. Cursing his stupidity he reached for his gun. The voice that came out of the darkness beyond the lights stopped the movement. He turned, his face bitter, as Captain Lodtz stepped into the light, smiling at him mockingly as he held out the cane.

'Your cane, I believe, Colonel,' he said. 'You may have it back if you promise not to hit any of us with it.' He paused and laughed softly, the sound filled with menace. 'We already owe you quite a few blows of our own.'

20

The Germans began the house searches at seven a.m. and continued until noon, dragging furniture into the street, breaking open trunks and chests of drawers, ripping up floors and smashing holes in ceilings. They found nothing. No guns. No knives. No ammunition.

Korina Mattel told Helga Strom later that it was a credit to the village considering that not only did they successfully hide almost fifty weapons ranging from Schmeissers to shotguns and more than two thousand rounds of ammunition; they were also successful in concealing a case of dynamite they had brought into the village from the explosives hut by the south logging camp. They also managed to conceal the entire supply of cognac and aquavit, and four barrels of lager which were buried in a snowdrift and froze, unfortunately splitting the barrel staves.

Sergeant Driker and Lieutenant Dobermann were in charge of the search and as the morning lengthened, so did their faces. Driker was positively mournful when he finally gave up, knowing deep inside that some of these women were probably responsible for the deaths of his men.

'We ought to shoot the lot of them,' he said bitterly, as the squads of men were paraded in the square before marching back to the Varennes. 'That's the only way.'

'Shooting civilians who appear to be co-operating is really not my style,' Dobermann said stiffly. 'Sometimes I wonder if you and the Captain are not more suited to the SS.'

Driker's cheeks went a deep red and he clicked his heels, saluting formally. Dobermann took his time answering the salute, making him wait. When he finally touched the peak of his cap he made no attempt to hide his distaste. 'You may take the men back, Sergeant. My compliments to Captain Lodtz and inform him that we have searched the entire contents of every room of every house and there is nothing here that represents any kind of threat to the German army.'

After the Sergeant had left with the men, Dobermann walked around the square to stop beside the truck, leaning against it to light a cigarette. Women were out in the square again, some of them drifting towards the church. There were two women sweeping the steps, watchers he supposed, and two more across the square standing talking but frequently glancing towards him. More look-outs, he decided.

Smiling cynicaly he strolled to the church, climbing the steps. One of the women dropped a bucket with a clatter. He clucked his tongue and shook his head in mock disapproval and went on into the church.

Inside he found some thirty women, many of them young, none of them more than middle-aged. They were kneeling, apparently praying. In the pulpit was a young woman he had not seen before with long blonde hair and fresh, attractive features. He smiled at her but she stared back coldly, as though he had violated them all with his presence.

'What are you people up to?' he asked her wearily. 'Why don't you return the weapons and the gold and be rid of us. All our Captain wants is the gold. The bodies of our men he can forget.'

There was silence in the church. The women remained on their knees, heads bowed.

Dobermann sighed. 'There is nothing you can do. Nothing. So please, return to your homes and forget whatever little fantasies you have. My men now have orders to shoot any woman who approaches within ten feet without being ordered to do so. Let this be an end to it.'

He turned and left them, his boots clicking crisply on the stone floor. When the door banged shut, Michelle Argent lifted her head and said in a furious voice, 'The arrogant pig!

Doesn't he know that five of us could have put a knife in him simply by opening our hymn books!'

There was a burst of laughter and the tension eased. Helga got to her feet and held up her hands. 'Let Tania have her say,' she told them.

Tania gripped the edge of the pulpit and gazed at them earnestly. 'We have to go ahead. Tonight. It's the only way.'

'Without Colonel Barrington?' Korina Mattel asked dubiously.

'We can do it,' insisted Tania. 'Charles told me the entire plan. We are ready to do it now.'

'And why should he tell you?' asked Karen waspishly. 'Or did he talk in his sleep?'

There were some giggles and Tania flushed angrily.

'You're just jealous, Karen,' declared Sonja. 'Let's face it, you're not exactly number one on anybody's list . . . male or female!'

'None of that matters,' interrupted Tania. 'What is important is that I know the plan and tonight the Germans will be off guard. They won't expect anything to happen. Not with Colonel Barrington a prisoner.'

'You heard the Lieutenant,' Anna Rekvarik said doubtfully, her forehead wrinkled with worry. 'Our whole strategy was based on the fact that they did not suspect us.'

'They still won't,' said Helga Strom. She made an open, helpless gesture. 'It's not for me to persuade any of you. It's a matter for each one alone. But don't imagine that because an officer says so these German commandos will open fire on young women. They'll hesitate. They'll wonder. They'll react just a second or two later than they would with a man.' She paused and grimaced. 'Except perhaps for me. With me they'll shoot two seconds early!'

Some of the women smiled grimly, but most were too concerned with Tania's appeal for unity and determination. In everyone's mind was the ultimatum Lodtz had given the village, the declaration that he would shoot every man, woman and child if necessary.

'If we act at all it must be today, tonight,' said Tania, sensing their mood. 'It will be the only time we have the advantage.'

'And what advantage is that?' snapped Mrs Jacobsen, who was a member of Lillie Group and collected information from the German soldiers who used her village store. 'They are patrolling the woods, guarding the square, planning to execute the menfolk first thing in the morning. They have the church under surveillance because it is obvious that too many of us are here. They have the English Colonel under arrest, and I'm sure they will be using their most brutal methods of interrogation on him. Where is this advantage? Our leader has gone, our element of surprise has gone, and our men are now more at risk than ever?'

'We're all at risk, Elsa,' said Helga sadly. 'Give them the gold and they will still want revenge against the village for the men we have killed. This man Lodtz is like that. Perhaps he would destroy our homes, or perhaps they would bring in the civilian secret police the way they did in Poland. The Gestapo, questioning us, torturing us, sending some to the labour camps, others to their headquarters. Is this what we want for our sons and husbands, for our young women?' She straightened her shoulders, putting an arm around Tania as she spoke. 'No, sisters. I am with Tania. I am for the Varennes, tonight, when they think we are confused and afraid.'

There was a rising murmur of agreement. Sonja stepped forward to the other side of Tania. 'I am with them. If it is just the three of us, we will still go!'

'There are more,' snapped Mrs Jacobsen, stepping forward with Korina Mattel beside her. 'Don't get too cocky my dear!'

In a moment the entire mood had changed and the church was filled with eager faces, clenched fists rising above the heads of determined women. When the babble of voices had finally subsided, they looked to Tania, accepting her leadership.

'You've all had your own instructions from Colonel Barrington during the past few days, but I'll cover them briefly now. Lillie is the first assault group and will attack the main entrance of the building using explosives which will be pre-set five minutes before the attack. Heidi will need twenty sticks of dynamite wired and fused to her arrows with support from two other people. I will be with this group which will be led by Helga. Her special squad which must take the entrance hall will consist of Korina Mattel, Mrs Tollinson and Mrs Jacobsen. They will use shotguns.

'Tania Group will take the rear of the hotel, using the mortars to dominate the road from the town. Sonja will lead the group with Michelle, who will be responsible for checking the elevation and firing the shells, as second in command. It will be necessary to keep back any German patrols trying to return to the hotel. You'd better read the notes on mortars that Colonel Barrington prepared. I think he also demonstrated the method?'

Sonja nodded: 'With cans of beans. But we are ready.'

'Michelle Group recovers as many weapons as possible from the first wave of the attack, then occupies the slopes on either side of the road from the village,' continued Tania. 'It will be their job to ambush German patrols who get through the mortar barrage. No one must get through until the men are free.'

She looked around the circle of faces, waiting for questions. There were none. She smiled wanly. 'Good luck, then. We rendezvous on the north ridge at midnight.'

They left, moving slowly in twos and threes, ignoring the Corporal and two soldiers beside the trucks as though they were of little consequence. Some went to their homes and sat before wood fires, thinking of the night to come and wondering if there would be a tomorrow. Others met in small rooms with drawn curtains and planned the detailed strategies needed for the attack. Pistols were cleaned, shotguns oiled and barrels sawn down until they could wreak carnage at close quarters. In the cellar of Mrs Mattel's butcher's shop, Korina, Heidi and Elsa Jacobsen carefully fixed detonators and fuse wires to sticks of dynamite and bound them tightly to the shafts of arrows.

In the vestry of the church Tania sat upon the bed and sobbed in helpless misery. Even when Helga came in and poured a glass of schnapps she could not stop the deep shudders of anguish.

'This is a great help to the Englishman, young Tania,' remarked Helga, sitting down beside her and proffering the glass of aquavit. 'It gives us all great confidence in your ability to put the plan into operation.'

Tania wiped tears from her cheeks with the back of her hand. 'I can. You know I can.'

'Ten minutes ago I thought you could,' said Helga. 'Now you're crying like a love-sick girl and I am filled with uncertainty again.'

Tania straightened and took the glass, spots of red appearing in her cheeks. She drank it down, closing her eyes and taking a deep breath as the strong liquor burned its way down to her stomach. 'When the time comes I will do everything that must be done, Helga,' she said stiffly. 'It's just the waiting. I know they're torturing him. I know he will never talk. So . . .' her voice broke again and she squeezed the glass in her hand. 'So I can do nothing but wait.'

'I know.' Helga patted her knee and placed the bottle on the table. 'Try to get some sleep. We will meet later to decide the final plan.'

She crossed to the door, then looked back and chuckled. 'I can just see that stubborn Englishman's face when you knock down his door and toss him a shotgun. "I gave instructions for you to be with Michelle Group!" he'll say. I just hope I'm there to see it.'

After she had gone Tania sipped her aquavit and said softly to herself, 'I just hope it happens.'

21

A vulture had been circling overhead all morning, crossing and re-crossing the patio area at the hospital in Mandalay, tasting the smell and the look of him and pretending it had the courage to land. Barrington detested the birds more than any other creature. It was not only the fact that they were carrion and associated with death; it was also their ugliness and ungainliness. Their eyes were sunken and their wings untidy and noisy, and the call of the bird sounded like rusty metal on wet glass.

As soon as he could walk he was planning to get a shotgun and amuse himself by blasting the vultures that came close enough. But they were strange birds, sometimes looking like people, and he could have sworn that the previous morning one of them floated across to his bed and gazed at him with alarming animosity.

The pain in his leg was like a slow-burning fire, a dull red glow that flickered now and then with incandescent agony. At those times he thought of Elizabeth, selecting favourite images of her that glowed and came to life. Elizabeth in Delhi, all pink and white and so beautiful that the teeming thousands always seemed to leave a small circle of space that was only hers. And there was Elizabeth in Jabalpur, eating rice cakes and playing with children who regarded her with such solemn brown eyes. There was Calcutta; the orange groves in the mountains near the hill station at Udaipur where the mess was always short of funds and the in-joke was never to get killed there; and Prince Raschid's Palace at Jaipur where they had endless days of peace during the month they spent there as his guests.

It had been the perfect summer, a summer of memories and a summer of optimism for the future. In 1935 the world seemed to be regaining its sanity and the British Empire seemed indomitable.

There were other images he kept locked in the corners of his mind, only rarely dusted off and savoured for his blackest depressions, and then Elizabeth was always grey, her eyes dull and even her blouse and bodice an empty, lifeless grey. She had wanted to remain at their home, lying on a chaise longue they had brought out onto the terrace so that she could look across the purple plains of Rawalpindi and west to the Khyber Pass. She had died like that. Gazing at the faraway mountains, a tear drying on her cheek. He had only left her for three minutes, but in that time she had left him forever.

The doctor who came to see him once a day was called Trotter and filled with transparent optimism and forced joviality. His view was that the leg should come off about six inches above the knee, but as long as the gangrene was being contained he was reluctantly forced to agree with Barrington that it was worth keeping it around for a few more days.

Occasionally, when the doctor appeared, the oddest thing would happen and he would look completely different, his hair close-cropped and fair and his eyes a quite ruthless blue. On those occasions Barrington called him Lodtz, though he had no idea who the devil Lodtz was meant to be, and the vultures would gather round with white capes and ugly faces that kept pecking at him, sometimes so badly that he went back to the Palace at Jaipur.

In the evening, as shadows lengthened along the terrace of the hospital, his Sergeant-Major came to visit and stood awkwardly to attention until Barrington told him to give him a hand with the bloody food and make himself useful . . .

'Begging your pardon, sir,' said the Sergeant-Major, doing his best to cut the lump of stewed lamb into bite-sized squares. 'Me and the lads . . . that is all the lads and Sub-Lieutenant Frobisher, sir, if you'll pardon the familiarity.'

'Yes, yes, Sergeant-Major. This is completely off the record.'

'Right, sir. Well, we sort of put our heads together and came up with a despatch which we sent off to HQ in Lahore, sir.' He passed the plate to Barrington and chuckled contentedly for a moment.

'And what was the despatch about, Sergeant-Major?' He was forced to ask.

'Ah, yes, sir. Well, we've informed the adjutant and the chief surgeon that you had a little mishap with your 'orse. Nothing drastic sir, just that the 'orse sort of stepped on you and bruised a few of the muscles and things around your knee. We thought it would be a month or so before you could ride again, so instead of making for Lahore before the rainy season, we're sitting it out here and will see them in six or seven weeks. 'Ow about that, sir?'

'It rather sounds to me, Sergeant-Major, as though you have placed yourself, and young Frobisher, in a position that could end up at a court martial.' He paused, clearing his throat in a tone that made the Sergeant-Major wince. 'However, as I am the victim it is hardly for me to take any active part in any disciplinary measures, and as I do have frequent fevers it would be inappropriate for me to assume that this conversation took place, let alone refers to a real event. Don't you agree, Sergeant-Major?'

'Oh absolutely,' he replied, looking totally baffled. 'You see me and the lads thought that with a knee like yours the Chief Surgeon wouldn't have much option but to send you back to Blighty with measurements for a bowler 'at.'

'I couldn't have put it better myself.'

'But seven or eight weeks from now, with a bit of exercise, maybe a walking stick to get you about, we could convince him that it's really only a bit of an 'andicap. I mean, you take over the regiment at Christmas and the M.O. isn't going to want to queer that, now is he, sir?'

'Let's hope not,' said Barrington, smiling up at him. 'There's just one problem, as I see it. Suppose this surgeon chap here decides to take the leg off? You have a problem then, Sergeant-Major. Hardly the treatment for a few horsey bruises.'

The Sergeant-Major's eyes went small and round, like black beads, and he spoke in a hoarse, conspiratorial whisper, reminding Barrington irresistibly of Long John Silver about to spill the beans. 'Well, sir, some of us had a little chat with old sawbones and we think he's got a completely new slant on your case.'

'What kind of blackmail or extortion did you decide on, Sergeant-Major?'

'Almost biblical it was, sir.' The Sergeant-Major's shoulders shook silently and it was a few minutes before he could wipe the tear from his florid cheek and continue. 'Sort of leg for a leg, you see, sir. We just told him that if he took off your leg, we'd take off his.'

Barrington groaned. 'He'll have us all court martialled.'

'No, not 'im, sir. We convinced him. He's the nervous type. Not too keen on life in India. Wants to get home to mum and the girl next door. There's just no way he's going to take your leg off.'

'Well that's good news,' said Barrington. 'At least now we only have two options. If I get better we go back to Lahore and pretend the old knee acts up now and then.'

'Absolutely, sir. I've seen it before. I used to have an S.-M. with his right arm so stiff he couldn't do a thing with it. Used to salute with his left hand and do you know, sir, nobody noticed. Not even the General when he came down from Delhi . . . course we did put a splint and bandage on it that time . . . Er, what's the second option, sir?'

'Oh, that?' Barrington speared a piece of lamb and waved it casually at the Sergeant-Major. 'That's the one where I die because the surgeon refuses to take my leg off.'

'Ah, yes. We thought of that one, sir. But then we thought of the kind of gentleman you are, sir. We all agreed, to a man, that we'd bury you here and you'd thank us for it, sir.'

He was thinking about the Sergeant-Major's words when the vulture came closer and this time managed to land at the foot of the bed. He ignored it, deciding that this was the best thing to do under the circumstances, but when it began to talk he started to watch surreptitiously from beneath half closed eyes. There were two white-coated figures by the bed and some soldiers in greenish uniforms. They seemed to be arguing with the vulture who turned out to be the surgeon, Lodtz, whom he didn't like at all. Barrington tried to concentrate, but his thoughts kept wandering to Mandalay and the lush green hills of Burma.

'Throw cold water over him. Break his fingers. Get the man's attention, damn you!' raged Lodtz.

The sergeant in charge of the interrogation of Colonel Barrington was called Jorgen Mellitz, a barrel-chested soldier who enjoyed putting his boot in on a Saturday night but was singularly unsuited for the finesse that was required in the present situation. Lieutenant Niemens, technically responsible for questioning Barrington, stirred restlessly and indicated the blood-stained bandage around the British officer's knee.

'Sir, the old wound has been opened due to the over-zealousness of Sergeant Mellitz. We now have the Colonel in a state of delirium, talking most of the time about Burma and India.'

'Listen to me, Niemens,' snarled Lodtz. 'I want him talking about the gold. Do you understand me?'

'I understand you, sir, but the English Colonel does not. We have no doctor so I suggest you order the village doctor out here as soon as possible.'

'We are not running a field hospital, Niemens. Can't any of you get it through your skulls that this Englishman, this pathetic Colonel, is responsible for us being here, for the loss of our men, the loss of the gold? He is the key to it all. Get him talking and we can be out of here and on the way back to Germany tomorrow.' His voice had risen to a shrill cry, almost a plea. 'Get him talking tonight!'

Sergeant Mellitz stamped to attention and nodded to his two assistants, moving back to Barrington with a length of chain which he began to wind around his hand. Niemens shook his head in disgust. 'Sir, the only way Barrington will talk tonight is by being revived by something a little more subtle than a bucket of water. We have two hours to midnight. At least let us use one of them to get the doctor to bring him round.'

Lodtz hesitated, staring at him suspiciously. 'Pain is the best way to sharpen the mind.'

'Captain Lodtz,' Niemens said patiently. 'Each time you inflict pain on this man, especially through his leg, you send him back to a hospital in Burma where he underwent great pain. You cannot separate the two. You cannot get sense out of a man who believes he is still guarding the Khyber Pass!'

Lodtz ground his teeth and glared at the figure lying on the bed. As he watched the head moved from side to side and Barrington spoke in a vague, dreamy voice. 'Sound the bugle, Frobisher. Bring out my horse. We'll have the devils before tiffin.'

'All right,' snapped Lodtz. 'Send for the doctor. But I want this man speaking lucidly in one hour, Niemens.'

Lodtz left the room, slamming the door. Niemens took off his hat and jacket and went to the desk and sat down, taking out a cigarette. He looked across at Sergeant Mellitz, who showed neither pleasure nor displeasure at the change of tactics.

'Go and get Jansen, Mellitz. And be gentle with him. You know, the velvet glove.'

He gazed pointedly at the heavy chain still wrapped around the Sergeant's fist. Mellitz mumbled an apology and dropped the chain on the table, leaving with his men. The figure on the bed was very still, as though listening. Niemens smiled and lit a second cigarette, crossing the room and sitting beside the bed. He held one out to Barrington.

'You feel up to holding this, Colonel?' he asked.

Barrington made no movement for a moment, then turned his head and opened his eyes. The pupils were still small and his features were bathed in perspiration, the pallor of old wax. He considered the cigarette, then reached for it with a steady hand.

'I get the feeling you had a tough time in Burma?' said Niemens. 'How long ago was it?'

'Thirty-six,' said Barrington, exhaling smoke. 'Things were a bit primitive.'

'That knee's a mess . . . even before Mellitz started on it. How did you manage to stay in the army?'

Barrington gave him a lob-sided grin. 'You have to lie a little.'

'Incredible,' said Niemens, shaking his head. 'And they sent you to get the gold.'

'They were busy. They thought the cane was more of a swagger stick. You say the Sergeant's name is Mellitz.'

'Yes. Red Company. Strong and stupid. Every company ends up having a few like that.'

Barrington nodded. 'Do you know what happened to my men?'

Niemens face went stiff and he turned away, stubbing out his cigarette. When he turned back his cheeks were very pale. 'I can only assume, Colonel, for I was not involved in the event.'

'Then assume.'

'There were some wounded, and quite a few unwounded. We withdrew, leaving them with some of Captain Lodtz's more fanatical comrades. The kind who live, breathe and worship the image of Adolf Hitler.'

'I thought you all did that,' said Barrington.

'No. Many of us are soldiers, taking part in a European war that has been inevitable for the past eight years. When we have finished it, the world will be a better place.'

'And so you make a start by murdering my men?'

Niemens stiffened, breathing sharply through his nose, about to walk away. Instead he took the cigarette from Barrington's fingers and stubbed it out, offering him another from a silver case. 'There will always be men like Lodtz. Men who take duty to extremes of barbarity. But if it is any consolation I believe that the Oberkommando will strip him of his rank when they read the reports.'

'It isn't any consolation. It wouldn't be if they hanged him, although they won't.'

There was silence between them for a while, Barrington blowing smoke at the distant ceiling and surreptitiously trying to flex the muscles of his left leg and assess the damage from the amount of pain it created.

'Is there much point in holding out until the end?' Niemens asked.

'Not really,' said Barrington. 'But all the same I shall.'

'Lodtz will execute the hostages.'

'Let him, they are nothing to do with me. And they have no idea of the location of the gold.'

'Who does have?'

Barrington looked at him, smiling without humour. 'You wouldn't believe me if I told you.'

'Try me?'

'The British Navy. The Admiralty in London. The War Office. The Bank of England . . . and me. I told the rest of them last night on your radio. Oh and then there's my men who hid the gold and are halfway to Trondheim by now.'

Niemens gazed at him without expression for a moment, then sighed and shook his head. 'I wish I could believe you, Colonel, but you have no men. The tracks in the snow were of yourself and four women. And the Radio Operator disturbed you before you had a chance to use his transmitter. No, Colonel, you are on your own. Your genius is being one step ahead of us all the time. From the moment we left the aircraft, with your convoy beneath us, your strategy was immaculate. Even here, to somehow move the gold, to persuade the simple village women to become your pawns. Remarkable.'

'You've got a great imagination, Lieutenant. I'll bet you believe in fairies too!'

Niemens laughed. 'If Lodtz had believed me yesterday we would have had all the proof we needed last night. But now, you must give it to him.'

Barrington lost his casual manner, his eyes taking on the glint of steel that brooked no argument. 'It was a pleasant chat, Lieutenant. Good night.'

He put out his cigarette and lay back, gazing up at the ceiling. Niemen's mouth tightened angrily and he debated shouting for Mellitz and his thugs until he remembered he had sent them for the doctor. He made one last try, knowing it was futile.

'Colonel Barrington, the gold is not worth all the pain, the torment, the innocent lives of men and women in this village. It is just metal, yet already it has cost the lives of your own men and some of ours. I beg you, just give us the location and I guarantee the safety of all the people of Borgas.'

There was no reply. After a moment Niemens stood up and crossed to the window, gazing out at the moonlit snow. He lit a cigarette, feeling tense and frustrated. At least the doctor would give him a little more time, he told himself. But then the beating would begin again and Barrington would return to India. Down the road the doctor appeared wearing an overcoat over his pyjamas. Mellitz and the privates trooped along beside him, warm by comparison. The snow had begun to fall, floating down in the still night in large flakes that began to stick to the window, distorting the world outside.

He watched the snowfall get heavier until the night was a dark grey blanket, white at the edges where it caught the light from the window. There were footsteps outside, then the door opened and Doctor Jansen entered, stamping snow on the floor, moving with his bag to the figure on the bed.

'I can't give you long with him, doctor,' said Niemens.

'Then why bother to call me?'

'He needs a stimulant. Something that will clear his mind, make him respond more easily.'

Jansen removed the blood-stained cloth from the Colonel's knee and looked up sharply, his lips trembling with anger. 'I will first dress his leg.'

'Doctor,' said Niemens quietly, 'I have taken some trouble to get you here. It is better for the Colonel if you give him a stimulant.'

'First I will bandage his knee,' the doctor said stubbornly, 'then I will give him a thorough examination. If he requires a stimulant I will administer one, but if he requires a sedative, I will administer that.'

'You will do as you are ordered,' snapped Niemens.

Doctor Jansen closed his bag and glared at the German officer. 'I may be your prisoner, Lieutenant. I may have been brought forcibly to this place of torture, but do not imagine for a moment that I am a part of your evil regime or that I will lift a finger to assist you in this inhuman activity!'

Niemens went very pale, turned on his heel and walked out of the room without a backward glance. Mellitz and his companions went to warm themselves in front of an oil stove. Jansen turned back to Barrington, opening his bag and taking out bandages and a tin of ointment. He cleaned the wound, shaking his head as he uncovered the lacerations and heavy contusions.

'It could be worse, Doctor,' murmured Barrington.

'If it gets any worse I can't guarantee that you'll have it much longer,' he replied furiously. 'For God's sake, man!'

'Sorry, Doc. Just take your time putting on the bandage.'

Jansen turned to his bag, took out a roll of cotton wool and something else which he slipped under the Colonel's pillow. 'There's a loaded luger under your pillow and a message from Helga. She says, all your women will be paying you a visit tonight. So try to stay awake.'

'Tonight?' Said Barrington. 'They can't do it tonight!'

Sergeant Mellitz stirred on the far side of the room and came over to the bed, staring at the Colonel with a suspicious expression. He mumbled something to the doctor in German, but Jansen looked vague and shrugged. Mellitz gave Barrington a punch on the shoulder, then lost interest and went back to the stove. When he was on the far side of the room Barrington spoke urgently through closed lips.

'You've got to stop this, doctor. They're not ready. Nothing's ready. Tell them I absolutely forbid it.'

'Tell them yourself,' replied Doctor Jansen. 'They'll be kicking that door down sometime in the next hour.'

Barrington opened his eyes and stared at him incredulously.

'Will you at least try to behave like a man in a coma,' snapped Jansen, 'or else I'll slip a needle in your arm and put you to sleep for the duration!'

22

Gusts of wind were blowing the falling snow into whirling spirals that marched along the north ridge like elegant ghosts in some vast, primeval ballroom. In twos and sometimes threes they advanced down craggy slopes and over undulating drifts of snow to embrace stately pines with a soft moan of contentment, before disappearing into the deeper shadows of the forest.

They were not alone in the shadows. Three groups of women in soft boots, ski pants and fur-lined anoraks sat around in small clearings within the pines, talking softly. There was the gleam of steel, the brief clatter of a weapon being put together, the click of safety catches and the sudden flare of a match as a cigarette was lit.

Magda Peters was trying hard to ignore the icy nausea in her stomach as she moved through the dark shadows between the trees. They'd moved her out of Lillie Group into Michelle, the group that would be attacking the rear of the hotel, taking the mortars. Her mouth was dry and her heart a deafening turmoil in her ears. Herman was guarding the mortars. He patrolled them every night. She licked her lips, hurrying through the darkness, bumping into trees and branches, yet not caring.

She hadn't wanted to get involved with Herman, she told herself for the thousandth time that day. But once she had encouraged him to go into the woods with her everything had happened so fast. They had kissed with growing fervour until the only thing she could think about was Herman and the deep, aching need she felt for him. He had laid his combat jacket on the ground with her anorak beside it, then oblivious to the cold they had taken off their clothes and held each other for a long time.

He had made love to her so gently it was as though he thought her to be made of fine porcelain, not knowing it was the first time until she cried out with the pain. And his tenderness grew, matched by his wonder, and somehow he drew her closer, moved deeper, so that she cried out again and again – only her voice was filled with joy.

For the rest of that night and the following day she had wrestled with a horrifying dilemma. Was love a part of war, or was it an entirely different state in which people could transcend the demands of generals? Could love be greater than King and Country? Could it excuse duty, ignore honour, deny the call to arms? She did not know. The questions were too deep. All she knew was that she was terribly in love with Herman Wilner.

Tania waited with Helga and members of Michelle Group halfway along the ridge, almost above the Varennes Hotel. The snow was falling heavily and they could only make out the vague glow of windows. Magda reached them, her face ghostly white in the gloom.

'Yes, Tania? They said you wanted me?'

'I thought I might have seen you at the church this evening,' said Tania, studying her closely. 'Are you all right?'

'I'm okay,' replied Magda, looking nervously at the faces around her. 'What is it you want?'

'The guard that patrols the mortars?'

Magda felt an icy clutch of fear in her throat. She nodded. 'Yes. His name is Herman Wilner.'

'Heidi was going to work her way round in the dark and put an arrow in him, but the snow is too thick and she has too much to do at the front.' Tania paused, gripping her arm sympathetically. 'You were a great help last night. We know what it must have cost you to take him into the woods like that. We understand the revulsion you feel.'

Magda gazed at her in astonishment. Revulsion? She had loved every minute. She wondered whether she should tell them, then realized they could not possibly understand. 'I didn't mind,' she said quietly. 'It was nothing at all.'

'Could you do it again?' asked Helga. 'Could you just walk up to him in the snow and charm him out of his jackboots?'

'Well yes,' said Magda, her pulse racing. 'I'm sure I could.'

'But this time there's a difference,' Helga said slowly. 'This time he has to be killed.'

The agonised 'no' was torn from her as she swayed unsteadily on her feet. Sonja gripped her arm, looking concerned. Magda stared at their earnest faces as though they were strangers, as though this was part of a nightmare. But it was all too real and Helga was already bending forward, peering into her eyes.

'Listen, child,' said the woman. 'The front of the hotel we can handle, but the rear is crucial. We have no more than one minute to kill that guard and grab those mortars. If we fail they'll take the mortars themselves and pull back to the trees. We'll never win then. They'll pick us off when they feel like it, destroy our village. But if we have that kind of fire-power it gives us the advantage. You understand?'

She nodded, wanting to scream that she didn't understand at all. She wanted to find Herman, to explain to him how important the mortars were and that they must run away, far away, before the war began and there was blood all over the snow.

'One of us can do it,' said Sonja, 'but his orders are to shoot any woman who approaches. You are the only person he would not shoot.'

He might, thought Magda. *Please God make him shoot me because that way I don't have to do anything at all.*

'When?' she asked with a mouth like dry tissue paper.

'Now,' said Tania. 'I wish it could be one of us, Magda, but he only knows you. And everything depends on his removal. You understand. If you fail, we all fail.'

'I understand,' she whispered. 'I'll go. Don't worry about it.'

She walked away from them through the trees and the dark, whirling snow and they watched with worried expressions until she was gone.

'She's very strange tonight,' said Sonja.

'Nerves,' suggested Tania.

'Perhaps,' Helga said, her face grim. 'We'll know soon enough. Pass the word to Heidi's team to get into position. We move on your signal, Sonja. As soon as Magda has taken out the boy friend.'

'You don't think that's it, do you?' Tania asked quickly. 'You don't think she's got involved?'

'Well it's too late now,' said Sonja. 'Let's check our watches.'

* * *

The snowflakes were like cool petals bursting against the heat of her skin. Magda pulled off her woollen cap, unzipped her anorak and flung her fair hair around her shoulders. She was on the road now, curving past the entrance to the hotel where she knew other guards would be. She walked silently, a slim shadow in the night, then climbed the sloping bank and slid down the other side into what was normally the car park. She cut across it, her eyes accustomed to the gloom, picking him out a full ten seconds before he saw her.

'Darling Magda,' he said, hugging her to him so that all the snow fell off his hood into her face. He laughed, brushing it away, and kissed her. 'You are as cold as the ice fairy and twice as beautiful.'

'Perhaps I am the Ice Fairy, the one that comes with winter and vanishes in summer. Perhaps there will never be another winter.'

'There'll never be such a beautiful winter, but spring is going to be better and in the summer you will come with me to Lanrop.'

'I never agreed to come,' she said in an empty voice. 'I made no promise to you.'

He kissed her, his breath hot and his young, hard body taut against her. 'Don't be cold, Magda. Don't tease me after last night.'

She leaned back in his arms, her face as pale as the snow that laid icy tears on her cheeks. 'I will go with you to Lanrop if you will run away with me now.'

He laughed. 'I cannot run anywhere. And neither can you in this blizzard.'

'I mean it,' she said in a strange, tormented voice. 'Come with me now, away from here, as far as we can go. We'll find friends. We'll survive.'

His laughter died and he moved his hands up to her shoulders, his eyes beginning to look deep. She turned her head away. 'Magda, I am a soldier,' he said. 'If anything is going to happen here you must tell me. I have my duty.'

'Yes,' she said in a choking voice, 'we all have our duty.'

The tears that ran down her cheeks were cold and clear, and the sob that burst from her lips was filled with such anguish that he wrapped his arms around her and leaned towards her lips. Only then did he feel the knife, slicing through the fabric of his jacket, piercing the abdomen and lunging upwards, searching and finding the vessels of his heart.

'Oh Herman!' she screamed. 'God forgive me Herman!'

And then he was slumping forward into the snow, the blood bubbling in his throat, the awful realization of her treachery only just beginning to reach his consciousness as darkness swooped in and overwhelmed all else.

23

The two guards on patrol at the entrance to the hotel paused beside the heavy pine post with 'Hotel Varennes' carved upon it. It was almost midnight and most of the lights were out on the upper floors, signifying that the majority of the soldiers were already asleep.

'Lucky bastards,' said Gunther Haas enviously. 'If this snow gets any thicker, they'll be digging us out in the morning.'

'We're a waste of time,' replied his companion, a thickset man called Rimmel. 'Nothing is going to happen now we've got the Colonel. And that's a pair of boots I wouldn't want to be in.'

Haas chuckled, lighting two cigarettes and passing one to Rimmel. 'They'll break him. Then we'll be out of here.'

They smoked in silence for a moment. From the hill beyond the hotel there was the distant cry of an animal in pain. They looked at each other. The sound came again.

'Probably a fox,' said Haas, trying to sound confident.

'More like a hare,' said Rimmel. 'Maybe an owl got it.'

'Maybe,' said Haas, peering into the night. The snow swirled around them so that it was difficult to discern anything against the trees, but it cleared for a moment and he could have sworn someone was standing just beside the road that swept up the hill past the hotel.

'I think I saw something out there just then,' he said. 'By the road.'

Rimmel leaned forward, staring into the gloom, rubbing snowflakes from his eyes. There was a brief gust of wind, whirling the snow into small white devils, but when it cleared briefly he saw a slim girl wearing a white anorak with the hood thrown back. Her hair was dark, cut short like a boys, and her arms were stretched oddly in front of her. With a shock he realized that she was holding an archer's bow.

'Jesus, Gunther, there is someone out there!' he said, unslinging his Schmeisser.

There was a swish in the air and a thud beside him. He turned to see Gunther Haas staring in horror at the shaft of an arrow protruding from his chest. He tried to speak, but his mouth filled with blood and he pitched forward into the snow. Rimmel turned back, the Schmeisser as cold as the shiver of fear that went through him. Even as he cocked the weapon he felt the thud in his chest and knew it was too late. He had a brief glimpse of the girl, so slim and young and harmless, and then he was falling into darkness.

As other members of Lillie Group, led by Helga, ran silently towards the entrance of the hotel, Heidi picked up the first of the dynamite arrows with its fuse hanging down like a tail. She stretched the bow, sighting over the knuckle of her left hand, moving the arrow head along the garret windows. 'Ready,' she said in a tense voice.

The woman beside her was Maria Hengel, a woman in her late twenties whose husband was one of the men in the cellar of the hotel. She and Loris Hagnar were support for Heidi so all she had was a luger, but she would have given anything to have been grabbing one of the Schmeissers from the dead sentries and running on for the hotel. Instead she had a smouldering piece of rope. With a sigh she blew on the ember until it glowed and touched the end of the fuse.

As the fuse spluttered into life Heidi released the arrow, watching critically as it arched through the falling snow to pierce the pine shingles between the top floor garret windows. She picked up the next arrow, notching it into the string. 'Quickly now,' she said, her voice lifting with confidence.

The fuse spluttered and Loris slapped her shoulder. She

drew back until her right thumb was behind her ear, the string of the bow taut against her cheek. She aimed at the centre of the space between the second and third windows and gently released the arrow. The falling snow deadened all sound, but the sputtering fuse was easily discernable. The explosive charge was in place.

'It's going to happen,' said Loris, a note of awe in her voice. 'It's really going to happen.'

'You mean you didn't believe it?' asked Maria, mockingly.

Heidi released another arrow and it sped into the night, thunking into the sloping roof of the hotel just beside the fourth window.

'Not this part,' replied Loris. 'I mean, sticks of dynamite on arrows. Crazy.'

'The first man to do it was Marco Polo,' said Heidi, and released the fourth arrow. 'Light the rest of them.'

The women did as they were told, watching with growing tension as the sputtering fuses got shorter. Heidi was working fast, notching an arrow, lifting and shooting in one fluid movement. Eight arrows were now sticking from the shingled side of the hotel, spluttering tails of fire beneath each one. The two on the ground smoked and crackled. Heidi scooped up the ninth, notched and drew it back. She released, scooping up the last before it reached its target.

'That went through the window,' said Maria. 'I've got a feeling you just blew it.'

'It doesn't matter,' Heidi replied calmly, aiming the last arrow. 'They've only got ten seconds left!'

She shot the arrow and watched with satisfaction as it slapped into the wood between the last two windows, quivering there with its burning tail. A light had come on and there were shouts of alarm, then a chair smashed through the window and a moment later the arrow with its stick of dynamite came whirling after it. Heidi just smiled and waited.

* * *

Mrs Tollinson and Helga Strom were flattened on either side of the main doors, Korina Mattel and Tania crouching down on the steps. Mrs Tollinson and Helga carried sawn-off shotguns, twelve bore, loaded with hand-made cartridges they had filled with the heaviest lead they could find. Tania and Korina held Schmeissers and all of them were armed with pistols.

Beyond the doors was the wide hall with its log fire, now smouldering into ash. Around it, stretched out on leather chairs, were the night guard under the command of a corporal. There were five men, two getting ready to relieve the sentries at the gate.

Helga checked her watch and turned to see an arrow flash through the night with its fiery tail. She gestured to Mrs Jacobsen, positioned at the corner of the building from where she could cover the rear gallery. She carried a sawn-off under-and-over pump action Remington shotgun and across her shoulder was a bag of twelve gauge shells. She ran along the side of the building and crouched beside them.

'We go in thirty seconds,' said Helga. 'How about Tania Group?'

'They've just pulled back with two of the mortars and two cases of shells, but Michelle has sent Karen and Magda forward to see if they can get more from the armoury. Sonja says to watch for them.'

'We will,' said Helga, studying her watch. She lifted her head, smiling grimly. 'All right girls. Let's go.'

They swung out from either side of the doorway, Mrs Tollinson kicking the double doors wide with a heavy ski boot, the shotgun held low as she lunged into the entrance hall with Helga beside her. The Corporal was the first to his feet, his eyes bulging, clawing for his pistol. Helga blasted him in the chest from ten feet, throwing him back with flailing arms to crash against a dozing soldier.

Mrs Jacobsen put her back to the wall beside the door, and pumped shot after shot until the gun was empty, then crouched down to reload as Tania and Korina Mattel came through with the Schmeissers ready to sweep the room. But even as they both swung towards the last man, Mrs Tollinson blew a massive hole in his chest. They stood and waited, letting the smoke clear, hardly daring to believe it was this easy. The five Germans were sprawled in bloody bundles, the walls behind them spattered with shot and streaks of blood.

Mrs Tollinson broke her gun and felt in her pockets for shells, gesturing to Helga to follow suit. There was a clatter of feet and a young soldier in shirt and trousers with a pistol in his hand came running out of the corridor, sliding to a halt with bulging eyes as he saw them. Mrs Jacobsen pumped a shell into the barrel and fired, blasting him back into the corridor.

Helga looked at her watch. It had taken twenty seconds. 'We have ten seconds,' she said.

They waited, the silence eerie. There were distant shouts, the clatter of feet on the stairs above. Tania moved closer to Mrs Jacobsen. The older woman gave her a bleak smile. 'You're sure about Barrington's room,' she said. 'There isn't going to be time for a search.'

'Room sixteen, second floor.' She said calmly. 'Doctor Jansen was quite definite.'

Mrs Jacobsen shrugged. 'All right. But keep wide of me when I start using this thing.'

There was a massive explosion that brought a dusty cloud from the ceiling. Helga snapped an order and they ran, Tania and Mrs Jacobsen for the stairs, Korina and Mrs Tollinson for the ground floor corridor. Helga took up a position beside the door leading to the cellar, waiting. There was a second explosion and she grinned. It shook the entire building.

The sticks of dynamite were going off at ten second intervals, blowing massive holes in the upper floor of the hotel. Dazed and wounded men, blown out of bed by the explosion, staggered through dense smoke to fall out of the gaping holes. Others were trapped under beams and rubble, crying for help as the roof and ceilings began to burn.

From the ground it was spectacular. Within two minutes the entire roof of the hotel was a mass of burning wreckage, the night filled with the shouts and screams of wounded men.

'My God,' said Loris, 'we've wiped them out.'

Clouds of smoke began to roll towards them, held low by the falling snow. As far as they could see most of the roof was on fire, but the south wing of the hotel was still intact. Heidi took another set of arrows with fused sticks of dynamite. 'Let's go and see what we can do about that.'

They crossed the road and worked their way up the hillside, coming to the corner of the hotel grounds. The wind was blowing the smoke away from them and it seemed to Heidi that the snow was not as heavy. It was a difficult position to get a clean shot so the arrows would pierce the woodwork and hold, so she slid down the bank and stepped out onto the clean white carpet of snow, which extended from the trees to the hotel.

She notched an arrow into the bow while Loris and Maria kept watch with pistols in their hands. Loris touched the smouldering piece of rope to the fuse and as it spluttered into life Heidi raised and shot the arrow into the woodwork beneath the eaves in the centre of the wing. She was fitting the second arrow when a window on the second floor dissolved in a shower of breaking glass and a Schmeisser chattered at them. Loris gasped beside her and staggered forward, her legs loose and rubbery. Maria began to fire rapidly at the window, but the range was too far for accuracy.

Heidi lowered her aim and placed the arrow cleanly through the broken window. A man staggered in the empty frame, crying out, the sputtering arrow in his chest. A moment later he had fallen back, out of sight, but another Schmeisser began to fire from the next window.

'Let's move back,' said Heidi, feeling a chill of fear as bullets exploded in the snow around them.

Maria was beside Loris who was on her knees, her face ashen, blood soaking through the sleeve and shoulder of the anorak. 'We can't leave Loris,' she said in a shrill voice.

They pulled the girl to her feet and made a stumbling run for the trees. More machine pistols opened fire and suddenly Maria sprawled in the snow, clutching her leg. Heidi pulled her back into the trees and studied the wound.

'It's not too bad,' she told her. 'If you can walk you can help Loris. Get to the church where Doctor Jansen is waiting. He's got help. You'll be all right.'

'I can't move,' gasped Loris, her face like old chalk. 'My whole side is on fire.'

Heidi pulled her roughly to her feet. 'Listen, if you sit here you'll die. I can't look after you. You'll both have to look after each other.'

Maria stared at the young woman with disbelief. 'You'd leave us?'

'You know what I've got to to do,' replied Heidi. 'Now move.'

Maria pulled herself upright, limping to Loris and putting an arm around her waist. 'We'll get to the church,' she said coldly. 'But I won't forget the kind of ruthless cow you've become, Heidi Terrel.'

Heidi watched them disappear into the darkness, then turned back to her bow in time to see the dynamite explode in the centre of the south wing. It blew a massive hole through the wall and roof, hurling pieces of wood and plaster into the sky. But there was no fire. She collected the sack of arrows and the smouldering piece of hemp and began to edge along the slope. Two Germans were running towards the trees, shouting to each other. She ignored them, working up the hillside to a place she remembered from the previous summer. She had shot a hare in the hotel grounds and received a telling off from the village Constable.

She wondered if he would tick her off now, smiling grimly as she notched another arrow into the bow and lit the fuse. She raised it, sighting between two pines, placing it accurately beneath one of the upper windows. She dug into the sack for another, wondering if they had managed to free the men.

Helga heard the pounding of feet on the stone steps long before the cellar door burst open. She let it fling wide before pulling the trigger on both barrels. Two men were blown back, one of them lifted right off his feet, his head a bloody ruin. The second took the blast in his chest and spun away down the stairs. She saw the third man too late, rising to the level of the doorway, a machine pistol in his hand. She broke the barrels of the gun, knowing she could not reload in time.

The German was confused, shocked by the blast of the shotgun and the explosions that were still continuing overhead. He found it difficult to relate the chaos to the stocky, grey haired woman before him, but his training took over and he swung the Schmeisser towards her, his finger tightening on the trigger. There was a quick burst of gunfire from the side and bullets tore into his chest, tossing him back down the stairs.

Helga looked towards the doorway finding Karen there, grinning at her. She had pulled back the hood of her anorak and unzipped it to the waist, unbuttoning her blouse low enough to reveal the full sweep of her breast which heaved now with unconcealed excitement. She was every inch a Valkyrie ready to die in battle.

'You're supposed to be covering the gallery,' snapped Helga.

'Michelle has moved in to get shells. Let's see if there are any more down there.'

As if in answer a burst of machine gun fire ripped across the wall above their heads. They flattened to the floor, Helga crawling forward until she could look over the edge of the doorway. The three bodies were sprawled down the steps. Where it turned the corner she could just make out the blue steel barrel of a machine gun. She fired, ducking back as bullets ricocheted off the wall.

'That's a pity,' she said. 'We can't get past him without a grenade.'

'Grenades!' exclaimed Karen. 'What a lovely idea!'

She fitted a fresh magazine into her gun and crossed the room to the door leading into the dining room. Helga started to call her back and thought better of it. If Karen got the grenades it would solve the problem. She raised the shotgun and fired down the stairs, flattening against the floor as the machine gun chattered back.

As Karen opened the door to the dining room and slipped inside she heard the sound of approaching footsteps that came to a stop somewhere on the other side of the far door. She froze, letting her eyes adjust to the dim light. There was a long dining table, some chairs and heavy furniture against the walls. There were maps and papers on the table and in one corner a large oak dresser lined with dishes. She wondered whether to switch on the light, but decided against it, moving soundlessly halfway along the wall.

There was a click from the door, an edge of light, widening rapidly as someone pushed it open. There was silence again, then a quick word in German. A figure was silhouetted briefly in the doorway, feeling for the light switch, and then the room was suddenly brilliantly lit. The four Germans who entered were in various stages of undress, some only in vest and trousers with magazines for their Schmeissers tucked into their trouser pockets. They were totally unprepared for the girl they saw standing against the wall. She was tall, beautiful with wild golden hair and her mouth was wide with soundless laughter as she swung the machine pistol in her hands and pressed the trigger.

The bullets ripped into the tight group of men. The first burst took the leading pair, sending them staggering into their companions as ugly red holes appeared in their chests. The second burst caught the other two as they lunged back towards the door, turning them round and round. The last stayed on his feet, trying to raise his gun. There was a hole in his arm pumping blood and another high in his chest, yet he still struggled, his eyes fixed on the woman across the room.

Karen changed the magazine in the Schmeisser, then walked up to him and stood with her hands on her hips.

'Big brave German soldier,' she said, sneering at him.

He took deep, rasping breaths, forcing the barrel of the gun towards her. At the last moment she slapped it from his hands and took the luger from her waistband. While he watched, unable to do more than totter backwards, she pushed the barrel into his stomach and squeezed the trigger.

Karen stepped over the bodies into the corridor beyond the dining room, looking for movement, but there was none. On the floor above were running footsteps, a burst of gunfire, then a massive explosion from the rear of the building. She ignored it and turned off the corridor into the kitchen. It was brightly lit, but deserted. She crossed to the store room, remembering that Michelle had said the soldier told her they kept all the ammunition together. The first room she entered was small and filled with pans and cleaning materials. The second was lined with shelves, some containing large tins of ham and sausages in brine. There were barrels of herring lining one wall and a meat slicer on a bench beside the door.

There was the clatter of running feet in the corridor leading to the dining room. She moved to the next door, opening it and stepping into a large room stacked with cases of ammunition, grenades and mortar bombs. In the centre of the room, pushing the last grenade into a loop on his webbing, was Private Klaus. He swung round, his eyes widening with astonishment when he saw her. She aimed the gun at his stomach and moved to him.

'Don't move your right hand at all,' she said softly. 'With your left hand unfasten that harness and pass it to me.'

He licked dry lips and reached up with his left hand, carefully unfastening the buckle. The shoulder straps loosened and he awkwardly shrugged out of it until he held it in his hand.

'That's a clever boy,' said Karen. 'Now give it to me.'

She took it from him, the barrel of the Schmeisser an inch from his stomach, and as she draped it over her shoulder he lashed out with a flat left hand, knocking the weapon aside as his right hand flashed down to his boot and came up with the cold gleam of steel in it. She jumped away from him, trying to swing back the gun whilst her right hand was occupied with the belt of grenades. The knife caught her in the side, cutting deep just above the kidney.

He came at her again, crouching low, his eyes small and afraid. The knife had blood on it. Her blood. She felt the beginning of rage, but checked it as he lunged for her. She had the trigger beneath her finger, swinging the machine pistol up with her left hand, firing it wildly as he lunged directly into the path of the bullets. They tore into him, gouging holes across his chest and stomach.

She laughed as he swayed unsteadily before her, his eyes glazing as his knees buckled. There was movement behind her and she swung round, expecting Germans. Olga and Michelle were there, looking at her with shocked expressions.

'What do you want?' she asked harshly.

'Mortar bombs,' said Michelle, staring at Karen's side as though hypnotised. 'You'd better sit down. You're wounded.'

'You sit down,' said Karen, turning back towards the kitchen. She was only vaguely aware of the blood that was pouring out of her side.

Michelle picked up one of the steel cases of mortar bombs and started towards the door. Olga, tearing her eyes from the horrifying wound, picked up another and began to follow. They crossed the kitchen to the gallery door where Anna Rekvarik was keeping watch.

'Nothing yet,' she told them. 'Hurry.'

'You take this,' said Olga. 'I must try to help Karen.'

Michelle opened her mouth to argue, then closed it and shrugged. Anna took the case of bombs from Olga and went out into the gallery with Michelle. Olga turned back into the kitchen. Karen was leaning against a table, her arm pressed against her side. It did nothing to stop the blood from pumping out and her left side was crimson down to her knee.

'Karen, come with us through the gallery. We can get you to the church.'

She turned and stared at her for a moment, as though not recognising her, and then she gave a crooked smile and reached unsteadily for her with a bloody hand. 'Ah, sweet Olga. Let me take you to the woods.'

She tried to laugh but stopped with a spasm of pain. Olga took the belt of grenades from her and then tried to guide her towards the gallery. Karen pulled away, suddenly angry.

'I'm staying here,' she said. 'They'll be coming for the ammunition soon.'

'No Karen, you mustn't,' pleaded Olga. 'You've done enough.'

'Get out,' said Karen harshly, 'You couldn't care less.'

'It's nothing to do with that,' said Olga helplessly. 'You don't have to die.'

'I don't intend to,' she replied. 'I just want to kill a few more men.'

Olga looked at her in horror. 'Is that what you're doing? Killing men?'

'As far as I'm concerned it's open season on them,' replied Karen, making no attempt to conceal her bitterness. 'And I intend to get my share.'

There was the sound of running feet and German voices on the other side of the door to the dining room.

'Please come?' said Olga.

'They'll be coming in here for the ammunition,' whispered Karen, her eyes bright beads against the chalk white pallor of her face. 'Stay and kill a few men, sweet Olga.'

The girl backed away from her, shaking her head. 'No, it isn't like that. They're Germans. The enemy.'

'Men are the enemy. Arrogant, brutal, egotistical men.' She laughed at Olga's shocked expression. 'I found out early. I was fifteen when I was raped in a ditch beside the road. That's when I found out about the enemy.'

'And when you raped me, Karen? Did that make *you* the enemy?'

Karen looked bewildered and started to shake her head. The door burst open and they both turned, pressing the triggers of their machine pistols simultaneously. A corporal and a private stood in frozen attitudes, their mouths gaping as bloody holes exploded in their bodies, hammering them back into the room beyond. Someone kicked the door shut and there was silence again.

'On your way, sweet Olga.' Karen said hoarsely. 'Let's hope there is a place for us both in Valhalla.'

'No,' the girl replied sadly, moving towards the gallery. 'I am not brave enough for that.'

Karen emptied her magazine into the door, then quickly replaced it with a fresh one. When she looked round Olga had left and she was alone in the lofty kitchen. The ammunition room was close by and she crossed to it, surprised at how weak she had become. Somehow she reached the case of grenades and put one inside her anorak, then went back into the kitchen and crouched in the darkest corner by the big old oak dresser.

The door from the dining room was the only way to the ammunition, unless the Germans wanted to fight their way across the grounds to the gallery. She smiled, feeling her spirits soar with the knowledge that they had to come to her. She checked the magazine in the luger, then placed a fresh magazine for the Schmeisser on the floor.

When the attack came the speed and efficiency of the Germans was shattering. The door was flung wide and two men dived into the kitchen at floor level whilst a third stood behind them, firing his machine pistol through the opening. Karen killed him with her first burst, then swung towards the two prone men, pressing the trigger. Bullets were exploding across the wall and the oak dresser, filling the air with splintered wood and broken china. She felt hot knives pierce her thigh and stomach, and heard the hammer click on an empty chamber.

She dropped the Schmeisser, knowing there was no time to reload, and plucked the luger from her belt. The room was full of smoke and from the doorway at least three machine pistols were firing. She felt herself sliding to the floor, the sound of bullets and the smell of cordite assaulting her senses, yet somehow she found the strength to take the grenade from her blood-soaked anorak and pull the pin.

There was a roaring in her ears and small hammers were thudding against her, knocking her from side to side. The grenade felt so heavy, its handle slippery like oiled silk, and the muscles of her arm were like strands of old rubber. But even as the blackness swooped down she flung it through the door beside her.

The explosion killed more than thirty soldiers, including Lieutenant Dobermann as he rallied his men for the charge into the kitchen. It detonated the mortar bombs and two cases of grenades, blasting out the rear wall of the hotel and part of the floor above. It sent a ball of fire into the sky that could be seen a mile away and stopped the returning patrols in their tracks, convinced that the entire hotel had been destroyed.

It also saved the life of Colonel Barrington.

24

When the first shotgun blasts echoed through the hotel Barrington was being doused by a bucket of ice cold water from a barrel-chested bear of a man he had chosen to call Fritz. Beside the bed, slapping him repeatedly across the face was his partner, a squat, dark-haired man whose features looked as though they had been chiselled out of rotting wood. Lodtz stood over the bed, a cigarette in his fingers, his eyes like cut glass.

'I have little patience left, Colonel,' he was saying. 'Unless you want the lives of fifty hostages on your conscience you had better give me the location of the gold.'

They pulled Barrington into a sitting position. He shook his head, his senses clearing, gazing at the German Captain with contempt. He had opened his mouth to reply when the shotgun blasts rang out. Seconds later there was a thunderous explosion above their heads and clouds of dust filled the air.

Lodtz crossed to the phone, speaking sharply in to it. A second explosion shook the building and the phone went dead. He flung it aside in disgust and came back to the bed, taking his pistol from its holster.

'This is your doing, Barrington,' he said thickly. 'You had better talk and talk fast!'

There was another explosion, the sounds of crashing timber and the cries of wounded men. Barrington stared at him without a flicker of emotion. Lodtz cocked the luger, aiming it at his right leg. Another detonation shook the room, then the door burst open and Niemens entered, buttoning his tunic.

'Captain, we are under attack,' he shouted. 'You are needed downstairs.'

'Who is attacking us?' Lodtz asked quietly.

'The women,' replied Niemens. 'They appear to be attacking from both sides.'

'Women!' Lodtz stared at him in contempt. 'We are being attacked by women?'

Niemens controlled his impatience with an effort. 'I tried to warn you, Captain. Barrington had to be using the women against us.'

'Then go and deal with them,' Lodtz said icily. 'Get the men together and wipe them out!'

Two more explosions came in quick succession, shaking the walls and bringing down lumps of plaster from the ceiling. There were distant shouts and cries for help.

'And you, sir?' asked Niemens. 'Will you be taking command?'

'Against women?' Lodtz sneered at the lieutenant. 'I leave that kind of fighting to you, Niemens!'

There was the rattle of shots from below, the rapid blasts of shotguns interspersed with the chatter of machine pistols. Niemens brought his heels sharply together, his face pale with anger, and left the room. Lodtz turned to the interrogators, gesturing towards their tunics and weapons.

'Prepare yourselves. It could be that the Colonel's women may be planning to rescue him.' He glanced at Barrington. 'Isn't that true, Colonel?'

'You know as much as I do about it,' Barrington replied blandly. 'Although they do seem to be making rather a mess of your headquarters!'

As if to support the words there was a further explosion from the end of the building and the sound of shattering glass followed by a burst of gunfire.

'You think women can be a match for my men? Trained soldiers at the peak of physical fitness?'

The door was smashed open and Mrs Jacobsen lunged into the room, her eyes wild, grey hair flying, the shotgun blasting out before the two privates could lift the machine pistols they had been loading. The first blast threw the huge barrel-chested man across the room with flailing arms, the second took his companion in the face as he pressed the trigger, killing him instantly, but not before one of his bullets had caught Mrs Jacobsen in the shoulder. She staggered back against the wall beside the door, dropping the shotgun.

As the older woman was dealing with the two soldiers, Tania had entered and moved to the right of the door, aiming her Schmeisser at Lodtz. Without hesitation he placed the luger against Barrington's head, staring back at her with a faint smile.

'The moment that weapon fires the Colonel is dead,' he said.

Barrington moved his hand, reaching for the pistol he had concealed beneath the mattress after the doctor had left. Lodtz's gun nudged him behind the ear.

'Move again and you're dead anyway,' he said softly.

Tania hesitated, her face tormented. There was the sound of running footsteps in the corridor and she edged away from the door, looking indecisive.

'Shoot him!' snapped Barrington.

'Drop the gun,' Lodtz told her. 'Or you will all die.'

Sergeant Driker stepped into the room, a Schmeisser in his hands, pointing it at Tania. 'Immediately, Miss,' he ordered.

With a defeated expression she let the machine pistol fall to the floor. Lodtz stepped away from Barrington and ordered the two women to stand against the wall. Mrs Jacobsen was very pale, holding her shoulder where blood was seeping through her fingers.

Barrington slowly moved his hand down the bed whilst Lodtz's attention was on the women, slipping his fingers around and beneath the mattress until they touched the butt of the luger. He relaxed, waiting.

'What's the position, Sergeant?' Lodtz asked.

'Small assault groups have hit the front and rear entrances of the hotel simultaneously, whilst explosive charges were fired into the upper floor.' He paused, as though wishing he could offer a different method. 'It seems they're using a bow and arrows, the charges tied to the arrows.'

There was a dull concussion from the south wing of the hotel. Lodtz gazed at Driker in disbelief. 'A bow and arrows! Women assault groups! What kind of nonsense is this, Driker?'

'Not nonsense, sir,' he replied patiently. 'All the sentries and the duty personnel on the ground floor are dead. The upper floor of the hotel is in chaos. Most of the charges blew holes in the walls and roof and this entire block is now burning. Our position is not good, Captain.'

'Don't be ridiculous,' snapped Lodtz. 'Niemens is forming a counter attack now. We must outnumber these women by five to one. Dammit, Driker, I want a positive report!'

'Sir, we have more than a hundred men dead or injured, at least half of them still trapped on the upper floor which, as I said, is on fire. Lieutenant Dobermann is forming a squad to take the kitchens where our ammunition is stored. We have no grenades and I think we can assume that the mortar battery has been taken.'

Lodtz stared at him with burning eyes, the skin stretched so tight across his face that it seemed like polished bone. 'A hundred!' He said with stunned disbelief. 'A hundred of my men lost!'

'At least that many, Captain. You must take command, regroup, before it is too late.'

Lodtz turned towards Barrington, his mouth twisting savagely as he raised the pistol. 'You are responsible for this. You have been the cause of it all, Barrington. Now tell me where the gold is or you die this instant!'

Driker looked at Lodtz in astonishment. 'Sir, there is no time for that.'

'I must have the gold!' screamed Lodtz.

The floor shivered beneath them and cracks rippled

across the walls as the hotel shook to a gigantic explosion. Driker staggered backwards, struggling to keep his balance. The very air seemed to be sucked from the room and every window shattered. Lodtz knew what it was, what it meant. He tightened his finger on the trigger of the Luger, swinging it towards Tania.

'Very well, Barrington, watch your women die!'

Barrington lifted his pistol from beneath the level of the bed and pulled the trigger. The bullet took Lodtz in the throat. He turned, unable to comprehend the gun in the Englishman's hand. Barrington fired again, hitting him in the chest. He staggered back into Driker's line of fire as the Sergeant pressed the trigger of his Schmeisser. Lodtz arched and spun round, his mouth wide in soundless agony as bullets tore into him.

Tania scooped her machine pistol from the floor and as the shocked Driker stepped clear of the falling body of the Captain, she fired a burst at point blank range, killing him instantly.

The shattered building was coming apart at the seams as they ran along the smoke-filled corridor to the stairs leading down into the hall. Above their heads the ceiling sagged, flames roaring from ragged holes, and the air was filled with the sound of falling masonry and groaning beams. There was no organised resistance on the second floor. What soldiers they saw were in a state of shock, trying to find their way to the stairs.

They came down the stairs into the main hall where a massive beam had fallen, blocking half the room. There were bodies of German soldiers sprawled in the rubble, but from beyond the beam were steady bursts of gunfire. Barrington crouched at the bottom of the stairs, easing Mrs Jacobsen down beside him. Tania checked the magazine on her machine pistol, ready to lunge across the room.

'Just stay where you are,' he told her sharply.

'I'm the only one who can get behind that beam,' she said.

He took the bag of shotgun shells from Mrs Jacobsen who

managed a grim smile, assuring him that she could manage on her own. He filled the chamber with three cartridges and put a fourth under the hammer. The soldiers behind the beam were firing at someone near the front door, and from the number of shots Barrington judged there to be three of them. He rose to his feet, putting all his weight on his stiff left leg, ignoring the waves of pain that came from the knee.

'I go first, you empty one magazine as cover, then reload and follow.'

'You can't clear the beam,' she said furiously.

'And you can't obey orders,' he snapped. 'You women are really beginning to get out of hand.'

He lunged forward, taking one long loping stride and launching himself over the beam, landing on a pile of debris on the far side. Two of the three Germans crouching behind the beam swung round, firing at his body as it rolled down the heap of rubble. He came to a stop behind a piece of masonry which luckily provided cover. From the stairs Tania opened fire with her Schmeisser, catching the soldiers by surprise. One was hit in the chest and spun round, falling. Barrington rolled out from behind the masonry and fired, working the pump action, watching a soldier lift up onto his toes as though trying to defy gravity before going over backwards with a choking cry.

The third soldier was in an awkward position at the end of the beam and the only way he could return fire was by getting to his feet. He had to take the chance, but as he rose to swing round his gun he was cut down from both sides.

There was silence, the air filled with the smoke from burning timber and the greyer, more acrid smoke from the guns. Barrington pushed himself to his feet, grinning crookedly at Helga who was crouched by the door, a streak of blood on her cheek and a spreading red stain on the leg of her trousers.

'So what kept you, English?' she said.

'If I'd known you were going to demolish this place I'd

have stayed somewhere else!' he replied, crawling over to her. 'What's the problem?'

'There's an idiot in the cellar with a machine gun,' she answered. 'Karen went to get grenades, but I think she decided to blow the hotel up instead.'

Tania arrived with Mrs Jacobsen who sat down against the wall beside the door as Barrington edged his way to the cellar steps. The moment he tried to look through the doorway the machine gun chattered and bullets ricocheted off the masonry an inch from his head.

'Will you please stop trying to get killed!' Tania said angrily.

'My dear Miss Arlberg, from your behaviour in that room upstairs I was quite convinced you were contemplating suicide. How you've managed to get this far without taking a bullet in your stubborn hide is a complete mystery to me.'

She glared at him. 'Don't call me Miss Arlberg.'

Helga looked from one to the other in astonishment. 'Children, children!' she exclaimed. 'Can we find a way to get into the cellar?'

There was a prolonged burst of gunfire from the grounds, then the thump of a grenade. Barrington raised himself sufficiently to look over the window sill to the grounds of the hotel. There was more firing and he slid down to the floor, frowning worriedly.

'That's Tania Group,' Helga informed him. 'They've been using the mortars for the past couple of minutes so I imagine the patrols are coming back.'

'You've got Michelle Group in reserve?' Barrington asked.

Helga nodded. 'They're on the hillside. We'll know when anything tries to get past them.'

'So we've got to have reinforcements and fast.'

There was more firing from the grounds, then footsteps running towards the entrance to the hotel. They swung round, guns ready. Sonja entered on the run with Olga and Heidi. They crouched beside the door, firing into the night.

'There's an officer with about ten Germans. They got out through the south wing before Heidi blocked it off,' Sonja informed them.

'What about the rest of you?' Barrington asked.

'Karen is dead, a few of the others are wounded and back with the doctor at the church. Mrs Tollinson and Korina Mattel are in the ruins of the gallery so we could get them in a crossfire if they move forward.'

'Good girl,' said Barrington. 'don't suppose you've got such a thing as a grenade?'

'A present from Karen,' said Olga, opening her anorak to reveal a brace of grenades.

Machine pistols chattered and bullets began to explode across the ceiling above their heads. From the staircase there was a crashing of falling masonry and a blazing section of the upper floor fell into the hall. Smoke began to billow around them.

'If you start throwing grenades down there,' said Mrs Jacobsen, 'you're likely to hit our men as well.' She looked apologetically at Barrington. 'It's just that my husband is down there and he's going to be pretty mad at me for getting shot as it is.'

Barrington was working on one of the grenades, carefully unscrewing the handle. 'Ma'am,' he murmured, 'I wouldn't dare to injure any of your men.'

He pulled the handle carefully out of the grenade, revealing the pencil-thin fuse. This he unscrewed, placing it on the floor before screwing the handle back into its original position. Sonja and Olga were busy beside the door, firing out into the night. Across the hall the staircase was well alight and flames were beginning to spread to the wall. The heat was intense, but so far most of the smoke was being blown away from them.

'Don't hurry on my account, English,' said Helga, 'but I think it's very close to checking out time.'

'Just about ready,' said Barrington. He picked up the shotgun and loaded it, then crawled back to crouch beside the door. He pulled the pin from the grenade and tossed it over the step, listening as it clattered down towards the cellar. He counted with it, waiting until it had hit nine steps before kneeling upright with the shotgun at his shoulder. The machine-gunner was in full view, reaching for the grenade as it bounced towards him. Barrington pulled the trigger and pumped a fresh cartridge into the chamber, but it wasn't necessary.

* * *

When Korina Mattel and Mrs Tollinson opened fire from the smouldering rubble of the gallery, Lieutenant Niemens found himself and his men effectively pinned down on the edge of the snow covered grounds. The ruddy glow from the burning hotel was beginning to show their position and from the road leading to the village there was further gunfire which told him some of the patrols were returning. Most of his men were low on ammunition and his best course seemed to be to link up with the patrols.

'Pass the word,' he instructed a corporal. 'I want every man on his feet and running down the hill road when I give the word.'

The man beside him was returning fire towards the hotel. His magazine ran out and he removed it, searching for a new one and cursing when he found he had none left. Niemens felt a chill of apprehension. His group of ten men was the only organised force and unless they could link up with the returning patrols they would have nothing to fight with in minutes.

'Save ammunition,' he ordered. 'Two of you give covering fire.'

His men, lying flat in the snow, raised gaunt faces and waited for his signal. From the slope behind the hotel came the dull thud of a mortar. The explosion came a moment later, searing the night with a ball of fire halfway down the hillside towards the village.

'They're using our mortars,' said the corporal bitterly.

'We ignore them,' Niemens replied with more confidence than he felt. 'They can't be accurate, not without training.'

There was another thump and seconds later an explosion lit up the trees along the road. It was followed almost immediately by the rattle of gunfire. Niemens rose to his feet, firing a burst towards the entrance to the hotel and began to lead his men at a run along the drive. They had taken no more than a dozen steps when a barrage of gunfire came at them from the hotel. Men cried out and fell around him. Others slowed, firing towards the burning building in confusion.

Niemens shouted for them to go on, turning towards the hotel. There should have been no more than two women firing from the doorway and with the smoke billowing from the hall he did not expect them to be a serious threat. What he saw filled him with a bitter despair. He swung his Schmeisser, shouting a warning to his men, firing a short burst before the hammer clicked on an empty chamber. Then he could only stand, watching the men pouring out of the hotel with pistols and Schmeissers in their hands, their faces etched with hate as they ran towards them.

As the bullets tore into him he had one last image of a young woman standing in the doorway, her long blonde hair glowing crimson from the light of the fire behind her. A machine pistol hung by her side and she was shouting, her eyes shining with triumph. Beside her was Barrington, looking at him as he fell beneath the hail of bullets.

25

The trucks left at noon the following day with every case of gold safely loaded and checked by Colonel Barrington. They bypassed Annolsetrene and took the main road from Valebru to Dombas and from there north through the mountain forests to the great fjord of Trondheim.

Mopping up had taken most of the night, but the women had been content to let the men take care of it. After their treatment at the hands of the Germans there were scores to settle and when the grey light of dawn filtered through the trees the hotel was a smouldering ruin and a small group of dejected prisoners all that remained of Captain Lodtz's commando force.

The prisoners were loaded on the trucks and taken with the gold for shipment to England, and the bodies of their companions were buried among the trees on the hillside above the town. Apart from the burned-out shell of the Hotel Varennes, there was nothing to suggest that the Germans had ever occupied the village of Borgas.

Although the convoy of trucks was driven by men from the village, all the women who had escaped injury insisted on making the journey and Barrington felt no inclination to dissuade them. He was still both elated and amazed at the success of the operation, and humbled by the determination the women had shown when he had tried to dismiss the idea as naive and unrealistic. Their courage had never been in question, only their ability to overwhelm Lodtz's Sky Wolves.

As Helga had said as she lay with her injured leg propped

up in the make-shift hospital Doctor Jansen and his helpers had set up in the church: 'We had God, luck and the Norse Valkyries on our side, English. With all that we were invincible.'

'Even so I get cold shivers when I think of what might have happened if Lodtz had taken you more seriously.'

Helga chuckled. 'You worry too much. Your plan was good. You always said that a woman was the equal of any man . . . once she had kicked him in the balls!'

Barrington smiled to himself, remembering her laughter that had followed him all the way out of the church. Tania stirred beside him, her blonde hair like perfumed silk against his cheek.

'What are you grinning at?' she asked.

'Oh just something Helga said,' he replied. 'If it ever catches on we could have a lot of female chauvinists on our hands.'

She looked at him questioningly, waiting for him to explain. He kissed her instead, nestling down with her between the stacked cases of gold as the truck rattled north through the last pass to Trondheim.

There had been a German air raid at the docks when they arrived and the Lieutenant Commander who met them at the quay was eager to get his destroyer away and out to sea. The gold was quickly transferred from the trucks and the German prisoners marched up the gangway.

'Will you all be going with us, Colonel?' asked the naval officer.

Barrington looked towards the group of women standing along the quay. 'I'm not sure,' he said slowly. 'I don't think they've had much time to think about it.'

'Remarkable bunch,' said the Lieutenant Commander. 'One could almost believe they knew how to use those German weapons they're carrying.'

'Yes, couldn't one,' said Barrington, and walked towards the women.

The men had driven the trucks to the end of the quay

where they were taking on supplies and weapons. The women stood apart, waiting for Barrington, their Schmeissers hanging from straps over their shoulders as though they had been carrying them for years. He considered them gravely, feeling his throat tighten with emotion as he looked at Sonja with her wild chestnut hair that probably still smelled of cordite, to young Heidi who had placed her arrows so well. There was Anna Rekvarik, a bandage around her wrist as though she had burned it against a kitchen stove instead of fending off a piece of blazing timber. And Korina Mattel, grinning at him with a filleting knife still in her boot.

And there was Magda, pale and composed, her eyes unreadable. Like all the rest of his women she would never be the same again.

'You're staying,' he said sadly.

'You've shown us what needs to be done,' said Sonja. 'There are villages to contact, an underground network to set up. We need to be ready for the occupation, ready to keep on fighting.'

'Some might say you've done enough.'

They smiled at him and shook their heads. He considered them gravely and thought of the blood and bodies sprawled in the blazing building the night before.

'All right, ladies,' he said, feeling the emotion well up as he cleared his throat selfconsciously before continuing. 'Just do what you have to do and do it fast. And for God's sake take care of yourselves.'

Tania walked slowly back to the gangway with him, her eyes on the ground. When he stopped she faced him, her smile tinged with sadness. 'What will you do now?' she asked.

He shrugged, leaning more heavily on the walking stick she had found for him. 'I don't think this war is for me . . . don't think the top brass will give me much of a chance, anyway.'

'So?'

'Perhaps I'll go back to India. There's a palace in Jaipur I want to see again.'

Tears came into her eyes and she took his hand, squeezing it tightly. 'Oh, Charles, if I could see it with you.'

'All you need to do is cross this gangway.'

She looked at him for a moment and slowly shook her head. 'No. And they'll never let you go to India, you're too good. Too important. I'd be sitting in a flat somewhere, wondering what you were doing, wanting to be with you and part of it. I couldn't take that.'

He nodded, touching her cheek to stop the tear as though the act itself would end the sadness. She leaned forward and kissed him with salty lips, then stepped back.

'When it's over, Charles,' she said. 'When it's all over.'

'Yes,' he said.

But he knew it already was.

Alistair MacLean

His first book, HMS *Ulysses*, published in 1955, was outstandingly successful. It led the way to a string of best-selling novels which have established Alistair MacLean as the most popular adventure writer of our time.

Fontana Paperbacks

Fontana is a leading paperback publisher of fiction and non-fiction, with authors ranging from Alistair MacLean, Agatha Christie and Desmond Bagley to Solzhenitsyn and Pasternak, from Gerald Durrell and Joy Adamson to the famous Modern Masters series.

In addition to a wide-ranging collection of internationally popular writers of fiction, Fontana also has an outstanding reputation for history, natural history, military history, psychology, psychiatry, politics, economics, religion and the social sciences.

All Fontana books are available at your bookshop or newsagent; or can be ordered direct. Just fill in the form and list the titles you want.

FONTANA BOOKS, Cash Sales Department, G.P.O. Box 29, Douglas, Isle of Man, British Isles. Please send purchase price, plus 8p per book. Customers outside the U.K. send purchase price, plus 10p per book. Cheque, postal or money order. No currency.

NAME (Block letters)

ADDRESS

While every effort is made to keep prices low, it is sometimes necessary to increase prices on short notice. Fontana Books reserve the right to show new retail prices on covers which may differ from those previously advertised in the text or elsewhere.